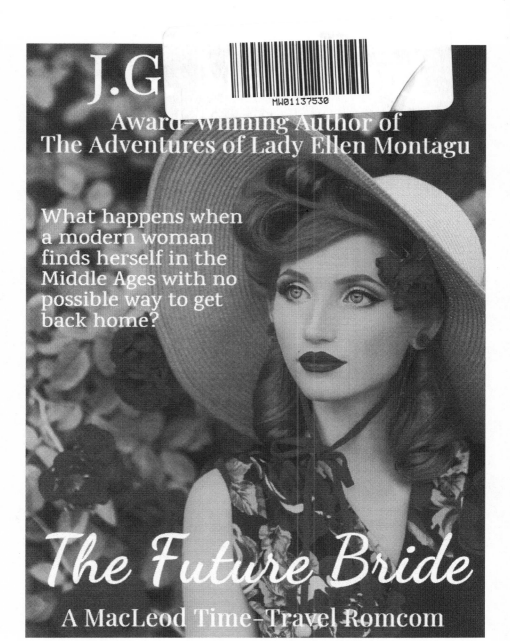

ISBN 9781687772091

jgmacleod.com

The Future Bride Acknowledgments

I am grateful for those special people in my life who continue to encourage me to pursue my passion of writing. Their support means so much to me.

- To my parents, Gail and Bill, and my brother, Shawn, who continue to encourage my writing.

- To my incredible daughters, Skyler, Mea and Avery, all published authors in their own right.

- To my ancestors, whose daily lives I have attempted to capture throughout this novel.

- To Ancestry.com for providing my DNA & family tree information to help me craft this tale.

The Future Bride
Notes & Disclaimers

- This is a work of fiction. Names, characters, businesses, places, events, locales, and incidents are either the product of the author's imagination or used in a fictitious manner. Any resemblance to actual persons, living or dead, or actual events, is purely coincidence.

- Some names and identifying details have been changed to protect the privacy of individuals.

- I have tried to recreate events, locales and conversations from my memories of them. In order to maintain their anonymity, in some instances I have changed the names of individuals and places. I may have changed some identifying characteristics and details, such as physical properties, occupations and places of residence.

- The information in this book is meant to supplement, not replace, proper linguistic training/expertise in Scottish Gaelic. I am not a native Scottish Gaelic speaker and, therefore, understand that many of the nuances that make this language so beautiful are simply "lost in translation" when using an online dictionary as a tool to bridge English and Scottish Gaelic for the purpose of a fictional story.

- While historical names, places, events and incidents are often seemingly referenced throughout this story, it is a work of fiction. The thoughts and actions of the characters used in this story are in no way meant to represent the author's own political views, nor provide an assessment of historical figures, locations, events or movements. The story is meant to entertain and does not draw any conclusions about the beliefs or undertakings of real individuals, alive or dead.

- This is a work of romantic historical fiction; as such, certain historical inaccuracies are present for entertainment purposes. For example, the wearing of the kilt appears much earlier than in any recorded historical records. Certain locations/castles on/near Skye were not inhabited/controlled by those families stated. Names of my actual ancestors have been changed in some cases, to protect my family's privacy. Some poems/songs presented in this story were not yet written in the time period captured. Please enjoy the story for its intended purpose: entertainment in the romcom/romantic suspense genres. Tropes are intentional.

Titles by J.G. MacLeod

Abalone: One woman's courageous journey through relationship abuse

The Adventures of Lady Ellen Montagu trilogy:
Lady Ellen (Book 1)
Two Paths (Book 2)
New London (Book 3) (Coming 2019)

The Future Bride: A MacLeod Time-Travel Romcom

A Moment in Time (Coming 2020)

O my Luve's like a red, red rose,
That's newly sprung in June:
O my Luve's like the melodie,
That's sweetly play'd in tune.

As fair art thou, my bonie lass,
So deep in luve am I;
And I will luve thee still, my dear,
Till a' the seas gang dry.

Till a' the seas gang dry, my dear,
And the rocks melt wi' the sun;
And I will luve thee still, my dear,
While the sands o' life shall run.

And fare-thee-weel, my only Luve!
And fare-thee-weel, a while!
And I will come again, my Luve,
Tho' 'twere ten thousand mile!

(Robert Burns)

For Skyler:
~Beautiful as Skye; Strong as Karatedo
Daughter of my Heart, Through Time ~

The Future Bride

Chapter One:

I crashed through the underbrush, taking cover in the canopy of trees off the beaten path I'd been traversing ever since escaping from the strangest wedding ceremony I'd ever attended. That was at least *two hours* ago. Since that time, I'd ridden as best I could upon a chestnut mare generous enough to transport me on very short notice. I had nicknamed her Selma after my co-worker back home – a small comfort from the terror of being hunted by three hostile groomsmen, also on horseback, who had pursued me as soon as they'd noticed I was missing.

When I'd heard them approaching, I had led Selma off the road and into the trees to hide. The men had shouted to one another as they'd raced past, but hadn't seemed to notice me crouching on the damp moss. It took ages for my heartbeat to return to normal. When I could finally catch my breath, I made the difficult decision to leave the road behind and follow the less-defined paths through the forest instead. They were scarcely visible in the moonlight that managed to filter through the leaves above me. I stubbed my toes several times on unseen rocks and tree roots. The shoes I was wearing were exceptionally soft, probably leather, but resembled ballet slippers, and did nothing to assist with such an arduous journey. I missed my cross-trainers.

I wrapped Selma's lead once around my wrist to make sure I didn't get separated from her in the dark. It was extremely slow going. I hated feeling so clumsy; I was normally graceful. I couldn't see enough detail in front of me to tell if it was summer here. My senses were confounded, being so used to relying on my eyesight. It was damp; I could tell that from the goosebumps upon my arms. Suddenly, I stepped in a puddle of water. *"Damn it!"* I hissed, clenching my teeth. If this was a dream, it was quickly turning into a nightmare. I didn't even want to *see* the state of my dress. It had been trod on numerous times, and even entangled by bushes and roots.

Now my feet were cold and I had left in such a hurry I didn't have matches *or* blankets. Come to think of it, I didn't have water or food either, and my throat was parched from exertion. I would lap up the puddles like a dog if it came to that, but I was hoping for a stream rather than a disease-infested stagnant pool. Selma whinnied unhappily beside me. "I'm *sorry*," I apologized, "we'll stop soon. I just want to get as far from the road as I can before I collapse."

We continued the slow plodding for at least another hour, accompanied by the hum of insects and the odd sound of a larger animal scampering away. I hadn't considered dangerous creatures, like bears or wolves. I had no idea where I was, so my knowledge of the local food chain was non-existent. Suddenly, I lurched forwards as my dress caught on something. I tried to stop myself from falling on my face and managed, just barely, to avoid a face plant by grasping a thin trunk to my right. "*Damn it!*" I repeated, but as I straightened I noticed it wasn't quite as dark ahead.

"*Fuck it!*" I whispered into the gloom, giving Selma a tug on her lead. She whinnied her displeasure, but followed me as I made for the lighter section of woods. It wasn't as close as I'd imagined; at least another twenty minutes of plodding was required to reach it, but the light became increasingly recognizable as a campfire. I clenched my hands into fists as I slowed even more, not wanting to alert the sleeping inhabitants of the site to my presence until I'd had a chance to appraise them. Please let it be a group of women. I wasn't getting my hopes up, but what a relief it would be after everything I'd been through tonight!

I decided to tie Selma to a tree a few feet away so I could investigate unencumbered. I inhaled sharply, keenly aware of how thirsty I was, and stepped soundlessly to the edge of the clearing. It wasn't a campsite like you'd see back home; there were no comforts. Trees and bushes still invaded the so-called *clearing*, but it had enough room to burn a fire without threat of destroying the entire woods. I observed a ring of rocks around the flames and could smell something wonderful cooking on a rack of branches criss-crossed in the centre. My stomach grumbled loudly as I craned my neck to locate the *people*, but I couldn't see a single one – man, woman, *or* child!

Perhaps they'd gone in search of more food, or firewood, or water. Whatever the reason for their absence, I had to take advantage of it. I was just about to step into the clearing, when a strong arm grasped my waist from behind whilst pointing a blade to the side of my neck. "*Na gluais!*" a gruff voice growled against my ear. Fear immediately prickled along the back of my neck and I could feel my heart pounding in my ears. I wanted to scream, or run, or sink to the ground, but I had been training for such a moment as this since I was six years old.

Sensei would tell me to use both my arms, since they work together – not alone. He would tell me to move quickly, in a circular motion, against the man's elbows. And he would tell me to run, since I neither knew my attacker or my surroundings well enough to be assured a victory if I tried to attack. "Co th 'annad?" he growled, louder this time. Before he had time to react, I rotated both my arms. "*Ifrinn!*" the man cried as the blade flew out of his hand. He dropped his arms, clutching his right elbow as I tried to turn in a tight circle to return to Selma.

The man was too fast; he stuck his foot sideways and I tripped, landing hard on my hands and belly in the soft earth. Before I could get back up, the man was already sitting on my backside with one heel pressed painfully into the back of my knee, his powerful hands pinning my wrists against the ground. "Co chuir thu?" he cried in my ear. I launched my head backwards and heard a loud crack as my skull smashed against his nose. "*Mo mhallachadh!*" he screamed, dropping my arms to cup his hands around his face. I quickly rolled left, successfully throwing him. Before he could react, I turned and kicked him as hard as I could in the shoulder. He bellowed again, but I had already scrambled to my feet and was running as fast as I could towards Selma. I struggled with the knot I'd tied to keep her from wandering away, so within seconds the man was coming at me again.

Sensei would tell me to attack now; he would advise quick, decisive movements, keeping my arms up for protection, while rendering the man incapacitated, or too frightened to continue. That was the goal, anyway. I'd never had to try this in *real* life; it had always been some hypothetical concept – a philosophy studied for years and now taught to ones as small as I had been when I'd entered my first session. The man's face was terrifying as he launched himself at me. His nose, chin, and cheeks were covered in blood. Muscles rippled in his biceps as he attempted to grab me around my neck, but I repeated my circular manoeuvre, freeing myself instantly. This time, however, I did not turn and run; instead, I stepped towards him, hitting him three times in quick succession with the palm of my hand: on his chest, throat, and nose. He swore again, in his unusual language, but I was already wrapping my arm around the back of his neck, sliding my leg between his, and taking a step closer to push him off balance. He fell, as intended, but he did something I had *not* expected: he grasped my dress around my mid-section as he lost his balance, which prevented my escape. I collapsed on top of him and found myself staring into a pair of shockingly blue eyes, the colour of peacock feathers. The rest of his face was unrecognizable because of the blood. I would have head butted him, but the sight of his eyes gave me pause for just long enough that he was able to wrap a single fist around my neck and force my head backwards.

He grasped one of my arms with his other. "Co thu an ifrinn?" he growled, "an do chuir MacDhomhnaill thugaibh?"[1]

"Let me *go!*" I shouted, thrashing my legs, "let me *go*, you animal!"

In the light of the campfire, I saw him frown when he heard me speak. He recovered himself and asked again, slower this time, "co as a tha thu? An do chuir MacDhomhnaill sibh air mhal?"[2]

"Do I look like an extra from *Outlander*?" I exclaimed, staring at the night sky while the man's fist held my neck upright, "I have no idea what the *fuck* you're saying!" Tears stung my eyes now. I had failed to get away. Would the man rape me? Kill me?

For a few seconds, he didn't reply. I could hear jagged breaths escaping his lips, and feel the rise and fall of his hard chest beneath me. I felt shame wash over me as the tears began to fall, dripping down my cheeks and onto the man's hand. Finally, after what felt like ages, the man tried again. "Chan eil mi a 'cleachdadh Beurla..."[3]

I sobbed. "Speak English, you *prick!*"

"Tha mi a – *Am tryin'*!" he retorted angrily.

---

[1] Who the hell are you? Did MacDonald send you?

[2] Where are you from? Did MacDonald hire you?

[3] I don't practise English.

I couldn't see his face, because of the angle of my neck, but the sound of those two words – *I'm trying* – gave me sudden hope. "You speak *English*?" I breathed, my chest still heaving.

"Nae often," he admitted gruffly.

"Thank *god*," I cried, my legs finally settling against his as exhaustion overtook me.

"Co-dhiu tha sinn ag aontachadh mu rudeigin," he responded, but his voice sounded less hostile.

"*What*?"

He sighed deeply. "God," he stated, "we agree on *one* thin' – thankin' *God*."

"I doubt that," I retorted testily, "will you let me go? You're *hurting* me!"

"Ah doobt *that*," he responded, using my own words against me.

"You're a fucking bastard, you know that?" I exclaimed, thrashing my legs against his again. I hoped he had bruises for *days*!

Suddenly, one of his powerful legs wrapped around both of my own in a grip so tight I thought I'd lose all circulation. I cried out loudly, more tears falling from the intensity of the pain. "*Please*!" I begged, "I can't take it!"

"If ye accept the job, feumaidh tu rud sam bith a ghabhail![4]" he growled back, clearly pissed I wouldn't relent.

"What *job*?" I cried, "what are you talking about?"

"MacDhomhnaill is mah guess…" he stated.

"It sounds like you're saying MacDonald," I replied, "but how would you know my *name*?"

---

[4] …you have to take anything.

The man relaxed his hold on my legs while he responded, "*yer* name? Yer a *MacDonald*?"

"If I say yes, will you kill me?"

The man laughed bitterly. "Is docha."

"*Is docha*?" I questioned, my voice high pitched, "what does *that* mean?"

"Probably. Aye. Mebbe. Nae," the man said, as if enjoying the sounds of the English words he was uttering without caring what they meant.

"You're playing with me!" I accused angrily, "you need to let me *go*!"

He laughed again. "And let ye lead them right *tae* me?"

"Lead *who*? The *groomsmen*?" I inquired, wondering if the three men who had been chasing me were after *this* man too.

Suddenly, the man released his hold on my neck. I allowed my head to crash onto his chest, the searing pain relenting slowly. Finally, I lifted my head gingerly to stare into the pair of brilliant blue eyes again. I swallowed hard and waited for him to answer. He was watching me closely, his gaze intense and hard to read. "Yer wearin' a weddin' frock," he mused, "how did ye get here?"

I shook my head sadly. "I don't *know*," I breathed, feeling tears welling in my eyes again. My cheeks flushed in embarrassment. Sensei would *not* approve of this!

The man's eyes flickered and his jaw twitched, but he otherwise gave no sign he noticed I was going to cry again. "Yer lyin'," he stated evenly, "but why? Who sent ye?"

Tears began to roll down my cheeks. "No one," I managed to reply, "honest. I don't know *how* I got here. One minute I was at work – the next I was getting married. I just want to go home."

The man frowned again. "Ah don't understand. Ye were taken? The marriage is co-eignichte?" I stared at the blood on the man's cheeks and chin, drying in the firelight.

"I don't know what that means," I said before the exhaustion, pain, fear, and uncertainty overwhelmed me and I began to sob uncontrollably. I collapsed against the man's chest, crying like a baby. I was beyond shame; I had no more energy to fight him, and I had no more energy to try to get away. I was even too tired to realize how awkward the moment was: lying on top of a tall, muscly man, dressed in what *should* have been a costume from an episode of *Outlander*, in the middle of a dark woods, in a place I hadn't travelled to of my own volition. Maybe I'd been drugged and kidnapped. I'd read about such cases.

"I'll take ye back with me," the man said quietly, "get some answers…"

"I want to go home. Please let me go," I sniffled, lifting my tear-streaked face.

The man pretended not to notice my distress. "Ah can't do that, Sasannach," he said gravely. I stared at him in disbelief for a second before I started giggling through my tears. His eyes opened wide.

"That's what Jamie calls Claire in *Outlander*!"

The man's eyes didn't register understanding. "Is Jamie yer brother?" he asked.

I giggled again. "*No*," I replied, "but I wish he was my husband."

"Tha e na dheagh eisimpleir de dhiadhachd?[5]" the man wondered, a curious expression upon his bloodied face.

"Whatever you say, Scotland."

The man frowned again. "*Scootland*?" he stated, completely confused by my statements. He paused and then tried again, "where are ye from?"

"Huntsville," I said, figuring it wouldn't hurt to be honest.

"*Huntsville*?" he asked, little lines appearing on his forehead, "is it far?"

"*Very* far," I agreed.

"And they took ye? *Air a ghlacadh*?"

"I'm not sure," I said, "I think so."

The man's jaw twitched again. "And ye were marryin' a MacDonald taenight?"

I hesitated. Everything seemed to hinge on that name. "I don't know *who* the man was."

"Ye had not met heem yet?"

"No. They dressed me, but I escaped when the ceremony was about to begin."

"Thug thu iomradh air groomsmen…"

"Yes, three of them. They pursued me on horseback. That's why I'm in these woods."

The man's expression was thoughtful as he listened to my tale. "How dae Ah know yer not a spy?" he finally asked.

"*Spy*?"

"Aye, Sasannach, a *spy*," he replied.

"In a wedding dress?" The man stared at me for a few seconds. Suddenly, I felt him lift his leg off mine. Relief flooded my body as my blood began circulating normally again. "You're very strong," I

[5] He is a good example of masculinity?

commented absent-mindedly, "men don't usually attack women – well, unless they're trying to *rape them*, I guess – " I stopped abruptly as I realized I might be giving the man ideas he'd not thought of yet.

He had a displeased expression upon his face as he said sternly, "na bruidhinn air na rudan sin.[6]" He shoved me roughly off him and stood. As I got to my feet, I observed him fully for the first time. He was at least six-two or three and dressed in an outfit similar to Jamie's on *Outlander*, except *this* man's kilt was a faded blue and green tartan. I imagined the pattern would be quite lovely when not so travel worn. I stood awkwardly before him, all five-feet-six of me, feeling small as well as sore, tired, and famished. He was staring at me, unspeaking, and I got that same nervous feeling I'd had when he'd first held his blade to my throat. I couldn't understand his language, so perhaps he was considering raping me after all.

"Can I go?" I asked in a small voice.

"*Nae*," he replied gruffly, "yer comin' with me til Ah can get more answers." He gestured behind him to the fire. "Meat's probably burned now."

"Sorry," I apologized, disappointment spreading through me.

"Perhaps we will have tae eat yer horse," the man said, an unreadable expression in his eyes.

My cheeks flushed. "Oh, *god*, that would be *horrible!*" I exclaimed, glancing behind me to where I had tied Selma.

"It was a joke," he said simply when I turned back to face him, "Ah wanted tae hear ye laugh again." I stared at him, wondering if I'd heard him correctly. "A-null an seo," he said gruffly, gesturing to a log by the fire.

---

[6] Do not talk about such vulgar things.

I paused, considering my options. One second later, I made the obvious decision to follow the Highlander to the resting place, if only to regain my strength, find something to eat and drink, and gather my wits before trying to escape again. He sat on one end of the log, taking a long stick and poking the fire, which had died down considerably during our altercation, while I stood awkwardly a foot away. He grunted and glanced up at me. "Ah hope they fed ye at that weddin'," he commented sarcastically.

My cheeks flushed again. "Of course," I stammered, "I didn't expect you to – "

"Suidh," he commanded, "ye look as if ye might turn and run – and Eh'd rather share mah food than chase ye."

I hurried over to the log and perched on the opposite end. He removed the meat from the fire and suddenly pulled a knife from a large pocket at the front of his great kilt. Clearly the blade he'd held to my neck was not the *only* weapon he was carrying. I watched as he cut a leg off for each of us and passed one to me. It felt strange to accept the man's generosity after fighting so savagely with him, but I was so famished my scruples had all but disappeared. "Thank you," I said softly and eyed the meat curiously, "what is it?"

"Coney," he replied through a mouthful, "Ah was tryin' tae catch another when Ah happened upon *ye*, cursin' like a luighiche-bana."

I paused so I could swallow a mouthful of the savory meat. "I was *not* cursing," I said defensively, "at least not like a – like a – "

"Luighiche-bana?" he suggested, his lips curling slightly at the corners.

"I take it that's not a nice word?"

"Just a hen who serves," the man explained, taking an enormous strip off the bone with his teeth.

"Of *course*," I retorted, rolling my eyes. I didn't feel like eating anything this man had caught, but I was starving.

When the man had swallowed, he turned to gaze at me, a small smile still upon his lips. "It was a *joke*," he stated, "Ah made ye laugh before, but Ah dae not know how. Ah was tryin' tae repeat the action."

I nodded, wondering why I felt so vulnerable. At home, I was confident and fierce. I trained small children in the art of self defense and had borne trials of my own. But here, I felt small and scared and awkward. "Ith – *eat*," he told me, pointing at the meat in my hand.

I finished the leg and waited to see what he did with the remains. When he tossed his into the fire, I did the same. He watched everything I did just as closely. "Ye are uncomfortable outside?" he questioned after a time.

"I haven't been in the woods since I was a child," I explained tentatively.

"Does Jamie not walk with ye?" the man asked curiously, his blue eyes lit by the embers dancing at our feet.

I stared at him dumbly for a second before realizing he still thought Jamie was a real live person. I shook my head. "No, I have no Jamie. It's just me now." He nodded slowly, but asked no more questions about my love life. He used his knife to peel more meat from the bone. He passed it to me, but I held up my hand and said, "you should eat it. You caught it. I can always pick some berries."

"Sgailean oidhche?" he questioned casually, still cutting strips off the rabbit carcass.

"I don't know what that is, but berries. *Small. Round. Fruit.*"

He laughed, but didn't turn to face me. "Ah know what berries are. Caora. Berries. Ah was askin' what *kind* of berries. What are ye goin' tae pick?"

"I'm sure there are many kinds. It's summer?"

He glanced at me sharply. "Ye don't know what season *tis*?"

I turned to look into the fire instead. "Of course I know what *season* it is. I was just thinking aloud." I paused and added, "I have picked wild berries before – when I was a child. My grandmother took me," I lied.

"And ye picked Sgailean oidhche?" he inquired again, "or Luibh Paris?"

"No, *blueberries*. There are many where I come from."

"Will ye recognize them in the dark?" he teased, throwing the last of the carcass into the fire and wiping his hands on the bottom of his kilt.

"Perhaps my horse can assist me. Thank you for the rabbit." I stood and took two steps away from the fire before the man's hand was pressed firmly onto my shoulder.

"Suidh sios,[7]" he demanded gruffly, an edge of frustration in his deep voice.

I turned slowly to face him and his hand dropped to his side. "*Please* – let me go. I need to find my home. I don't want to lose time," I pleaded, feeling my pulse accelerating again.

He eyed me warily as if he believed I would either run or attack him again. "Ah already told ye – yer comin' *with* me."

"What if they come back?" I questioned, trying to reason with this man in the faded kilt and bloody face.

---

[7] Sit down.

"The *groomsmen*?" he asked, a small smile tugging at his lips again, "Ah can handle a couple MacDhomhnaill." He suddenly grinned fully for the first time since I'd met him, a macabre sight with his strong jaw splattered red. "Except the boireannach." I could tell he was teasing me, but I had no idea what he'd said. When he saw my blank stare, he cleared his throat and explained, "ye said ye were a MacDonald. After seein' how ye fight, Aam inclined tae be wary of the *girl* members of yer clan. *Boireannach*."

"Oh," I said, feeling guilty for reasons I couldn't explain. "You had a knife to my throat," I said, "I was only defending myself."

"Ye did a good job," he complimented me, "never seen anythin' like it – from a *woman*." He paused, as if wondering how much he should admit. "I've never seen anythin' like it – from man *or* woman, which is why Aam takin' ye with me. Yer not just some Sasannach MacDonald from Huntsville. Yer a puzzle. Aam gonna figure ye out."

Chapter Two:

I followed the man reluctantly back to his camp after he'd retrieved his knife from the ground. He had a bed roll under a nearby tree he said he usually used as a pillow, since his great kilt (the upper part of his clothing) functioned as a warm blanket when he was travelling long distances, but he unrolled it, and suggested I rest upon it and get some sleep. "We have a long journey ahead."

"Where are we going?" I asked, as I sat upon the makeshift blanket and watched as he spread his kilt upon the knoll beside me.

"Ah cannot tell ye – in case yer a spy."

I gaped at him. "You *still* think I'm a spy?"

He shrugged and reclined upon his own blanket, which overlapped my own. "Ah don't know *what* ye are. Spy. Barmaid. MacDonald. Runaway bride. Mebbe all four." He opened a small pouch strapped across his front and removed a drinking flask. It appeared to be made of leather, but I wasn't certain in the darkness. He unscrewed the top and poured a mouthful down his throat before passing the container to me.

I had some difficulty figuring out how to hold it, as it jiggled all over the place and wouldn't stay steady. Suddenly, the man was leaning across my blanket and grasping the container. I thought he was punishing me for my ignorance by taking back his bottle, but instead he held it steady and lifted it to my lips so I could have a drink. "Thank you," I breathed, wiping my chin, "I was so thirsty."

He frowned. "Ye shouldn't be out here if ye don't know how tae find water." I felt as if I was being scolded by a teacher or father, but I didn't reply. The man stood and moved a foot off his blanket. He poured a small amount of water into his hand and began to wipe his nose, cheeks, and chin. From where he was standing, I could see the handsome features emerging I had witnessed while lying on top of him. He replaced the cap on his container and tucked it inside his sporran. He hesitated and then said in a husky voice, "don't be frightened."

I looked at him questioningly in the darkness. "Of *what*?"

"Of *me*," he replied and returned to his blanket. I gasped when the embers illuminated a large scar running from the top of his cheek bone all the way past the bottom of his chin until it disappeared inside his tunic.

"What happened?" I questioned.

"The MacDhomhnaill," he answered simply. He reclined on the blanket again and propped his head up with his hands on the back of his neck.

"That's terrible," I gushed, "why would they *do* such a thing?"

"Ye realize yer talkin' about yer *own* family?"

I blushed scarlet in the darkness. "Not *my* family!" I protested vehemently, sitting up to glare at him, "my relatives would never *do* such a horrible thing to you!" I folded my arms across my chest.

He stared at my determined face in the last of the firelight. "Yer a MacDonald. Ye'd dae *anythin'* tae seek revenge. It's in yer blood." There was a finality to his words that would have shut down an ordinary woman.

"You don't know *anything* about me," I said defensively, "I've known what it's like to be homeless – bullied – *alone*! I would never hurt someone in that way – *never*!" The urgency of my words rang out in the clearing and surprised even me. I clamped my lips shut, knowing I'd said more than I'd intended. I blinked back tears and rolled onto my side so I wouldn't have to see his scarred face.

The sounds of insects filled my head as silent tears rolled down my cheeks. I curled my hands beneath my head, but the ground was hard and uncomfortable. I hated this fucking place – its landscape, its language, and its men most of all!

"Oidhche mhath," the man whispered from his blanket, "Rosa...[8]" I had no idea what he'd just said to me, but I was too angry to ask.

I tossed and turned for ages, unable to find a position that felt right. I had removed my shoes and placed them next to the fire, but as the night deepened, so too did the chill. The silly undergarments they had dressed me in at the wedding did nothing to keep out the damp from the dew settling over the forest floor. Before I knew it, my teeth were chattering and nothing I thought about could take my mind off the cold. Suddenly, I heard movement beside me and the sound of twigs breaking. I turned to ascertain the source and saw the man stooped in front of the fire, tossing in small branches to relight the embers. In a short time, he had a small fire going. He turned away and caught me watching him in the dim light. "Tha mi an dochas gun cuidich sin,[9]" he said softly, sitting beside me on his blanket.

"I don't understand," I admitted quietly, staring at the scar running along his face.

"Sorry," he apologized, "Aam not used tae speakin' in yer tongue." He hesitated. "Ah hope the fire warms ye." He glanced my way, saw me staring at his face, and rolled onto his side to hide it. "Good night."

"Good night," I whispered to his back and settled myself down in front of the fire. It didn't eliminate the chill completely, but it made my toes toasty, which helped some. At least my teeth weren't chattering anymore.

---

[8] Good night, Rose.

[9] I hope that helps.

I stared at the man's back, the firelight flickering on his tartan. I traced the blue and green stripes with my eyes, sure I'd seen the pattern back home – in Scottish tourist shops most likely. I wondered what his name was. He still hadn't asked me mine.

Chapter Three:

I was awake just before dawn; I must have fallen asleep for a few hours, but I missed my comfy bed back home with my over-sized pillow and comforter. I would give *anything* to sleep in a hotel with room service, but I'd take a campsite with running water and electricity at the very least. I heard movement at the edge of the trees and rolled over to see the man skinning a rabbit with his bare hands! *"Oh my god!"* I cried, and turned back over.

The man finished removing the fur and knelt at the ring of stones again where he quickly started a fire and placed the rabbit's lifeless body on a stick in the middle. "If ye want tae eat, ye have tae be willin' tae kill," the man said calmly.

"Good morning to you too," I retorted sarcastically, "it's not every day you witness a poor rabbit getting his skin ripped off!"

"Nae," the man corrected, "not his *skin*; Ah left it on. Ah like mine tagh agus aotrom.[10]"

I rolled my eyes and sat on the damp blanket, wrapping my arms around myself for warmth. "I bet that's something disgusting," I accused. I stretched my toes towards the fire again, the heat chasing away the cold.

"Feumaidh mi aire a ghabhail dhomhsa,[11]" the man told me, a serious expression upon his face now, *"stay here."* In the early morning light, I could make out his scar more readily. It was a faint pink, indicating the injury had occurred some time ago.

"Okay," I responded, distracted by his face.

He seemed to notice and marched angrily into the bushes behind our campsite without a backward glance. I stood and slipped on my shoes,

[10] Nice and juicy.

[11] I need to take care of myself.

stretching my arms over my head to ease the muscles in my back. I rolled my neck side-to-side, and then did several side twists to limber up. Sleeping on my back in a damp forest had aged me twenty years.

When I was finished stretching, I moved away from the fire into the clearing and started with a simple Fukyugata San Kata to warm up. I moved through the sequences slowly, annoyed by how restrictive the wedding dress was. I bent to examine the hem. It was caked in mud, and ripped in two places. I pulled on one spot and it gave way fairly easily. I continued pulling until the hem reached the middle of my thighs. I redid Kata Fukyugata, pushing myself to do each move faster, sharper, and stronger – like Sensei had taught me as a child. I had been doing this kata for so many years, the moves were ingrained – as natural as breathing and walking. When I could feel my heart beating faster, I moved to the more advanced Wankan Kata. It had always been one of my favourites; I deeply admired its perfect blending of both grace and strength.

I was on my third rotation when suddenly the man exclaimed from behind me, "*de a tha thu a 'deanamh?*[12]" I turned gracefully around only to see him rushing towards me. "What are ye doin'?" His glare was so hostile I planted my feet firmly upon the ground and held my hands in front of my face, prepared for an assault. I was too nervous to respond. He was a foot in front of me now. "Who are ye? What are ye plannin'?"

"*Take it easy!*" I finally managed, but I remained in defensive posture.

"*An do chuir an Diabhal thugaibh?*[13]" he shouted, lunging at me. This time, I was ready. It was easier to see in pale morning light. I easily

---

[12] What are you doing?

[13] Did the Devil send you?

leapt back, moving into a cat stance, waiting for his next move. His cheeks were red and a vein in his neck was pulsing. "Are ye a witch?"

"*Oh my god!*" I cried, incredulity washing over me. Was this guy *serious*? I was lost in the woods with a Quaker.

Suddenly, the man pulled a dagger from his stocking and launched it at me so fast I barely had time to react. Fortunately, I was already in cat stance so I did the only thing I could think of in such close proximity: I kicked him in the elbow to dislodge the weapon. The knife flew out of his hand and he grasped his arm. "Aam goin' tae *kill ye, witch!*" He was completely overcome with rage. He ran towards me again, but I leapt back a second time.

"*I'm not a witch!*" I screamed, leaping away from him two more times.

The next instance, I wasn't so lucky; instead of lunging, the man barrelled towards me and didn't stop. When I tried to leap out of his path, he kept going, his arms outstretched as he clobbered me to the ground. His knee pressed into my chest, pinning me to the earth, but I was so dazed from the fall I couldn't hear anything he said at first. Suddenly, something wet covered me and I blinked through the water, registering the man's face hovering over me. "*What are ye?*" he was crying, "*answer me! Who sent ye?*"

I sucked in a deep breath, feeling my lung inflating after the wind had been knocked out of me. "No one," I moaned, "*please…*"

When I came to, I was lying underneath the tree, my hands bound together with a thick coil of rope. The man was eating what was left of the rabbit he'd caught, and my horse was grazing in the trees to my right. "You untied her," I tried to say, but my voice cracked from thirst.

"Which Aam *never* gonna dae with *ye!*" he retorted, tossing the empty carcass into the fire and standing. He rolled my blanket up and strapped it to Selma.

"That's *my* horse!" I accused, "you can't take her!"

"Ye stole her – and now Aam stealin' her back!" he cried, glaring at me as he hauled me roughly to my feet. He pushed me towards Selma's saddle and forced my right foot into her stirrup. "*Get on,*" he demanded, shoving my bound hands onto the horse's back. I heaved my leg over her side and clung to the saddle horn with both hands. "*Bu choir dhomh fhagail aig na madaidhean-allaidh!*[14]" he said angrily as he tugged on Selma's lead and turned into the woods in the opposite direction I'd come the previous night.

"You *know* I don't know what that means!" I accused.

The man glanced over his shoulder at me. "Ah said Ah should feed ye tae the wild animals."

I gasped. "I was only *exercising!*" When he continued weaving through the trees, completely ignoring me, I felt as if my head was going to pop off. "Are you completely *daft?*" I taunted, "a witless wonder? How did you make it to adulthood? *Hmm?* Does your mother still change your diaper?" He pretended he couldn't hear me. I curled my hands into tight balls, my face flushed deep crimson. "Maybe *you're* the Devil! Did you ever think of that? You see a woman exercising and you're so fucking

---

[14] I should leave you to the wolves!

sexist – so god-damned *jealous* – you attack her!" He scoffed and kept walking. "*No*! You *assault* her! Well, forgive *me* for trying to stay fit! Forgive *me* for stretching after sleeping all *fucking* night on the ground and eating your shitty-assed rabbits!"

Finally, the man stopped dead in his tracks. I exhaled and waited. He turned to face me in slow motion. "Are ye finished?" he asked.

I gritted my teeth, infuriated by his response. "I want an *apology*!" I shouted.

He shook his head. "Ah suggest ye keep quiet, unless ye want yer groom's *friends* tae find ye." He stared at me meaningfully while I processed his words.

"I'm not a witch," I pouted, changing the subject.

He smirked. "Ah *know*," he said simply, and turned back around.

"You *know*?"

He sighed deeply as he began to walk again. "Aye, Ah knew as soon as ye passed out."

"*Took you long enough*!" I complained, "I told you at least *three* times!"

I heard him chuckle. "And dae ye think a real witch would confess what she was?"

I hesitated, unsure how to respond. I didn't believe in *real* witches, so how could I reason with a man so superstitious he'd performed his own mini exorcism? "I guess not," I replied diplomatically.

"And Ah don't believe a real witch could be taken down so easily," he added, an undertone of amusement in his voice.

My defenses shot up again. "*Easily*?" I retorted, "I was trying not to *hurt* you!"

"A bheil mi a 'coimhead goirt, Rosa[15]?" he laughed.

"Why can't you speak English?" I asked peevishly, already annoyed by the constant bumping up and down in the saddle.

"It does not come as naturally tae me," he replied, "why don't ye speak *mah* language?"

"I don't know how!" I exclaimed, "*obviously!*"

The man glanced over his shoulder at my annoyed expression and laughed. "Ye could learn. Ah could teach ye. We have a long way tae go."

"I don't think that's possible," I hedged.

"Why not?" he inquired, his voice frustratingly cheerful, "are ye a – how did ye phrase it? – *witless wonder?*"

"*Of course not!*" I cried, "I'm a quick learner. I've always done well in school…"

He glanced back at me sharply. "*School?*"

I hesitated, wondering what the right answer was. "I've had a few teachers – *yes.*"

He pondered that for a few seconds and then nodded. "Ye've been fortunate."

"Did you go?" I asked softly.

The man didn't answer right away. After a few seconds, he replied, "nae – mah parents taught me at home. Mah older brother went though."

"You have a brother?"

"Two," he answered, but gave no details.

"Wow," I murmured, "that's a large family."

"*And* a sister," he added, turning halfway around to see my reaction.

---

[15] Do I look hurt, Rose?

"*Really*? That's so lucky."

The man fell into step beside Selma so he wouldn't have to walk backwards to see my face. "Ye think so?"

"Yes, of course!" I replied easily, "*four* children? That's very lucky."

"Dae ye have siblings?" he asked.

I looked down into his curious blue eyes and swallowed. "No, I was given away when I was a baby. I never knew my parents. I don't really know if my mom or dad have other children. If they do, I've never been contacted."

The man watched my face intently as I spoke. "Who raised ye?"

"I – I lived in homes," I answered tentatively, feeling suddenly ashamed, "I had people take me in – and then sometimes they moved or had babies of their own, and didn't want me anymore." I shrugged, pretending it wasn't a big deal.

"A difficult life fer a child," he commented astutely.

I laughed ruefully. "It was nothing. I survived."

"Ah can see that," he stated, still watching me with intense eyes that saw through me. I glanced ahead and cleared my throat.

"It's why my karate teachers became my family," I explained, "my Sensei – the other members of the Dojo. They accepted me and taught me how to respect myself and others, even when I didn't feel so loveable."

"*Karate*? *Sensei*?" the man asked, his brow furrowing in frustration.

"Sorry," I apologized, "karatedo is an art. I studied it from the age of six. Now I teach it. It's helped me in so many ways. I can't even *begin* to describe them all to you..." I could feel my energy changing as I spoke about karate. The dismal cloud that had clung to me back at camp was slowly lifting with each word about my adoptive family back home.

"What dae ye mean – *art*?"

I smiled at him unexpectedly. "A way of life. I was lost when I started karate and it showed me a path to self-acceptance and discipline I hadn't been taught anywhere else. The Dojo welcomed me in – an *orphan* – and gave me a family to return to each week. I learned how to be a good person, and how to heal pieces of myself that had been broken by others." I realized perhaps I'd described too much, so I abruptly stopped talking.

The man had listened intently to everything I'd said. "*Karate*," he said, as if practicing the word. We walked in silence for a few minutes before he spoke again. "Ye've given me much tae think aboot. Ah hope ye don't mind if Ah don't speak fer a while."

"Okay," I said softly, wondering if my admissions would be important later, or if my story was just another step towards getting to know my captor while we journeyed to a mysterious destination of his choosing.

Chapter Four:

The land began to slowly incline, making our path through the trees even slower. I wondered if there was a faster way to reach our destination, but I stayed silent as the man led us through the tangle of weeds, over steep hills, and around (and sometimes through) small ponds. I wondered what the man's boots were made from, as they seemed well constructed and waterproof. After two hours, I finally couldn't hold it any longer and had to ask to stop so I could go to the bathroom. I hadn't camped since I was a kid, and I'd never gone outside. I was consumed by embarrassment when I requested the stop, and further mortified to have to ask the man for suggestions. "I have no idea where to go," I hedged, my cheeks flushing as he helped me slide out of Selma's saddle.

"Don't wander tay far," the man instructed, "ye don't want tae get lost in the woods."

"Okay," I said, my eyes flitting everywhere but his, "but by a tree — *or* — ?"

A smile tugged at his lips. "Ye've never gone outside before?"

I shook my head emphatically. *"Never."*

His eyes ran down the length of my torn wedding dress. "Well, it should be easier now ye've got rid of half the thing," he teased.

My cheeks burned. "Will you at least unbind my hands? I don't want to make a complete debacle of it…"

"Aye, Rosa," he agreed and began untying the rope.

"Thank god," I breathed when it slipped off, "that was hurting." My wrists were red when I turned them over to examine them.

"Hurry," he said, glancing at the sky instead of my hands, "it looks like rain."

"What will we do then?" I asked.

"Try not tae step in any puddles, Sasannach," the man said with feigned gravity.

I rolled my eyes and stomped towards the edge of the trees. When I pushed though, I found myself in a strange clearing. Paths flattened in the grass wound every which way, flanked by hills on either side. Directly in front of me were a number of smooth, grey stones, weathered from what looked like hundreds of years. Was this a graveyard? Why hadn't the man warned me? To my left was another patch of trees. I decided to do my business in there. It was an ordeal I won't describe fully here, but going to the bathroom in a wedding dress is not something I had much practice with. Even with the bottom cut off, the gratuitous undergarments made it difficult to squat. I eventually decided to remove the dress altogether. I felt relief for the first time in twelve hours! I kicked some dead leaves onto the spot and moved back into the strange clearing. I wondered what had made the paths and stones. Did humans live here? With the hills on either side, the scene was majestic. I hugged my dress to my chest and observed everything. This was the first time since the wedding ceremony I could honestly say I was intrigued by this place I'd somehow been dropped into. Beyond the stones, I could make out a large circle in the dirt with six or seven smaller circles emanating from its centre. It reminded me of throwing a stone into a river and watching the ripples it created. *"De tha thu a 'smaoineachadh a tha thu a' deanamh?*[16]" a deep voice growled from the trees.

I whirled around and saw the man emerging, a dark scowl deepening the scar on his face. "It's lovely, isn't it?" I asked, pointing to the beauty of the scene in front of us.

---

[16] What do you think you're doing?

The man started, and I thought his eyes were going to explode. His cheeks turned bright red and he gestured to my dress. "Why are ye unclothed?" he exclaimed angrily. I stared at him wide eyed, my brain becoming muddled as I watched his hostility grow. *"Cuir air e!*[17]" he yelled, turning his back and clenching his fists at his sides. I unfolded my dress with trembling fingers and managed to tug it over my head and brush the skirts down to cover my legs again. "Are ye *decent*?" he asked, his back still to me.

"Of course," I replied.

He swivelled to face me. His cheeks were still red. "Dae ye come from a *britheamh*?[18]"

"No, I come from Huntsville. I already told – "

"Get back on the cuddie!" he commanded, *"we're leavin'!"* His voice was so gruff I felt tears start in my eyes. I blinked them back as hard as I could and trailed after his angry figure. The majesty of the Fairy Glen was all but a memory.

---

[17] Put it on!

[18] brothel

Chapter Five:

The man had bound my hands again despite the angry red marks clearly visible on my wrists. He hadn't spoken a word since the Fairy Glen, and that was over an hour ago. He had been right about the rain too. It had started to spit, but so far hadn't gotten any worse. It actually felt nice upon my hair and face, counteracting the closeness of the forest we were picking our way through. I wanted to ask him if he always travelled this way, or whether he sometimes used more established pathways. I wanted to ask if he ever used an umbrella, when it got *really* stormy, or if he just let his clothes get soaking wet. I wanted to ask him why he'd been so angry at me in the clearing. I wanted conversation with another human being, but he was moody and uncommunicative. I could tell he was still angry, because he walked in front of Selma the whole time and never turned to look at me. I wasn't sure why, but I wanted that most of all: for him to *see* me. I was so far from home, but had no idea *why*. I had no idea how to get back to Huntsville, or what had caused me to enter Scotland in the *first* place. It made me sad, and took all my energy not to break down and weep.

I hadn't eaten since the leg of rabbit the night before. My insides were like a deflated balloon. I was also thirsty. The man didn't stop, however, and never took any provisions for himself either. Perhaps he wasn't aware I was hungry or thirsty. I considered asking him for a drink from that strange container he had, or asking if he had any dried meat stuffed inside his great pockets, but I clamped my lips shut and stared at the conifers closing in on both sides. The paths were becoming narrower, and if I'd been by myself I wouldn't have even noticed there *were* any paths. Finally, the man stopped abruptly and started to head into the cover of the trees. "I'll be back," he stated without further explanation.

I sat atop Selma, my hands bound in front of me, my wedding dress casting a faint glow in the dim woods. I sighed, looking around for anything to eat. I was famished and couldn't rely on this man for survival. I managed to shimmy sideways in Selma's saddle, gripping the horn for dear life. When I felt my foot touch the stirrup, I flung my other leg over her side and planted both feet upon the ground. It was tricky to balance without the use of my arms individually, but I shuffled towards the edge of the trees on the opposite side from where he had disappeared. I knelt down in the dirt, eyeing the foliage for signs of nuts or wild berries. The air was still misty, but eventually I discovered a patch of green and black berries. I guessed the black ones were ripe; they were a dark purplish black – probably wild blueberries. Just as I was about to start picking them, I heard the distinct sound of another horse's hooves pounding along the road outside our forest sanctuary. I hunched lower, listening closely. The horse did not slow its pace when it neared my position, and had soon receded into the distance.

I tried to get closer to the bushes, but my bound hands made it difficult to manoeuvre. Finally, I gave in and knelt in the earth. The dress was ruined anyway, and wasn't even mine. I stared at the plant, noticing its pretty, white, star-shaped flowers. If I could just get a mouthful, the man wouldn't be the wiser and I could travel for a longer distance without fainting. "What are ye doin'? Did Ah tell ye tae get down?" I was so startled by the sound of his voice behind me that I jumped and fell sideways into the dirt. I sat back up with great effort. The man was glaring at me, his scar directly in my line of sight.

"I was – I was *hungry*," I stammered, my face feeling hot under his gaze.

The man's eyes darted to the bushes in front of me and he exploded. *"An do dh'ith thu iad?*[19]*"* He quickly knelt beside me, grasping my jaw and yelling, *"co mheaud?*[20]*"* His vehemence was alarming. I started to cry, despite how ashamed it made me to do so. He used his free hand to stick a finger inside my mouth, peering inside while he rubbed the inside of my cheeks. His skin tasted bitter, like dandelion leaves in a wild-root salad. I shook my head and glared at him. He removed his finger and pulled his flask from his pocket. *Finally*! He was going to give me a *drink*! But instead of pouring water down my *throat*, he doused his fingers and ran them around the outside of my lips! This man was unbelievably obtuse! Could he not see I was *thirsty*?

He was so close to me I could smell his musky skin. He was a combination of leather, trees, and sweat. I was still crying, but I had the sense to lean towards the man's other hand – the one holding the flask. *"Please!"* I begged, *"water!"*

"Just a tiny drink," he advised, bringing the flask to my lips. He tipped a small amount down my throat and I swallowed greedily.

"Oh, *come on*!" I cried, more tears falling, "I'm *thirsty*! *Please*!"

"How many did ye eat?" he questioned, leaning back on his heels so he could see me clearly.

"I haven't eaten *anything* since the rabbit last night. I'm *starving*! *Please*!" I sobbed, hot tears coursing down my cheeks. I wasn't even embarrassed anymore. I just wanted food and water and my own bed at home. Netflix would be a bonus, but I wouldn't complain if I just got the first two. In fact, I'd sleep on the ground for *two weeks* if I could just get a long drink from this guy's container!

[19] Did you eat these?

[20] How many?

"Nae berries?" he inquired, his brow furrowed with distrust.

"I didn't have a *chance*!" I exclaimed, blinking hard to push the tears away so I could see his face clearer.

He sighed with what looked like relief and nodded. "We can go then."

"*What*?" I cried in disbelief, "can I have a drink first?"

"Ah already *gave* ye a bevvy," he reminded me. He avoided my gaze as he grasped my arms and hauled me to my feet.

"Can I wipe my face?" I asked, my voice trembling.

"Ye cry tay much," he stated, pulling me towards the horse, "Aam not used tae it."

"I actually *don't* cry too much! I hardly cry at *all*. Until I met *you*!" I was so angry, I wanted to punch the man in his smug little face. He ignored me and lifted my foot into the stirrup instead. I pulled it back out and glared defiantly at him. "You're an asshole, you know that? I said I was *thirsty*! Are you deaf?"

He sighed and finally met my gaze. "Ah don't have much left. Aam goin' without. Ah didn't expect tae be sharin'. I'll fill it at the next stream."

I bit my lip to stop it from trembling as I processed his words. His eyes were such a pretty colour. "Okay," I managed, shame flooding through me again.

"We should save it," he said less gruffly.

"Mmmhmm," I murmured, still lost in his eyes.

"Will ye get in the saddle now?" he asked.

"Maybe," I breathed, still staring at him. I felt suddenly lightheaded. "Docha...[21]" I added absentmindedly.

[21] Maybe

The man's eyes widened. "'S docha?"

"*Hmm?*"

"Are ye sure ye didn't eat any berries?" he questioned, frowning again.

"*Mmmhmm,*" I answered distractedly.

He shook his head and lifted my foot into the stirrup again. "Come on – we still have a long way."

I swung my leg over Selma's side and held on to the saddle horn. "Where are we going?"

"Tae get answers," the man said vaguely as he took hold of Selma's lead.

"Someone else was in a hurry too," I commented, "I heard him racing by on his horse. Or she. I couldn't see the rider."

The man whirled to face me. "*What? When?*" He dropped the lead and came to my side. "De cho fada air ais?[22]"

I shrugged. "When you went into the trees. *Twenty minutes?*"

"*Ye should have said something right away!*" he exclaimed, the angry expression back upon his face.

"I *would* have if you hadn't freaked out about the berries!" I said defensively.

The man threw his hands into the air in exasperation. "*Sgailean oidhche!*[23]"

"You know I can't understand you, right?" I retorted in frustration, "things would go a lot quicker if you'd just speak *English!*"

The vein in the side of the man's head started to pulse again. Maybe he was going to have an aneurism and I'd be set free! One could

[22] How long ago?

[23] Night shade!

---

only hope for small mercies in such situations. *"Night shade!"* he said through gritted teeth, "ye can thank me by keepin' yer gob shut the rest of the way!" He yanked on Selma's lead to get us moving.

"Thank you for *what*? Shoving your dirty fingers in my mouth? You are utterly revolting, you know that?"

He stopped abruptly and glared at me over his shoulder. "Fer savin' yer *life*! The berries are *poisonous*!" He rolled his eyes as if it was the most obvious fact in the whole world.

"Well, *excuse* me!" I shot back, "I'm sorry we can't all be rangers of the god damn north!"

"De tha ifrinn a 'ciallachadh?[24]" he spat.

"We ought to name you Aragorn, mister '*I'm so amazing in the wilderness*'! All bow down to the King of Gondor!" My cheeks were flushed with anger as I shouted at him.

He stared at me, speechless, for a few seconds and then yelled, *"tha thu craicte!*[25]"

---

[24] What the Hell does that mean?

[25] You're crazy!

Chapter Six:

We plodded along in a stony silence for about an hour before the rain finally made its real appearance. The forest became so dark, I could hardly see the man just a few feet in front of me. The trees sheltered us from much of the deluge, but the places where the foliage thinned became miserable. My hair, braided and coiled upon my head by some woman at the castle, was dripping into my eyes. Finally, the man stopped walking and pulled Selma into a denser part of the forest and tied her lead to a branch. He helped me out of the saddle and said gruffly, "we'll wait here fer it tae die down."

He arranged his great kilt upon the ground and motioned for me to sit. I managed to fall into a seated position, since my bound hands made graceful movements impossible. I was still angry as I watched the man collect stones for a fire pit. Soon, he had lit a fire and the flames warmed me some. I was still famished, however, and it was becoming harder to think of anything else. Even the man's arms were beginning to look like tasty chicken legs. He suddenly glanced my way and saw me examining him. His lips were a tight line as he barked, "*stop starin'*! Ah don't need a constant reminder!"

I was taken aback. "A reminder of *what*?"

"*Ah told ye tae be quiet!*" he responded testily, and sat upon a large boulder on the other side of the fire, rubbing his hands together for warmth.

I averted my eyes, feeling stung. What had I done to offend him so deeply? "I was just watching you make the fire," I stated softly.

I stared into the flames, feeling crushed. I missed my co-workers and their laughter. We always made it fun, even when customers frustrated us. I could picture each of their faces – their smiles – and an aching loneliness throbbed inside my chest. Sudden movement to my side startled me out of my thoughts. I glanced to my right and saw the man holding something out to me. I took it gingerly from him and looked down: it was a handful of nuts, seeds, and berries. "Thank you," I whispered in surprise, bringing both hands to my lips so I could eat the snack like a horse grazing upon grass. It was a fragrant mixture; I'm sure I probably swallowed lint from the man's pockets as well, but I didn't care. The urgency of my hunger made me amenable to whatever was offered. I glanced towards the man's position on the stone when I'd finished, and he was watching me with interest. "No poisonous berries?" I said to make conversation.

The man's eyes didn't smile, but his tone was not unkind. "Nae." He watched me for a moment and then added, "Ah have more, but I'll save it in case Ah can't catch anythin' tonight."

"Okay," I said softly. I felt suddenly shy. Silence descended and I sensed the ache spreading through my chest again. I was desperate for connection, no matter what form it took. "Do you think we'll be here long?"

"The sky is dark. We'll see."

"Okay," I repeated, feeling disappointed I didn't know how to engage the strange man. After a few minutes of silence, I said hesitantly, "I'm sorry, but I need to use the bathroom."

He sighed and stood, coming to my side to untie my hands. I gasped as the rope slipped off. The skin was raw and smarting. Tears stung my eyes as I examined them. "Thank you," I breathed, trying desperately not to cry.

"Leave yer frock *on*," the man said gruffly.

I glanced at him and his eyes were stern. "I just didn't want to soil it," I said in embarrassment.

"Dae yer best," he stated firmly, "if mah sister ever took *her* frock off outside, mah father would lash her."

I blushed. "I wasn't *undressed*. I had a foot of other stuff on!" I protested.

"Ye were naked," he insisted.

"No, I – "

"Ah said stop talkin'. Dh'fhaodadh tu feum a dheanamh de mhath a 'briseadh ort fhein.[26]" His voice was as hard as steel.

I turned quickly from him and disappeared into the trees. I pushed through several to distance myself from him before hiking up the stupid wedding dress and undergarments so I could try to go to the bathroom without getting urine all over myself. It took a great deal of finesse to manage, but I finally did the deed, covered the spot, and pulled the gown back down. Just as I was about to head back to our campsite, I heard the sound of a horse's whinny. I froze, listening intently. It came again, but it was off to my right and not back at camp. "A bheil uidh agad anns an t-salchar?[27]" a masculine voice questioned. I turned slowly, and there he was: about thirty years old, maybe five-ten, dressed in a faded kilt of red and black. He was holding what looked like a sword in his right hand, although I'd never actually seen one in real life.

"I don't understand," I said cautiously, "do you speak English?"

"Sgrios thu an dreasa,[28]" the man commented, taking a step towards me.

---

[26] You could use a good lashing yourself.

[27] Fancy a roll in the dirt?

[28] You destroyed the dress.

"I'm sorry, I don't understand. My friend can help translate," I explained, but the man was eyeing me with disdain.

He took another step towards me, and pointed the sword at my feet. "Bha thu a 'call na brogan.[29]" He lifted the blade and pointed it at my privates. "Bha mo bhrathair deiseil gus sin a dheanamh an-raoir![30]" He spit upon the ground. "*Ungrateful*!" he finally said in English.

"No, I'm *not* ungrateful – just lost," I said, hoping he'd understand.

"Thig a-nis,[31]" the man ordered, gesturing with his sword to the edge of trees he had entered through.

I shook my head. "I'm sorry – I don't understand your language," I began, but he was already walking towards me, his sword still drawn. My eyes opened wide. "*Please* – put that away!"

The next thing I knew, the blade was pointed at my throat. "Come now, ungrateful wench. Tristen is waitin'…"

"Who is *Tristen*?" I asked, staring down the edge of the blade into the man's furious green eyes. He might as well have been my brother, they were so similar to my own.

"Bu choir dhomh do ghearradh direach beagan…[32]" the man threatened, and I felt the tip of the sword touch my throat. I didn't dare speak, or move, or even swallow. "*Ye shamed heem*!" I held my breath, staring into his eyes, waiting for a moment to act. The man pulled the tip of the sword back an inch and remarked, "bidh mi a 'cordadh riut mar

---

[29] You ruined the shoes.

[30] My brother was ready to take that last night!

[31] Come now.

[32] I should cut you just a little.

mhuc agus cha bhith fios aig duine sam bith…[33]" His lips curled into a cruel smile.

I seized the moment by taking a quick step back, swivelling sideways, and kicking the hilt of the sword hard to dislodge it. The man was so startled, he just stared at his empty hand instead of retaliating. That gave me time to rotate to my other side and kick him as hard as I could in the face. He stumbled backwards, tripping over a tree root. While he scrambled to stand, I came at him again, kicking him two more times in quick succession. The final blow rendered him unconscious. I was breathing hard, sweat glistening on my brow. What had just happened? Who was this man, and who was Tristen? I gathered he was one of the angry groomsmen, but I hadn't understood half of what he'd said. Suddenly, I froze, my senses honing in on the sounds of the forest. Had the man come alone, or were there more? I glanced from side-to-side, but couldn't make out any movement in the trees. I walked as gracefully as I could in my bulky dress, heading back to camp in a wide circle to avoid being seen.

As I got closer, I heard a loud crash followed by a series of words I didn't understand. I emerged on the opposite side from our fire, but unfortunately that's exactly where the man who was leading me and a new figure were fighting. The other man was dressed in a similar red and black kilt to the man I had fought, but he was shorter and more muscular. He held a sword at his side and was facing the man I knew, who held nothing but a small dagger. He glanced up when he saw me, not difficult in a white gown. His brow furrowed and he shouted, *"go back!"*, which alerted his assailant to my presence. The bulky man glanced over his shoulder to observe me, giving the man *I* knew a chance to attack. He danced from

[33] I'll have you like a pig and no one will know.

51

side-to-side, jerking the dagger every which way to keep the man guessing where it would land. The bulky man tried to back up, but the forest was too dense. He had his back to the trees and had only one choice: to slash at my man with his sword. It caught him on the shoulder, tearing the top of his tunic. To my utter amazement, he didn't cry out; instead, he punched the side of the blade out of his way, and stabbed the bulky man in the bicep. The bulky man bellowed, and used the side of the blade to smash the man's wrist. His gamble worked, since it dislodged the dagger. The next thing I knew, my man was standing with both his hands in the air, a sword pressed to his throat just as one had been against mine moments earlier.

I inhaled sharply and took a cautious step towards the bulky man who was panting like a dog. "*Please,*" I said, holding my own hands in the air, "I'll come with you."

"*Mar ifrinn bidh thu!*[34]" my man shouted, despite being in mortal danger.

"Yes, I *will!*" I exclaimed, taking another step towards the bulky man who was eyeing me cautiously.

"*Na falbh le Domhnallach!*[35]" my man hollered.

"*Duin do chab!*[36]" the bulky man ordered peevishly, glaring from me to the man and back again.

"Take me with you, but don't hurt him," I pleaded. I was almost within range of the bulky man.

---

[34] Like Hell you will!

[35] Never go with a MacDonald!

[36] Shut up!

"*B 'fhearr leam basachadh!*[37]" my man spat, his face red. He glared at me and shouted, "*go back! Run!*"

"*Please*," I said, addressing the MacDonald, "I'll go with you. Just don't hurt anyone, and I'll go. *Please take me!*"

"*Are ye crazy?*" my man screamed, the scar on the side of his face as livid as he was.

"I *want* to go. I *want* to marry a MacDonald," I said sweetly, moving one step closer.

"*Boireannach gorach!*[38]" my man exclaimed, which provided just the diversion I needed.

The bulky man was in the middle of telling my man to shut up again, when I switched from having my hands in the air in a helpless posture, to moving into a cat stance for less than a second before kicking the unsuspecting man's wrist as hard as I could. The sword crashed to the ground and, while my man was picking it up, I had already kicked the bulky guy in the throat, then launched a series of swift punches to his chest, throat, and forehead. He was stunned, but he shook his head to clear it and pulled a dagger from his stocking. He wasn't quick enough; my man slashed at the bulky man's arm with the sword. What happened next will be forever burned into my brain: blood spurted into the air as the man's hand was severed! I was so startled, I just stood gaping. "*Tiugainn!*" my man was shouting, but when I didn't react he grasped my sleeve and hauled me across the clearing to our fire. He retrieved his great kilt and lifted me into the saddle in less than ten seconds, pulling Selma out of the cover of trees into a grassy area. The sky was grey and the rain torrential

---

[37] I'd rather die!

[38] Stupid woman!

as he unexpectedly leapt into the saddle behind me and whipped Selma to signal her to gallop.

The man urged Selma to run as fast as she could, for as long as she was able. When she began to tire, he moved her to the opposite side of the road from where we had been trekking all this time, and we entered the cover of trees once again. I could hear the man's heavy breathing behind me, and see the ripples of his forearm muscles as he directed the reins around my sides. Despite the dense trees, the man forced Selma to carry us around trunks and over roots for another hour. When she finally began to resist the urgent pace, he dismounted and walked in front, holding her lead and manoeuvering past rocks and vines. Neither of us had spoken to one another since leaving the gruesome scene, and I still felt so nauseous each time I remembered it that I was grateful he didn't address me.

Chapter Seven:

We pushed on, the rain drowning us every time the trees above opened even slightly to let the sky in. I hadn't wandered through the wilderness before, but something told me we were no longer headed in our original direction. By nightfall, I was starving again and my thirst was becoming unbearable. Several times I caught myself nodding off, and finally I actually slid out of the saddle and almost toppled off Selma. Fortunately, the man noticed and caught me before I could fall. "*Co!*" he murmured to Selma. She stopped abruptly, whinnied quietly, and looked around for grass to eat.

"*Sorry,*" I apologized to the man as he set me firmly upon the ground and released me, "I tried to stay awake."

"We'll make camp, but Aam not lightin' a fire taenight," he told me, pulling Selma to the side of the forest and securing her to a trunk.

"Okay," I said quietly, not wanting to complain about how cold my toes were, or how hungry I was.

The ground was damp from the misty air inside the forest. The man laid his great kilt upon the ground and then undid the bed roll too. He placed them side-by-side, as we had slept the previous night, but he also spent a half hour cutting several branches and criss-crossing them above our spot to form a shelter. It protected us from the elements, but inside it felt rather intimate – like being in a room rather than in the great outdoors with all of nature. I sat on the far side of my blanket, feeling shy and self-conscious in his presence. I tried not to observe parts of him I found interesting, such as the well-made leather boots he wore, or the stockings that reached the bottoms of his knees, revealing a few inches of toned thighs when he was seated beside me. He wore a tunic with ruffled sleeves that were visible when he had the great kilt off. "Would ye like a drink?" he suddenly asked to break the silence.

I glanced at his face and he was looking at me with what appeared to be concern, but perhaps I was imagining it. "Is there enough?" I asked hesitantly.

"Aye, Ah can collect rain," he told me quietly, reaching inside his sporran to remove the drinking container.

He unscrewed it for me and passed it across the small space. It was dim, but I could still see the scar on the side of his handsome face. His hair was a dark brown, almost black in this light, but flecked with red. I had always wished for brown hair, or something more subdued. Mine was the equivalent of screaming, "*I'm here!*" to everyone in the room. I held the floppy bottle and moved it tentatively to my lips. The man reached out to steady it, and I took a long drink. "Oh my god, *thank you!*" I breathed, opening my eyes. When I looked at him, he was watching me with those same intense eyes he'd used several times since we'd met. I wondered what he was thinking.

"S e do bheatha,[39]" he murmured, still studying my face.

My shyness returned and I found myself blushing. I glanced down and noticed, for the first time, I had blood splattered on the side of my dress. "*Oh god!*" I cried, sitting up straight, "*oh god!*"

The man leaned towards me and said, "tha e ceart gu leor" in a soft voice.

I stared into his eyes, my heart racing and my hands trembling. "I'm covered in someone else's *blood!*"

"Ye'll be okay," he assured me calmly.

---

[39] You're welcome.

"Why am I freaking out then?" I asked, showing him my shaking hands.

Suddenly, he grasped them in his own and held them against the blanket. His were large, and strong, and warm, and within his mine couldn't tremble anymore. He waited for a few seconds and then asked, "*better?*"

"I think so," I responded softly. He removed his hands and I looked at mine. They were no longer shaking. "*Thank you,*" I whispered, feeling vulnerable. Again, thoughts of home threatened to overwhelm me.

"Nae, thank *ye*," the man said in a husky voice. I glanced at him sharply.

"What do you mean?"

"Ye saved mah life," he told me, his expression serious, "if ye hadn't come when ye did, Eh'd be wearin' more than a scar…"

"Oh, that," I mumbled, "I don't want to talk about it. It makes me feel sick."

"Okay," he said quietly.

"How could you *do* that?" I asked, despite telling him I didn't want to discuss it.

"They would have *killed* me, or taken ye back tae be married. Is that what ye wanted?"

"No, of course not," I replied in a small voice.

"So ye were deceivin' him?" the man pressed, a hint of curiosity in his voice.

I met his gaze again. "When I told him I wanted to go with him?"

"Aye," the man answered, his eyes never leaving my face.

"I was buying time," I explained carefully, "distracting him so he would be more vulnerable…"

"Ah see," the man mused.

"I fought with one other man," I suddenly said, "but I couldn't understand anything he said. He spoke *your* language, mostly. He was carrying a sword and mentioned Tristen. Do you know him?"

The man's jaw twitched. "Why dae ye always hide important things?" He seemed irritated.

"*What*?" I exclaimed, "we were racing away from there, and not talking. You didn't speak a word either until we got *here*!"

He stared at me for a few seconds, and then sighed. "Aye, that's true."

"Oh my *god*, that's the first time you've ever agreed with me – on *anything*!" I cried, feeling strangely triumphant.

The man looked at me, not seeming amused. "'S docha," he said evenly.

I laughed. "'S docha," I agreed.

"What's yer name?" he suddenly asked.

I couldn't hide my surprise, but I answered him honestly. "Brigid."

"*Brigid*?"

"*Aye*," I said, imitating him.

He actually laughed too. "Brigid *MacDonald*?"

"Yes." He nodded thoughtfully. "Aren't you going to tell me *your* name?" I questioned.

"Nae."

"That's not fair!" I accused, "I just saved your life! I should at *least* know your name!"

"Aye, but Ah already saved yers."

"Oh, *really*? And when was that?"

"Nightshade. *Remember*?"

"The *berries*?" I asked, "they really *were* poisonous?"

"Aye." His expression was soft in the darkness.

"Those other berries you fed me, what were *they*?"

"Wild rose," he answered. "*Rosa,*" he murmured, staring at me intently again.

"You've said that to me before," I commented, recognizing another word from his dialect, "what does it mean?"

"*Rose,*" he repeated.

"Why do you keep saying it?"

"Because Ah didn't know yer name before," he explained, "and it seemed a good word fer ye."

I stared at him blankly. "*Rosa*? For *me*?"

"Aye," the man said.

"I don't understand," I admitted, feeling stupid, "how am I a rose?"

The man grinned in the darkness and pointed at my hair. "Ah could see ye in the forest, all red and white ye were."

I blushed. "You're making fun of me!" I complained.

"Nae," he said, his tone serious again, "not at all…"

"I was bullied for it," I found myself saying, "they made fun of the colour; called me names…"

"Other bairns?" he questioned with a frown.

"Yes," I responded, trying not to remember too much from the past, "they would make up songs and chants. Then if I defended myself, they got physical."

"Mah youngest brother has red hair, but his is *ghastly*. Looks like a pumpkin." He chuckled.

"*See*? Now *you're* mocking the colour *too*!"

"Aye, but he's mah *brother*. It's mah *job* tae dae it. Ah don't know why the kids'd tease *ye* fer it; yer hair is darker – like a rose. It's bonnie."

I stared at him in silence, my throat choked with words I couldn't manage to speak. The man seemed instantly embarrassed as well, and quickly changed the subject. "Mah name's Ferghus, if ye must know..."

"Ferghus," I repeated. I found myself smiling. "Nice to meet you, *Ferghus*. I've never known anyone with that name before..."

"*Really*? It's common on the island. Known two or three mahself."

"We're on an *island*?" I blurted without thinking.

Ferghus frowned. "Ye don't remember where ye *are*?"

I blushed, wondering how much to admit. "I don't remember *anything*. Like I said, one minute I was at work – the next I was being fussed over by some woman before the wedding."

"They brought ye over on a *boat*?"

"I don't know – I can't remember *anything*."

"Ye said ye live far away – in *Huntsville*?"

"Yes."

"Never heard of it."

"It's not *in* Scotland."

The man leaned closer, staring at me intently. "Where is it?"

"Canada."

"What's that?" he questioned, his eyes registering confusion.

I hesitated, trying to think back to my high school history and geography classes. When had Canada been discovered? If Ferghus had never heard of Canada, then I must be somewhere *years* before 1867! "It's a *really* new country across the ocean," I explained.

Ferghus stared at me, as if doubting everything I was saying. "Ah don't see how that's possible."

"Which part?"

Ferghus sighed. "Ah know enough about politics. Ah might not have gone tae *school*, but Ah always have mah ears open fer news. Eh'd know if a new country had been formed..." His tone was accusatory.

"Maybe we shouldn't talk about it then; you sound angry."

"Aam not *angry*," he said defensively, "just don't like bein' lied tae."

I could feel my skin growing hot. I sat straighter and pursed my lips. "I'm *not* lying. Think about it logically!"

"*Logic*?" he scoffed, "now we're into *philosophy*? Nae thank ye. Give me *facts* – somethin' Ah can see, or hear, or smell."

"Okay, *fine*!" I exclaimed, my eyes flashing, "I'm not going to be attacked by a man who slices *other* men's hands off! How's that for factual? *Hmm*?"

Ferghus stared at my angry face for a few seconds before lashing back, "so ye wanted me tae let ye die? Would that have suited ye? Leave ye tae the MacDonalds?"

"I rescued *you*, remember?" I reminded him, "and that's not philosophy! It's the *facts*!"

"If ye don't stop, Aam goin' tae bind yer hands again!"

"I'd like to see you *try*!" I shouted and the next thing I knew, Ferghus had grasped both my shoulders and shoved me down against the blanket.

I could hardly see his features in the dark shelter. His breath was hot against my face, his torso pressed against my chest. My own breath was coming out in little gasps as I tried to catch my breath. Neither of us spoke and, a few minutes later, when our pulses were almost back to normal, Ferghus suddenly released me and rolled onto his side, facing away from me. Emotions flooded my system; as the anger began to dissipate, fear and sadness replaced it. I felt like crying as I stared at Ferghus's back. What must he be thinking? What would *I* think if I met a complete stranger who told me they were from a place that hadn't even been discovered yet? I wondered if he was frightened, or possibly even doubted my humanity. I swallowed hard and whispered into the darkness, "I'm *not* lying, Ferghus. I wish you believed me…" I turned onto my side and faced the other wall of our shelter, my heart heavy in my chest.

***

I woke some time later to the sound of rain still pattering against the treetops. The ground was cold and damp, and my hands and feet were numb. My teeth started chattering and no matter what I imagined to ground myself, I couldn't get warm. I heard Ferghus shift beside me; I felt guilty for waking him. I was just about to tell him so when he sat in the pitch dark shelter and slid his bed roll out from under him. I wondered if he was still angry and planned to find somewhere quieter to sleep, when he suddenly laid back down beside me on the edge of *my* blanket and threw *his* blanket over top of both of us. I laid frozen beside him, unsure how to react. I stared at the criss-crossed branches above my head. *"Warmer?"* Ferghus asked softly.

I swallowed back my nerves so I could answer, "yes, thank you."

Silence settled over us again. Ferghus turned on his side and I could feel his bicep and thigh pressing gently against my wedding dress. "Ah won't hurt ye," he suddenly said.

"Okay," I answered automatically, still staring at the branches above my head. I could feel my heart pounding inside my chest.

"Ah won't hurt ye, Brigid," he repeated, "get some sleep."

I nodded, but didn't say anything else. It took forever to fall back to sleep, despite how warm it had suddenly become.

Chapter Eight:

When I woke early the next morning, some light was filtering inside the shelter. The rain had finally stopped. When I turned, I saw Ferghus was no longer inside with me. I sat and stretched, lifting the blanket off my lap and starting to fold it. I had an urge to be useful to Ferghus, since he was going out of his way to protect me from the MacDonalds. There was little I could do though, since I relied on him to hunt and I didn't know which berries and nuts were edible. I wished I had access to my bank account here; I could offer him some money for his time. I crawled out of the shelter and carried the bed roll to tie onto Selma. There was a ring of stones in the clearing that hadn't been there last night. When I turned away from Selma, Ferghus emerged from the woods across the way. "Madainn," he said, nodding his head at me. He was carrying a stack of wood, which he dumped in front of the circle he'd made.

"Madainn," I repeated. He smiled up at me for a second before lighting the fire. I hesitated and then went back to get the great kilt from our shelter, which I folded and laid across Selma's saddle. There didn't seem to be anything else I could help with, so I stood awkwardly behind Ferghus. "I thought you weren't going to light a fire?" I asked curiously.

He stood and brushed his hands on his kilt. "Ah wasn't, but we need tae eat. I'll have tae risk it." He pulled a knife from his pocket and nodded towards two dead rabbits piled next to a tree. "Ye might not want tae see this next part," he warned me.

I gulped. "Thanks," I said, and turned to face the fire while he skinned both rabbits. "You caught *two*?" I asked, trying to be enthusiastic despite my squeamish stomach.

"Aye."

"That's nice," I complimented him. I heard him chuckle. I turned around without thinking just in time to see him cutting a perfect circle around the second one's head so he could easily pull the fur off. *"Oh god!* I didn't need to see *that* so early in the morning!"

"Nae, probably not," he agreed in good humour and brought the rabbits over to the fire. He propped them up with large sticks and wiped his hands. "We're near a river; we can get water there."

"Okay," I said.

"Yer quiet this morn'," Ferghus commented, eyeing me curiously.

"I *am?*"

"Aye. Aam not used tae it." His eyes crinkled at the corners, but the rest of his face remained serious.

"Are you trying not to laugh?" I questioned.

"Ah wouldn't dare laugh at ye, *Rosa*," Ferghus said.

"You'd better mean that in the way you described last night," I told him, pretending to be affronted.

"What way was that?"

"Well, not the *pumpkin* way – the way you talked about your brother," I explained.

Ferghus laughed. "Eh'd never talk about ye that way. Yer far from boyish, Brigid."

I blushed and laughed self-consciously. "Okay." Ferghus went over to the fire and turned the rabbits. "What's your brother's name?" I asked to change the subject.

"Which one?" Ferghus joked.

"The red-haired one."

"Anghus," Ferghus replied, "mah oldest is Doughal. Mah sister's name is Mirna."

"Are you close?" I wondered.

"Sometimes," Ferghus answered vaguely.

"What does that mean?"

Ferghus looked into the fire when he replied, "Mah parents are busy findin' Mirna a husband. Doughal's the eldest, so he'll inherit everythin'." He shrugged. "Anghus is still young. He has time tae figure out what he wants tae dae with his life."

"And what about you?" I inquired gently, "what do *you* want?"

Ferghus looked at me in surprise and then laughed ruefully. "Ah get chosen fer clan business," he said, "or volunteer. Eh'd rather be away, so it suits me fine." There was something about his tone that said otherwise.

"Do you miss home?" I asked, "are you far away?"

"Nae, it's not far," Ferghus replied, "Ah was takin' ye there, but the MacDonalds forced me tae change plans…"

"Oh, I would have liked to see it – your home."

"Ye *would*?" Ferghus said in surprise.

"Yes," I answered, "I bet it's beautiful. Everything here is pretty."

Ferghus practically snorted. "It would be if people stopped tryin' tae take what isn't *theirs*…"

"Like *what*?" I asked curiously.

"Their land – their homes – their livestock – their *women*." He looked at me pointedly when he said the final one.

"I'm not sure he was taking me from someone *else*; I just wound up in the wrong place at the wrong time and they must have thought I was the bride…"

Ferghus stared at me incredulously. "*Tha sin craicte*!⁴⁰" He shook his head. "The MacDonalds are all thieves. They stole ye, and tried tae get a forced marriage out of it. Ye would have improved the whole lot of em tay!" There was a definite edge of anger in his voice now.

"I don't remember them *taking* me. I was at work, and I stepped away from the counter to check the storage room. When I came back out, this woman started to put undergarments on me. I was dazed and had no idea where I was..."

Ferghus paused, listening to my description. "Sounds like a powerful drug," he concluded, "they put somethin' in yer drink, and ye can't remember the truth."

I shook my head. "No, I don't think so. I have too many memories from before I got here. It doesn't make sense. Nothing does..."

"What did ye mean when ye said work? What was in the storage room?"

"Lots of things," I told him, "boxes of supplies. Coffee filters. Coffee beans. Paper. Cups."

Ferghus's brow furrowed. "Ye had a job – as a *bar maid*?"

"No, I worked in a *coffee* shop," I explained.

Ferghus snorted. "Ye won't find one of *them* around here. Nae one drinks *coffee* – whisky and beer. And don't tell nae one ye worked in a *shop*. *Nae one*..." His voice was firm and laced with scorn.

"*Why not*?" I questioned.

Ferghus took the meat out of the fire and began to cut it. "Because it sounds like ye were a servin' wench."

"Please don't call me that," I said quietly, feeling a strange emotion bubbling up inside me.

---

40 That's crazy!

Ferghus glanced up from his kneeling position. "Ah meant nae offense," he declared, "but ye don't want other people tae get the wrong idea. If ye work in a *tavern*, yer not going tae marry well…"

I frowned. "Who said I'm trying to get *married*? I'm here by *accident*!"

Ferghus laughed. "Tha a h-uile duine a 'feuchainn ri posadh[41]. It's what boireannaich *dae*!"

"You sound kind of sexist," I commented.

Ferghus shrugged. "Ah don't think so. Ah just know what Ah see." He passed me half the meat on a large leaf and we sat together in silence while we ate. After a few minutes, he said, "mah mum talks about nothin' else. She's always arrangin' visits so Mirna can meet different men. Ah bet she'll have somethin' arranged by the time Ah get home…" He rolled his eyes.

"That must be hard on Mirna," I observed.

"Na, she just wants someone tae take care of her."

"Well, I don't have anyone to find men for *me*," I laughed ruefully, "that's not how we do things where *I'm* from."

Ferghus looked at me with keen interest. "How dae they dae it in Huntsville?"

"Most people meet in school, or through a friend. And if that doesn't work, you make a profile on-line and go on a coffee date to see if you're compatible."

Ferghus stopped chewing, his eyes widening. "Ah didn't understand any of that, but it sounds balbh.[42]"

"I don't know what that means."

[41] Everyone's trying to get married.

[42] Vulgar

Ferghus sighed. "Mebbe we should stop talkin' aboot this. We should get movin' again. Ah don't want an ambush."

"Where are we going?"

"A friend's."

"Does this friend have a *name*?" I inquired, feeling annoyed.

"Sloane," Ferghus replied. He kicked dirt onto the fire and it hissed as the flames struggled to stay alight. "Uine ri dhol.[43]"

"I wish you'd stop doing that," I complained as I trailed after him to Selma.

"Doin' *what*?" he asked as he untied Selma's lead.

"Speak words you know I don't understand."

Ferghus looked at me incredulously. "Ah don't dae it tae *offend* ye. It's mah language. I've been speakin' it since Ah was a leanabh. What dae ye expect me tae dae?"

"Make an effort. I feel like you're always saying rude things to me behind my back."

Ferghus laughed. "Nae." He gestured to the stirrup. "Up ye go."

"I'll do it myself, since I actually have my *hands* free. You left marks on me you know."

"That's what people *dae*," he stated simply as he pulled Selma deeper into the woods.

---

[43] Time to go.

Chapter Nine:

Soon after we left camp, we stopped at a shallow river to drink and refill our water containers. With a belly full of food, my thirst quenched, and the sun shining above us, I didn't feel quite as unhappy. Ferghus had led Selma from the front after leaving camp, not saying much, but at the river he broke the silence. "If we make good time taeday, we'll just have tae camp one more night before we reach mah friend's."

"Okay," I said. "What do we do once we get to Sloane's?"

"We tell heem what happened and ask for his help," Ferghus explained as we set out again, moving back into the cover of the forest.

"Do you think he'll say yes?"

Ferghus turned to look at me over his shoulder. "*Aye*." His voice was absolutely certain.

"Why would he risk his life for you?" I questioned, thinking about my own friends back home. Would my co-workers take on a dangerous mission for *me*?

"Because Ah would do the same for *heem*," Ferghus replied easily.

"Is that how you got your scar?" I inquired before I could take it back. I could see Ferghus's shoulders tense. He didn't reply, continuing to lead Selma over tree roots and difficult hills. "I'm sorry, Ferghus," I said after a minute, "I shouldn't have asked." He still didn't say anything, so I stared morosely into the trees and bit my lip to keep from crying.

We plodded on for more than *three* hours. My muscles ached from the bumping, and I could only imagine how tired Ferghus must be after walking the whole way. He never complained though – about being hungry, thirsty, *or* tired. I thought I should take a page out of the book of Ferghus more often. When a lake became visible through the trees to our right, we tied Selma to a branch and drank some more of the fresh water.

The sun was hot and I longed to clean myself. It had been much too long since I'd last showered, especially after being exposed to the dirt and damp of constant travel. "Is there time for me to bathe?" I asked when we had eaten some nuts and berries Ferghus had found.

He stared at me incredulously. "Why would ye want tae dae *that*? It's less than a day tae Sloane's and ye can bathe in a tub of hot water."

"I promise I won't be long," I said, "I just want to rinse my hair. It's been coiled so tightly and my skin is grimy. I'm not used to this."

Ferghus sighed. "Fine. Ten minutes. Then we leave." He hesitated and then slid his hand inside his sporran. He handed me a thin sliver of what looked like glycerin. "That's all Ah have."

I took the soap from him and smiled happily. "Thank you."

"*Ten* minutes." He turned and climbed the hill to the forest, disappearing into the trees to give me privacy.

I slipped off my shoes and pulled my torn dress over my head. I waded into the cool water, enjoying the contrast with the hot sun overhead. I dipped the gown in the river and ran the bar of soap over the material, folding it to create a lather. Soon, I had it lying on the shore to dry while I waded further out. I kept the undergarments on, in case any MacDonalds should happen upon me while bathing. The glycerin washed away all the grime and blood from my skin and didn't do a bad job of cleaning my hair either. I rinsed it and combed it with my fingers as I headed back to the pebbly sand. I felt the dress; it was still wet, but would probably dry fairly quickly in the sun. I stretched my arms over my head to ease the kinks in my muscles. I'd been sitting much too long; perhaps when we started out again, I would ask Ferghus if I could walk for a while. I slid my shoes on and collected my dress, still clutching what was left of the glycerin. At that moment, Ferghus came ambling along the shoreline from a short distance down river. I smiled and held the soap out to him, but suddenly his entire countenance altered when he got close enough to see me clearly. "*Thuirt mi riut a bhith a 'cumail ort a' aodach*![44]" he shouted.

My smile faded from my lips and I lowered my hand. "I don't understand," I said.

He quickly turned his back to me and continued to holler, "*cuir an dreasa air*![45]"

"What are you saying? Can you please speak English?" I pleaded, my voice trembling.

"*Get. Dressed. Now.*" His voice was also quavering and I could see he'd balled his hands into fists.

"Okay," I said and hurried to pull the damp gown over my soaking wet undergarments, "I was just trying to dry off a little – "

"Are ye decent?"

"Yes, I – "

Ferghus whirled around, his face a frightening shade of purple. "*Tha thu mar chleasaiche*![46]" he spat and grabbed me roughly around my arm.

"*Ferghus!*" I cried, dropping his soap onto the sand.

"*We're leavin'!*" he growled and hauled me up the hill to the trees.

"*Let me go!*" I cried, "*you're hurting me!*"

"Are ye a bar maid or a quine?" he questioned as he shoved me towards Selma.

---

[44] I told you to keep your dress on!

[45] Put the damn dress on!

[46] You're acting like a whore!

I stared at him aghast, my mouth falling open. "I told you – I work in a *coffee shop*, not a *bar*!"

"Nae, yer actin' like a clarsach![47]"

"A *clarsach*? I don't know what the *hell* that is!" I exclaimed.

"Get on the cuddie before Ah tie ye tae her!" Ferghus shouted.

"Why are you so angry?" I asked as I started towards Selma.

"Someone could have come by and seen ye naked!" Ferghus yelled, "is that what ye want?"

"Of course not! I never took my – "

"*Ah* saw ye naked! Ah can't undo that, Brigid!"

When I turned to look at him, his face was scarlet. He avoided my gaze and pointed at Selma. "Get on her. And don't speak tae me ever again. I'll get mah answers and figure out where tae put ye."

"*Put me?*" My voice squeaked like a small child's. Tears immediately filled my eyes. I'm not sure why his statements affected me so deeply. Perhaps they reminded me of my childhood – of being sent from foster home to foster home, never belonging anywhere. Perhaps they confirmed what I'd been feeling ever since finding myself here: that I didn't belong and had nowhere to go. And the thought that frightened me the most was what if I could never get back home? What if I was stuck here forever, without a safe place to stay? What if Ferghus dumped me somewhere I'd be raped or assaulted? What if he took me back to the *MacDonalds*?

"*By God's bones, get on the cuddie!*" he cried, losing all control over his emotions. He suddenly punched the trunk of the tree Selma was resting beside, which incensed him even more. I had just placed my foot into the stirrup when he came running over and grabbed my hands. He

[47] harlot

shook them and yelled, "I'll never let ye free again, dae ye hear me? That way ye'll stay pure til Ah find somewhere tae leave ye!" He pulled the coil of rope from his sporran and started to twist it around my wrists. The sensitive skin immediately smarted.

"Ferghus, *no*! *Please*!" I begged, tears falling freely onto both our hands.

When he had tied them together, he hurried me onto Selma's saddle and tugged her through the trees as fast as he could. He never looked back and we continued like that until the last light faded and he finally had to make camp.

***

Ferghus didn't light a fire, and he didn't make a shelter for us either. He also didn't set his blanket down next to mine; this time, he laid near Selma's tree and made me lie further down the clearing. As soon as my head fell against the blanket, I started crying again. Within seconds, I was sobbing. I had never felt so miserable in all my life, and that was saying something. The warmth of day soon faded and a dampness spread through the forest. I curled onto my side, hugging my body to stay warm. Nothing worked. My teeth were chattering, and tears kept flowing no matter how much I pleaded with myself to stop. Finally, after what felt like a couple hours, I managed to stand with my hands bound. I hesitated, unsure what to do. I couldn't stay here, hated in this way. I didn't want to meet a MacDonald or a wild animal on the road, but I couldn't stay here. I turned in the opposite direction from where Ferghus had laid and crept slowly through the trees. I stumbled a couple of times; it was difficult to balance with my hands tied. The night breeze ruffled my hair, which I hadn't had a chance to put back up after my bath. There wasn't much of a moon either, making it extremely hard to see in front of me.

Suddenly, a footfall crunched in the leaves behind me. "Where are ye goin'?"

I turned slowly and could discern Ferghus's shape in the murky forest. I swallowed nervously. "I had to go to the bathroom," I lied.

He stared at me in the gloom for a few seconds. "Nae, ye didn't," he stated quietly, "ye've been cryin' all night…"

I inhaled sharply, trying to steady my breathing so I wouldn't start sobbing in front of him. "Please, Ferghus, I have to go. I can't stay with you. I don't need your friend's help. I don't want to trouble any of you. *Please* – just pretend you never met me." The words tumbled out of my mouth until I had no more to say. I hung my head and waited for his reply.

"Go back tae bed, Brigid," he said calmly.

I shook my head and started crying again. "I can't. I *won't*. Please. I'd rather marry a MacDonald than be treated like this…"

I heard Ferghus suck in his breath. I braced myself for a series of expletives, or his hands on me to teach me a lesson, but neither response occurred. I stared at his outline, wondering what he was thinking, or what he was going to do to me. "Ah can't let ye dae that, Brigid," he finally said.

"Why *not*?" I questioned, my voice filled with desperation, "why do you *care*?"

"Dae ye think Eh'd let ye marry the man who did *this* tae me?" he asked, his voice trembling as he pointed at the side of his face, "the man who took any chance of happiness away from me?" He sucked in his breath again and I heard his chest shudder. "Go tae bed," he told me again, "and that's an order."

I lifted my chin in his direction, feeling an overwhelming sense of loathing as I spoke, "you think you're better than them, but you're not.

You're just as bad, or worse. I wouldn't treat my *dog* the way you treat me!" I shook my bound hands at him. "I'm your *prisoner*. Why would I need any help from your stupid friends? Can it get any *worse* than this? You're already a fucking masochist. If you take me to your friends, what then? Are you taking me to Sloane so he can *rape* me? *Torture* me? I'd rather go to Tristen! He has to be better than this!" I felt as if I had a huge hole torn in my chest and everything was flowing onto the forest floor at Ferghus's feet.

"Tha mi duilich[48]," Ferghus mumbled and stepped forward. I braced myself, having no idea what he'd just said, but he unexpectedly started to untie the rope. When my hands were free, he grasped one and pushed the rope against my palm. "Thoir maitheanas dhomh.[49]" Then he turned abruptly and disappeared into the trees.

I stood rooted to the ground, half from shock, and half from complete exhaustion. I brushed away my tears and tried to decide what to do. Should I strike out alone, trying to find someone who would take me in for a while, until I could figure out how to get home? Or should I try to make my way back to the MacDonalds' castle and agree to marry Tristen so the awful men would stop pursuing me? I bit my lower lip and brushed my hands down the front of my ridiculous dress. Had Ferghus forgiven me for taking my dress off outside? Had he sent me on my way? I had no idea what the words he'd uttered *meant*. I wrung my hands, listening to the sounds of insects and small animals in the brush. I had started out alone, when I'd first run from the castle. Perhaps I was strong enough to make it on my own out here. Perhaps I had been over-relying on Ferghus for my survival, not trusting my own instincts enough in this strange place. Part

48 I'm sorry.

49 Forgive me.

of me knew that was indeed true, but the other part had been happy to have the company. The aching loneliness was back, filling me with an emptiness that made me wonder if I would slowly go crazy. I couldn't understand almost anything people said. It made me feel isolated and invisible. When Ferghus had tried to speak some English words with me, and we had shared a few stories about our pasts, it had started to connect us. I longed for that feeling, but I wondered if it was too late. Did he plan to return to his home tomorrow, or continue on to Sloane's without me? My head was throbbing and my bones were weary. I felt as if I might collapse. Finally, I decided to try to find my way back to our campsite and sleep as much as I could tonight. In the morning, I'd say good-bye to Ferghus and figure out what to do next.

I took careful steps through the darkness, using my free hands to grasp branches for support. I thought I was going the right direction, but after five minutes I still hadn't found the clearing *or* my blanket. Maybe Ferghus had packed everything and left by another path. The thought of being abandoned made my throat constrict. I took several jagged breaths, trying to capture a full breath, when suddenly a pair of strong hands wrapped themselves around my bicep. I jumped and was about to switch into defensive mode when I recognized Ferghus's scarred face in front of me. "I'm lost," I admitted, hearing the fear in my own voice.

"Ah know," Ferghus agreed softly.

"I tried to find the blanket," I said, but my voice faltered.

"Ah know," he said again. His hands were warm on my bare skin, causing goosebumps to appear on my arms.

"I'm sorry I shamed you," I gushed, "I didn't mean for you to see me. I was trying to get clean. Back home, our bathing suits are different;

we have different rules. I don't *know* yours…" I knew my words were jumbled, probably sounding ridiculous and impossible to interpret.

"Ah was angry at mahself; Ah came down tay soon. Ah was anxious," Ferghus said honestly.

"I'm not a whore; I don't even have a boyfriend," I persisted, wanting desperately for him to understand my point of view.

"Ah was worried," Ferghus continued, "Ah didn't wait the ten minutes."

I met his gaze. "Why *not?*"

Ferghus hesitated. "Ah didn't want anythin' tae happen tae ye."

"It didn't. I just used your soap." I pressed my palm against my face. "Oh no, it's *gone!*"

"What's gone?"

"Your soap. I dropped it in the sand when you yelled at me. I'm so sorry. It was all you had."

Ferghus let go of my arm and pulled my palm gently off my face. "Ah was angry at mahself. Ah saw ye naked. Ah wronged ye. Ah can't undo it."

"You didn't *wrong* me, Ferghus."

"Yes, Ah did. Ah saw ye."

I could feel his warm breath against my face. "No, it's okay. You just saw my undergarments. They're almost as long as my dress…"

Ferghus shook his head. "Aam ashamed. Ah can't look at ye. Ah can't undo what Ah saw."

"It's *okay*," I said emphatically, "*really*. You didn't do it on *purpose*, and neither did I!"

Ferghus sighed in the darkness. "We cannot speak of this tae anyone!" His tone was solemn.

"I won't tell Sloane if you don't." I pressed my hand over my chest as if pledging allegiance.

"Ye still want tae go with me?" Ferghus questioned.

"Do you still want to take me?"

"Aye," he replied as he placed his hand onto my sleeve and added, "it's this way."

Ferghus led me back to my blanket, which was still spread upon the dew-covered earth. "Dae ye need a fire?" he asked awkwardly.

"No, it's okay. It's too late," I replied quickly.

"How aboot a shelter? Ah can build ye one."

"No, Ferghus. You should sleep. You walked all day. You must be tired."

He didn't deny it; instead, he cleared his throat and asked hesitantly, "would ye mind if Ah moved closer tae ye? In case we're ambushed by Tristen's scouts..."

"No, I wouldn't mind..."

Ferghus nodded once and left me for a minute to retrieve the bed roll. I laid down on my blanket while I waited for him. When he returned, he joined me as he had done the night before and spread his blanket over top of us. Once again, it felt incredibly intimate to have a man lying directly beside me. I could feel the soft hair on Ferghus's arm tickling the bare skin on my own. "Ah hope ye can get some sleep now," he said. We were both lying on our backs, staring at the canopy above.

"Thank you." I didn't know what else to say.

"Ye can relax," he told me softly.

I felt myself blushing and was thankful it was so dark. "Okay."

"Ah would never touch ye, or dae anythin' improper," he added.

"I know," I said, feeling embarrassed.

"Mah friends would never hurt ye either," Ferghus continued, "what ye said before – "

"About that," I interrupted, "I was angry – I didn't mean it…"

"Mah friends and family – they'll protect ye with their lives if Ah ask them," Ferghus stated.

"I hope it won't come to that," I said, "I don't want anyone else to get hurt…"

"If we make good time taemorrow, we should be at Sloane's before noon."

"That doesn't sound too bad…"

We laid in silence, staring into the dark sky. "Aam sorry Ah made ye think it would be better tae go back tae Tristen than stay with me," Ferghus suddenly said.

"Tristen never did anything bad to me; I never even met him."

Ferghus sucked in his breath. "He's a cruel man. Will be the head of his clan one day. Then things will get *really* fierce."

"Will *you* be the head of *your* clan?" I asked curiously, having no knowledge of clan rules.

Ferghus actually laughed. "Nae, Sasannach, mah brother Doughal is next in line."

"That must be quite an honour…"

"Aye, tis."

"Do you wish it was *you*?" I questioned.

Ferghus hesitated and then answered, "doesn't do any good wishin', Rosa."

"Does that mean *yes*?"

He sighed. "Ah try tae focus on survivin' each day and mindin' mah elders…"

"Are you *happy*?" I wondered.

"We should get some sleep, Brigid. It's late…"

I could sense an unwillingness to converse any more on the subject. His resistance heightened my curiosity even more, but I knew better than to push him. "Okay, I'll try."

"Ah won't hurt ye. Ah promise," he repeated, which made me curious too. Was he trying to convince *me* or himself his intentions towards me were pure?

Chapter Ten:

Ferghus woke before dawn and caught us a rabbit. While he was lighting the fire, I asked if he ever caught anything else. He laughed and replied, "aye, but when Aam on the move Ah avoid large animals; don't want tae waste any of it."

"Makes sense," I said thoughtfully as I helped pack our blankets.

While the meat cooked, Ferghus and I sat side-by-side on a nearby log. He shared some of his water and then suddenly asked if he could see my hands. I looked at him quizzically. "My *hands*?" I asked, but held them out to him. "Are you checking for signs I'm a strong worker? Going to sell me to Sloane?"

He glanced at me sharply. "Don't say such vulgar things aboot yerself," he scolded.

I looked at him sheepishly. "I was just joking," I said.

"Sloane's not gonna buy ye; *plus*, yer not mine tae sell *anyway*," Ferghus said, his blue eyes emphatic.

"Okay, okay," I said, "I was only teasing. Why do you want to see my hands?" Ferghus turned them palm up to examine. He eyed them for a minute and then removed a small bottle from his sporran. "What's that for?" I questioned. He didn't answer, just twisted the cap off and poured a small amount onto the tip of his finger. He began to spread the fragrant mixture onto each of my wrists. It was thick, like honey, but much darker. "What *is* it?"

"Ye ask a lot of questions," he commented while he pulled a strip of cloth out of his great kilt and tore it in half. He wrapped a piece around each wrist and gently secured them.

"I like to understand things," I said defensively.

Ferghus laughed. "Ah never said it was a *bad* thing, Rosa."

"Like my hair?"

Fergus put the balm away and met my gaze. "Yer hair needs tae go *up*. Ye shouldn't have it untied like that…"

My hand involuntarily flew to my locks, still hanging loose after bathing in the lake the day before. "Is that not acceptable?" I asked.

"Only in private," he told me, "yer husband might enjoy seeing ye like that…" He turned towards the fire and rotated the rabbit, avoiding my eyes again.

"I'm sorry. I didn't do it on purpose," I assured him quickly.

He actually smiled. "Ah know."

I had saved the pins from the wedding, but without assistance, not to mention a mirror, it would be rather difficult to tame my hair that way. "Do you have any more of that cloth?" I asked, "I could use it like a ribbon…"

"Ah won't have any supplies left by the time Ah get back home," Ferghus teased as he pulled out another strip of cloth.

I blushed. "Thank you," I said, taking the offered material and gathering my hair into a ponytail. *"Better now?"* He appraised me for a second and then pulled the meat out of the fire and started to cut it. "I take that as a *yes*?" I pressed.

"Nae, but ye can fix it after breakfast." He handed me a helping of cooked rabbit and started to eat.

I frowned. "What's wrong with it?" I questioned, feeling irritated at being judged.

Ferghus didn't hurry to answer me; he chewed slowly and swallowed before responding, "it's still undone."

"No, it's not."

"Then why is it hangin' down?"

"Because I put it in a *ponytail*." I gave my hair a flick with my hand.

"Well, pony hair or nae, ye can't wear it like that when we see Sloane." Fergus tossed a leg into the fire.

"Why not? Will he be overcome by *lust*?" I asked peevishly.

"Are ye going tae eat anythin', or can Ah have it?" Ferghus gestured to my untouched rabbit.

"*Will he*?" I asked, "is that what you're so afraid of?"

Ferghus frowned. "Aam not *afraid*; Ah just want ye tae look respectable."

"And right now you think I look *dis*respectful?" I asked incredulously.

Ferghus sighed. "Brigid, ye need tae trust me on this. Ye said yerself, things are different where ye live."

I had suddenly lost my appetite. "You basically just met me – *what*? – *two days ago*? And already you've told me I can't exercise, or bathe, or style myself the way I'm used to. I've had to change *everything* about myself."

"Aam just tryin' tae help advise ye. Someone else might not be so forgivin'…" He eyed my meat. "Ye gonna eat that? We need tae leave soon…"

I gaped at him. "It's all yours," I snapped, shoving my portion onto his lap, "take it all – and my identity with it…" I stomped over to Selma and waited with folded arms for Ferghus to finish eating and putting out the fire. When he approached, I tilted my chin and said, "I'm going to walk this morning."

His eyes opened in surprise. "It would be faster if ye rode," he stated.

I rolled my eyes. "Women can *walk*, Ferghus, or am I not allowed to break a *sweat* in your world?"

He opened his mouth as if to reply and then decided against it. "Let's go," he said, "we have about a four-hour journey left."

"Yes, my king," I said sarcastically as he began to lead Selma past our campsite.

"Ye'd best hold yer tongue or a wild animal might bite it off," he retorted, "and Aam not gonna save ye." I burst out laughing as the tension evaporated. Ferghus looked at me over his shoulder for a minute and then shook his head. "Aam not used tae that sound, or the ways of hens." I laughed harder. "Tha boireannaich craicte![50]"

I hurried to catch up with him. "I see how it is – you speak in *your* language so I won't know what names you're calling me."

He stared straight ahead, a flush of colour creeping up his neck. "Yer a scholar, ye are. So smart, Sasannach."

"I am pretty smart, aren't I?" I joked.

His lips curled slightly. "Aye – and a lot of other things tay."

"What's that supposed to mean?" I inquired, glancing down every few seconds to make sure I didn't trip on a tree root.

"Nothin' of import," Ferghus answered vaguely. He cleared his throat. "Are ye betrothed tae Aragorn?"

"*What?*"

"*Aragorn.* Ye mentioned him before. Ye said he's competent in the wild..." He looked at me curiously.

"*Oh god*! That was just a *story*, Ferghus."

He frowned. "A *story*? Ye made Aragorn *up*?"

---

[50] Women are crazy!

"No, - not *that* kind of story," I said quickly, "someone *else* made him up. It's an epic tale. You know – adventure – quest – that sort of story…"

He was silent for a few seconds and then said, "a *legend*? The legend of Aragorn?"

I smiled at him. "Sort of. It's more like the Legend of *Frodo*. Aragorn joins in his quest."

"It sounds complicated," Ferghus commented.

"I told you it was epic."

Ferghus smiled too. "Aye, ye did."

"You must have stories of your own," I said.

"We dae," Ferghus agreed. He paused. "Dae ye remember the place we were attacked yesterday?"

"Yes."

"There's a giant who lives there," Ferghus stated matter-of-factly.

"A *giant*?" I repeated skeptically.

He laughed. "Aye, and Ah bet it was heem who scared off our attackers."

"No, it was both of *us*. I saw you cut a man's *hand* off, Ferghus."

He glanced sideways at me. "Aam sorry if it scared ye."

"It didn't *scare* me," I began, but then I sighed and decided to be honest. "It *shocked* me. I wasn't expecting it. I always try to do no harm."

"Ah thought ye said ye fought with one of the other groomsmen?"

"Yes, he sounded like he was threatening me. I couldn't understand the words, but he had a sword and kept pointing at my body."

Ferghus frowned. "He deserved tae have it used on *him* then."

I shook my head. "In karate, we never strike first. My hands are my weapons; if I use them irresponsibly, it's a sign of disrespect."

"Even if he was disrespectin' ye *first*?"

"Yes, even then. I used words and tried to reason with him, but I'm not sure he understood me." I paused and then continued, "I knocked him unconscious. I had no choice. I'd tried everything else first."

Ferghus was looking at me thoughtfully. "I've never seen another lass fight before. Ah thought ye must be a witch when we first met…"

I laughed. "No, just years of hard work…"

He nodded and fell silent. We walked for a few minutes and then Ferghus asked, "the exercises ye were doin' – the karate – it's tae prepare fer battle?"

"I guess that's one way of looking at it, but I like to see it as strengthening my body and mind."

"Ye miss it?" he asked as he led us around a particularly tangled section of weeds.

"Yes, very much," I answered.

He nodded, but didn't comment. We continued in silence for a while. It was much colder, but walking helped keep me warm. After a solid hour, the forest thinned and we came to a large body of water. "This is called *Inner Sound*," Ferghus told me, "we won't have the cover of trees fer a few miles. It's a dangerous stretch."

"Have you been attacked here before?" I asked.

"Aye. There are *two* MacDonald settlements south. Hopefully Tristen hasn't sent word tae either of them yet." Ferghus pulled his water flask from his pocket, took a drink, and then handed it to me.

"I don't understand why he cares so much," I said before I took a sip. I passed the flask back to him.

Ferghus began to lead Selma along the narrow stretch of grassland. "Because ye were meant tae marry him," he responded simply.

"I understand he went to some *expense*, but I never consented to the wedding," I stated.

"*Someone* arranged it," Ferghus said, "and ye left him just before yer vows." A chuckle escaped his lips.

"What's so funny?"

"Ye humiliated him."

"I didn't *mean* to," I said defensively.

He laughed again. "Don't feel *bad*, Brigid. Ye have mah complete support…"

"I think you're looking at this all wrong," I told him.

"Is that so?"

"*Yes*! What we need to do is convince Tristen I'd make a *terrible* bride. Then he won't feel so bad and – "

"That won't *work*, Rosa," Ferghus interrupted.

"Why not?"

"Yer *not* a terrible bride," he said.

"I don't know *anything* about getting married. It wasn't even on my radar before two days ago." I could feel my heart rate increase at the mere *thought* of settling down with a husband. Ferghus laughed. I stared at the back of his head as he walked. "What's so funny?"

"Yer the *perfect* age tae get married," he stated.

"Not where *I'm* from," I protested, "if I got married, everyone would think I'd gone crazy."

Ferghus looked at me over his shoulder. "Ah think yer friends are the crazy ones."

"My friends are *not* crazy!" I said vehemently.

"They support ye *servin'* people," Ferghus said, "yer tay good fer that."

"How do *you* know? I like my job."

Ferghus shook his head and turned back around. "Ah didn't say ye didn't *like* it, but ye still shouldn't have tae *dae* it."

"I have bills to pay. I have to earn money to pay my rent."

"Ye should let yer husband worry about those things," Ferghus commented.

"I don't *have* a husband!" I retorted peevishly.

Ferghus chuckled. "Gu direach![51]"

"What does *that* mean?"

"Yer the perfect age tae get married," he said again.

"Let's talk about something else," I suggested.

"Ye could bear some bairns; make a man proud," Ferghus stated.

I snorted. "That's when the men *I* know take off. Girl sees a pink line and suddenly – *poof* – he disappears."

Ferghus actually stopped walking. "Ah don't understand. *Pink line*?"

"Nevermind that," I said quickly, "men in *my* part of the world don't view a pregnancy the same way."

"They aren't happy?"

"Sometimes. Not always. If the girl is as young as *I* am, they don't usually stay."

Ferghus frowned deeply. "A man would leave ye with child? He would walk away?"

"Yes. Move on to the next one."

"*Next one*?"

---

[51] Exactly!

89

"The next *woman* – conquest. It's all a game they play."

Ferghus shook his head. "Yer men sound like bairns themselves."

"That's why I'm too young to get married. It takes them *ages* to grow up."

"Ye shouldn't have tae wait fer em tae be ready." He shook Selma's lead and urged her forward.

"We have no choice; there aren't many stellar ones," I said morosely, "*get this*! One of my co-workers started dating this guy. At first, he had a home and a job, but after *two weeks* he got laid off, and within *three months* he suddenly lost his house!"

Ferghus stopped walking again. "Brigid, Ah don't understand. *Date a guy*? Dae ye mean *court*?"

I shook my head. "No, not really. People date, but they don't always want to *marry* each other. They go on short outings first, see if they like each other enough to continue, and sometimes they date long enough to want to get married."

Ferghus stared at me in disbelief. "This practice sounds cheap and unfulfillin'. It has nae honour in it."

"Cheap is right," I said, "some guys don't even buy you dinner!"

"Ah don't think ye should subject yerself tae such a practice. It is the reason why ye unclothe yerself in public and consider goin' back tae Tristen. Ye have not been taught tae value yerself enough. Yer men sound inferior."

"I don't *unclothe* myself, Ferghus," I corrected him, "I *told* you – the first time I was trying not to soil my dress; I'd never gone to the bathroom outside before. And the second time, I was *washing* my dress. I'm sorry if you don't believe me, but I *do* value myself..."

Ferghus sighed. "Brigid, ye need tae get married; a good man would never let ye be treated in such a way. He'd defend yer honour and take care of ye. Ye shouldn't have tae work. Ah haven't known ye very long, but none of this sounds like what ye deserve…"

"I have no choice; I don't have any family. I have to live somewhere…"

Ferghus stared at me, his peacock-blue eyes piercing into mine. "Ye should be aware none of mah friends are married yet…"

I blinked. "I don't understand…"

His intensity didn't waver. "They're all lookin' fer a woman of quality…"

I blushed. "Are you *warning* me?"

"Not a warnin'; mah friends are all quality. Ah told ye before: ye have nothin' tae fear from any of em…"

My cheeks were burning under his gaze. "I don't know what they could possibly see in me; I'm not ready to get married. I'm just a girl who works in a coffee shop and – "

At that moment, something whistled past my head, missing my ear by a fraction of an inch. The next thing I knew, I was lying upon the ground on my back with Ferghus kneeling over me, scanning the shoreline on either side of us. I stared into his face, a panicked expression upon my own. He spoke evenly, in a quiet voice, "when Ah say run, yer goin' tae get onto Selma's back." He reached for my hands, grasping them in his own. Another arrow whistled past us, narrowly missing Ferghus's shoulder. "*Run!*" he ordered, hauling me to my feet in one motion. I felt dazed, but I obeyed his command and ran towards Selma. I threw my leg over her back and pulled myself up at the same time Ferghus leapt into the saddle behind me. He kicked Selma's side and we raced forward. Just then, a third arrow pierced the bed roll tied to Selma's back.

"*Oh my god!*" I cried, covering my head.

"Stay calm, Rosa," Ferghus whispered against the top of my head, "two on the west bank and three on the east; nae horses – probably on foot from Dunscaith or Armadale..." Selma galloped along the grassy terrain while I tried to process his words. I didn't understand the names, but I took strength in his confidence. I stayed hunched over for a few more minutes until Ferghus slowed Selma and touched me gently upon my back. "Yer safe now," he told me.

I slowly lifted my head and looked around. The space wasn't nearly as narrow, making an ambush impossible here. Ferghus kept Selma at a steady pace. "Why were they trying to *kill* us?" I finally managed, my voice quavering.

"Aam not sure if they were Tristen's men searchin' fer *ye*, or other MacDonalds comin' fer *me*."

"How can there be so many rivalries you can't keep them all straight?" I questioned.

Ferghus shrugged. "Somebody's always doin' somethin' tae someone. Hard tae remember the exact moment it all started."

"That's ridiculous. This whole *thing* is ridiculous! I need to turn myself in – go back to Tristen, introduce myself, and tell him I'm sorry I ran away from his *stupid* wedding ceremony!" I exclaimed, feeling as if I was having a panic attack.

"Breathe, Rosa – yer safe. Ye need tae trust me," Ferghus said.

"Did you hear anything I just said? We can *fix* this – I just need to speak to Tristen – make him listen to the *truth*."

"That's fear talkin'. Ye'd change yer mind once ye'd met heem. He's arrogant – entitled. He gets what he wants no matter who he hurts." Ferghus's voice was laced with bitterness.

"I can't do this," I gushed, "I thought I was stronger than this. I've trained my whole life, but in the middle of a *real* battle, I panic!"

"Mmm, Ah disagree," Ferghus said, much to my annoyance.

"I could barely *breathe* I was so scared! When you told me to run for Selma, I thought I was going to *faint*!"

Ferghus actually laughed. "But ye *didn't*. Yer just fine in a crisis. Other hens would have needed tae be *carried*, Brigid." He paused and then continued, "have ye forgotten how brave ye were in the woods?"

I could feel my pulse slowing and tears forming in my eyes. I didn't understand why I suddenly felt so damn emotional. "God, I'm crying *again*! What's wrong with me?"

Ferghus's voice was gentle when he replied, "yer overwhelmed. It's normal…"

"But *you're* not crying!" I sobbed, feeling utterly foolish. Ferghus had been calm the *entire* time.

"Yer not used tae this. Yer body's tryin' tae adjust…"

I let myself cry quietly for a few minutes while we continued along the grassy road. Finally, I wiped my cheeks with my palms and inhaled. My breath was shaky, but no more tears were falling. "What were they shooting at us – *arrows*?" I asked to break the silence.

"Aye."

"Can you *die* from an arrow?" I wondered.

"Aye – tis possible."

"How could you stay so calm? It was life or death!"

"Ah swore an oath tae serve mah clan, Brigid…"

"But you didn't swear an oath to protect *me*! You threw me on the ground – you covered me with your *body*!"

"It was nothin'…"

"It wasn't *nothing*!" I could feel my pulse racing again, "you saved my *life*!"

"It was instinct," Ferghus suggested.

"Some instinct," I said sarcastically, "you have a death wish."

He was quiet for a minute before he responded, "nae. But Ah couldn't just leave ye helpless, Sasannach."

"What if you had *died*?"

"Yer askin' all the wrong questions, Rosa," Ferghus told me matter-of-factly.

"Oh, is that right?"

"Aam not one of yer bairns from back home," he said, an edge of irritation in his voice, "if Ah had died protectin' ye, then Ah would have died with honour; ain't nothin' wrong with that…"

"But you don't even *know* me – not really. Why are you helping me? What's in it for *you*?"

Ferghus was quiet for a minute. "Ah don't have an answer fer ye, Brigid. All Ah know is if Ah can help ye, Ah will."

Chapter Eleven:

We didn't dismount for some time. I was keenly aware of Ferghus's hard body in the saddle behind me. I could smell his musky scent and feel the muscles rippling through his forearms where they pressed against the tops of my thighs. We rarely spoke; he seemed intent on watching the edges of the roads, especially when woods appeared again. He led Selma into the canopy. "We're close."

Within a few minutes, it grew hilly and Selma started to protest. "Does she need a rest?" I questioned.

"Aye," Ferghus said, "we need tae check her hooves fer stones, but Aam not stoppin' til we get tae Sloane's."

"I can get off," I offered, "I'm okay. I can walk…"

"Ye sure? Ye had quite a fright," Ferghus said.

"I'm okay, Ferghus." He nodded and helped me climb down. We continued along the winding paths, the hills steadily increasing until a sheen of sweat glistened upon my forehead. Ferghus pulled his flask from his pocket and handed it to me without speaking. "Thank you," I breathed, taking a long drink.

"Almost there," Ferghus told me when he'd put the container away.

"Okay," I said.

"Yer in good shape," he commented with a half smile, "these hills are steep."

"I won't be if I stop exercising," I complained lightly as we started climbing again.

Ferghus's lips twitched. "Yer exercisin' right *now*," he responded as we navigated around two enormous boulders.

"When I get back home, I'll have forgotten all my katas," I told him.

"Is that the name fer yer exercises?"

"Yes. I teach them to younger students at my Dojo."

"Yer a unique one," he said as the trees began to thin again.

Eventually, the woods ended and were replaced by a vast clearing of waist-high grasses and wild flowers. "This is beautiful," I breathed, observing navy water in the distance.

"Aye," Ferghus said, watching me closely. He pointed towards the water. "The castle's on the bluffs," he explained, "we'll get food and a hot bath there…"

I smiled. "Can I take my dress off for that?" I teased.

Ferghus's cheeks actually flushed. "Ye shouldn't say such things, Brigid."

"I won't say it in front of your friend – *promise*."

"Aam a man *tay*, Rosa," Ferghus said gruffly, "ye shouldn't talk about bein' naked."

I glanced at his earnest expression. "Sorry," I apologized, "I was only teasing. I'll be more careful from now on…"

He didn't reply, just urged Selma down the path towards the outline of a large home. It was made entirely of charcoal stone. I could see an outer circle protecting the inner walls, which rose into the air. It seemed to be a two-storey structure with underground passages. Suddenly, the sound of an explosion close by made me jump. "Whoa," Ferghus cried to Selma.

"What was *that*?" I exclaimed, "are we being shot at?"

Ferghus was watching the grass to our right, a small smile tugging the corners of his mouth. "Nae, just mah cousins showin' off their terrible huntin' skills," he joked as two men emerged from the meadow and ambled towards us.

One was just a couple inches taller than I, but looked strong as an ox: barrel-chested with large biceps. He had sandy hair and dark eyes, and was carrying an old-fashioned rifle over his shoulder. The other man was taller, but lean. As he got closer, I could see his features were boyish with a large grin spread across his face. He had blond hair as well, but his eyes were a clear version of Ferghus's. "Mura he mo cho-ogha a tha a 'coimhead coltach ri radan a chaidh a bhathadh![52]" the muscular man called.

"Chan eil a h-uile duine again fhathast a 'biadhadh le mathraichean![53]" Ferghus shot back with a mischievous grin.

"Co an Domhnallach a tha thu air a 'pholadh an-drasta?[54]" the blue-eyed one teased as we met them on the grassy meadow. He was carrying two dead birds on the back of his blue and green kilt, and his eyes were appraising me curiously.

"Cus dhiubh gu leor airson cunntadh![55]" Ferghus told them as Sloane pulled the arrow out of the side of the bed roll.

He held it up and grinned. "Co-ogha teann caol,[56]" he joked, but his eyes had also come to rest upon me.

I blushed in the presence of these strange Highlanders – all dressed traditionally and sporting muscular calves, thighs, and arms. I couldn't

---

[52] If it isn't my cousin looking like a drowned rat!

[53] Not all of us are still spoon-fed by our mothers.

[54] Which MacDonald have you been pissing off now?

[55] Too many to count.

[56] A narrow escape cousin.

understand a word any of them was saying, and I worried they were all discussing what to do with me. "Nam bithinn air a bhith nam aonar, bhiodh e air a bhith na dheagh spors," Ferghus boasted, smiling in my direction.

"I don't understand," I whispered, my cheeks still red.

"Ah, tha i sa *Bheurla*," the boyish one grinned, "an e taisbeanadh co-la-breith a th'ann?[57]"

"Nae," Ferghus replied tersely, finally speaking English, "it's complicated. I'll tell ye after ye've fed us."

"Sick of coney?" Sloane teased, as he gestured towards the castle. Ferghus grasped Selma's lead and we all began walking along the path.

"Aye," Ferghus laughed, "and pissin' intae the wind."

"What's yer name?" the boyish one asked, "mah name's Nyle. Ye came at the right time…"

"Brigid," I said shyly.

"He doesn't live here," Ferghus explained, "just wants a party…"

"Oh," I said, "a party for what?"

"Mah birthday," Nyle replied, "we'll be celebratin' taemorrow night."

"We'll be gone by then," Ferghus said with a sideways glance at me, "going tae take her tae Dunvegan."

"Co i[58]?" Sloane questioned, eyeing me curiously as we walked.

"Minichidh mi nas fhaide air adhart,[59]" Ferghus said gruffly.

"And what's *your* name?" I asked the thicker man.

---

[57] Ah, she's English. Is she a birthday present?

[58] Who is she?

[59] I'll explain later.

"Sloane," Ferghus interjected.

"Oh, so *this* is your friend," I mumbled. I felt truly out of my element, not sure what to say in the presence of any of these brawny men.

"He was exaggeratin', lass," Sloane joked, "we're *cousins*, but Ah don't know about *friends*."

"*Sgriobadh dheth!*[60]" Ferghus said and unexpectedly punched Sloane hard in the side. Sloane actually laughed and returned the punch, but landed his on top of Ferghus's bicep. Ferghus laughed too.

"Please say ye'll come tae mah ceilidh," Nyle said, smiling widely at me, "ye can leave the day after."

"It's just a *birthday*," Ferghus commented irritably, "she has more important things tae worry about right now."

"How old will you be?" I asked Nyle.

"Twenty-two," he answered proudly.

I returned the smile. "Well, happy *almost* birthday. I turned twenty-one in May."

Sloane glanced at me, but didn't say anything. Nyle beamed. "Then this shall be a belated party fer ye as well."

I laughed. "After the past couple days, a party is much needed!"

Ferghus frowned as we reached the enclosed yard leading to the castle. "We should stay focused," he said meaningfully.

"If ye haven't already noticed, Ferghus is a tad uptight," Sloane commented as he unlatched the gate.

Ferghus scowled. "I'll take Selma tae the stables," he stated peevishly and continued around the side of the property.

---

[60] Screw off!

Nyle laughed. "Ye poor lass. Ye slept outside with the likes of *him*?" Ferghus heard and glanced over his shoulder at me, his brow creased.

"I'm just sorry to impose on Sloane with no notice," I said diplomatically.

"Tis nae trouble," Sloane assured me as a man with greying hair and sideburns pulled the front door open for us. The entrance was narrow and dim. A portly woman bustled over and curtsied. "Cha robh fios agam gun robh aoighean again a 'tighinn an-diugh.[61]"

"Cha robh sinne nas motha,[62]" Sloane told her before switching to English, "this is Brigid. She'll need a room and clothes. Mah sister should be able tae assist with that…"

"Of course," the housekeeper said, and left immediately.

"First, ye need a drink," Nyle suggested.

"I've been told my choices are whisky or beer," I joked, remembering back to my conversation with Ferghus.

"Aye," Nyle agreed, "mah cousin was right. What's yer drink of choice?"

I shook my head. "I have *no* idea. I usually drink coffee."

Sloane laughed and turned to the butler. "A round of whisky fer all of us. We'll take it in the sittin' room."

I followed Sloane and Nyle down the hall. The sitting room was about the size of the coffee shop I worked in, but brighter than the hallway due to several large windows letting in the grey light of early afternoon. "I don't want to ruin your sofa," I protested when Sloane gestured for me to take a seat, "my dress – "

[61] I didn't know we had guests arriving today.

[62] Neither did we.

"Mah sister can lend ye somethin'," Sloane assured me, "and take nae mind of the furniture. Tis old anyway…"

"It looks like ye were at a weddin'," Nyle suddenly noticed, his voice curious.

I flushed, unsure how to respond, when the butler returned and saved me from speaking. He was carrying a tray of glasses and a full bottle of amber liquid. He set it upon a side table and began pouring us each a drink. Nyle took two glasses and passed one to me before joining me on one of the sofas. Sloane took a glass and sat facing us. "Cheers tae good health."

"And tae belated birthdays!" Nyle added with a grin.

Both tipped their glasses and swallowed the whisky in one drink. "Tis nae other way tae drink good water o' life, lass," Sloane advised me with a smile, "go on…"

Just then, Ferghus entered the room. He rolled his eyes when he saw the three of us. "Didn't take ye long tae start celebratin'," he chastised his cousins.

"Yer just upset we have a head start," Sloane teased.

Ferghus poured three more glasses and handed one to each of his cousins. "It will make all yer worries disappear," Ferghus joked as he took a seat across from me and lifted his glass in the air. The three of them stared at me, waiting for me to follow them in a drink. "Gus na lamhan a thoirt air falbh bho scum MacDhomhnaill![63]"

Sloane and Nyle laughed heartily. "Ye didn't?" Nyle questioned, his blue eyes alight with mirth.

---

[63] To severing the hands off MacDonald scum!

"Aye," Ferghus nodded, still holding his whisky in the air. His vibrant eyes settled upon me. "Come *on*, Brigid, we haven't got all day. There's a tub of hot water callin' mah name."

Sloane chortled and said, "ah, give the lass a moment; she's had tae put up with the likes of *ye* fer how long?"

"Just a couple days," Ferghus replied defensively, "believe me, I've *earned* this drink."

Nyle leaned forward in his seat. "Innis dhomh gu bheil I mar mo cho-la-breith agus is urrainn dhut m 'ol cuideachd.[64]"

Ferghus's eyes grew stormy. "Shut up and swallow, ye wee bairn; it may be yer last if ye don't sheathe yer bod[65] in front of the lass."

"Gawd, Ferghus," Sloane chastised, his face growing serious for the first time since we'd arrived, "drink up; ye need it more than us."

Ferghus tipped the glass and drained it. Then he stood, refilled it at the sideboard, and drank that too. I heard him slam the empty container against the table, but my back was to him. Both Nyle and Sloane exchanged a look with one another before Sloane cleared his throat. "I apologize on behalf of mah cousin. Tay many days in the wild."

Nyle shifted uncomfortably in his seat beside me. "Ye gonna drink that, Brigid?" he asked quietly.

I inhaled. "I'll try," I replied, smiling at him nervously. I pressed the small glass to my lips and touched my tongue to the liquid; it burned. "*Oh god*," I breathed and both Nyle and Sloane chuckled.

"Come on, lass, tis the smoothest on Skye," Sloane urged gently.

"Right," I said, readying myself. I counted to five inside my head and tipped the glass. The whisky burned all the way down and continued

---

[64] Tell me she's my birthday present and you can drink mine too.

[65] Penis

to warm my insides when I'd finished. "*Oh!*" I threw my head back and forth rapidly, "how can you *stand* it?"

Nyle drained his second glass and grinned. "Lots of practice."

"Aye, and that's the truth," Sloane agreed.

Just then, the housekeeper entered the room and curtsied. "Aila is ready fer the young quine."

Sloane rolled his eyes and stood. "Dh'fhaodadh I co-dhiu a bhith a 'coinneachadh rithe an seo.[66]"

The housekeeper's cheeks flushed. "Tha mi duilich. Cha tigeadh i.[67]"

"Did I do something wrong?" I asked, looking at each face to try to ascertain the reason for the change in mood.

"Nae," Sloane said, "I'll show ye tae the bathin' room mahself. Mah sister's probably poutin' over havin' tae share one of her frocks."

"Oh, I can just wear this!" I protested, standing shakily, my own cheeks red with embarrassment, "I didn't mean to inconvenience anyone; I'm very sorry!"

Nyle stood when I did and said encouragingly, "we're happy ye came; ye'll make a bonnie addition tae mah ceilidh."

"I hope I can stay," I told him earnestly.

He nodded and went to refill his glass while Sloane led me from the room with the housekeeper. We continued down the hall to a narrow staircase that lifted two stories into the air. "Ye can get Brigid's bath ready," he told the housekeeper, "and I'll deal with Aila." He stomped up the stairs.

---

[66] She could have at least met her out here.

[67] I'm sorry. She wouldn't come.

"Follow me, miss," the woman said and directed me to a back entrance that led into a walled garden.

The gardens were expansive and contained shade trees, as well as vegetable patches. In the far corner of the garden, I could see what looked to be a small tent hanging strategically atop a large wooden tub. It reminded me of a miniature hot tub from my own home town. "It's been sunny the past few days," the housekeeper said cheerfully.

As we neared the tented bath, I could smell something fragrant emanating from it; smoke rings were floating into the blue sky. "What's that smell?" I asked curiously and heard a loud splash in response.

"Ferghus, miss," the housekeeper answered.

"Take her inside," Ferghus's deep voice demanded from the tent.

"What's going on?" I wondered.

"*Get inside*," Ferghus repeated angrily, "ye shouldn't be bathin' outdoors. Take her into the *bathin'* room."

"Aye, sir," the housekeeper replied and nodded towards the house.

I trailed reluctantly after her, turning to watch the smoke lifting into the air. "What's he *doing* in there?" I asked.

The housekeeper looked at me quizzically and laughed. "Have ye never seen a *tub* before?"

I blushed. "Of course," I said, "just not in quite the same design."

The housekeeper smiled sympathetically. "Yers won't be quite as warm."

"Why *not*?" I asked.

"Ah told ye – it's been sunny the past few days," she repeated slowly as if I had brain damage.

I bit my lip and didn't reply. I soon discovered my bath was taking place in a dingy room with very little natural light. Instead, the housekeeper lit several candles around the room and helped me remove what was left of the tattered wedding gown. "Dae ye want tae keep this?" she inquired, staring at the dress in disgust.

"No," I said in embarrassment, "it can be thrown away."

"Good." She tossed it onto the floor and gestured for me to get into a tub of water. I climbed in and almost screamed. It wasn't exactly *freezing*, but it was certainly much colder than I had expected.

"God, this is *awful*," I complained.

"Tis," she agreed, "once yer clean, miss, don't go traipsin' into the woods and ye can avoid this unpleasantness fer weeks!"

"*Weeks*?" I said doubtfully.

"Aye." She handed me a bar of glycerin soap and said, "wash up. I'll check on Aila and a frock."

When she'd gone, I hurried to wash my body and hair as fast as I could. My teeth were chattering by the time the housekeeper returned. She had an armful of clothing she set on a wooden chair by the tub. She handed me a towel, which I wrapped around myself. The outfit consisted of several layers. First, I had to put on a pair of cream underwear that stretched almost to my knees. Then, the housekeeper placed a corset around me and fastened it so tightly, I could hardly take a breath. Layered on top of *that* was a white blouse with sleeves that gradually flared, dangling almost to the middle of my thighs. "How will I eat?"

"*Hmmm*?" she responded absentmindedly.

"Never mind," I mumbled as she helped me step into a floor-length wool skirt in a bright yellow tartan. The dress already felt heavy, but I was *still* not fully dressed. The final detail was a tank-style gown of black velvet that sat on top of the rest. It parted in the centre to show off the yellow plaid print beneath, and had three bows down the centre of my chest. I had never worn anything so elaborate in all my life.

"What about this hair?" the housekeeper questioned.

"I haven't had a brush in a few days," I said defensively.

She nodded and produced a comb that she ran through my tangled locks. I gritted my teeth, but eventually the hair lay flat. She gathered it on top of my head and secured it with pins before tying on a hat that resembled a thick, velvet headband. "Ye look bonnie, miss. Ye wear it even better than Aila in mah opinion."

"Thank you for all your help," I said.

***

When I emerged from the bathing room, I asked the housekeeper where I should go. She smiled and said, "I'll show ye tae the guest chambers. Ah prepared one fer ye." I followed her up a narrow staircase to the second floor containing six chambers. "Ah put ye in the first one, away from our other guests," she said pointedly.

"Will there be many visitors tomorrow night?" I questioned.

"It will be a small party," she said, "Sloane's father is away on clan business."

"I see," I responded, but I had no idea what any of this meant.

She curtsied and said, "I'll leave ye tae rest. Dinner will be served in an hour."

I glanced around the small room. To the right of the door was a small wooden table and chair. There were no pictures on the walls. In the far right corner was an enormous spinning wheel like the kind I had seen in illustrated versions of *Sleeping Beauty*. I found its presence almost creepy. Soft grey light was pouring in through one large window in the exact centre of the chamber. It contained no curtains, but had shutters like those on the outsides of houses in Huntsville. Beneath it was a long bench one would find in a locker room. The four-poster bed was pushed against the far left wall and reminded me of something out of a live theatre production of *A Christmas Carol*. There were two steps just to get into it, and drab tan drapes on both sides were held open with ties. Finally, a large, ornately-carved chest of drawers filled the final corner. It had a vase of white lilies upon it, which were just beginning to open.

I wandered over to the window, having nothing to unpack, and gazed out. It didn't afford views of the garden *or* water; instead, it faced the path we had traversed to get to the circular stone wall surrounding the front of the castle. I soon grew bored inside my chamber. I had nothing to occupy me: no meaningful work, or hobbies I could practice. A gnawing hunger plagued me as well, since I had given my breakfast to Ferghus. Just the thought of him made me angry. Why had he been allowed to bathe in the sunshine, while I had been forced indoors? My water had been freezing, while he had enjoyed a cigar in a hot tub! It was with these thoughts that I exited my chamber and descended the stairs. Just as I was rounding the banister at the bottom, a young man with jet black hair was passing by. Luckily, I still had my hand upon the railing so I did not lose my balance. "Tha mi duilich. Cha robh I gad fhaicinn ann an am," he said, his coal eyes deeply apologetic.

"I'm sorry, but I don't understand," I told him, my cheeks flushing in embarrassment.

He smiled kindly in realization. "I'm sorry I didn't see you in time," he repeated, "are you okay?"

I returned his gentle smile. "Yes, I'm fine. Thank you."

"We've not met before," he observed, "I'm Owyn – cousin to Sloane."

"Another cousin? How many of you *are* there?"

He laughed. "Too many." He paused and then commented, "are you a distant relation of Sloane's?"

"No, I'm Brigid. I came with Ferghus."

Owyn nodded. "I did not think Ferghus would be joining in the merry making. It's nice he could make it. Are you travelling with a large party?"

"No, just the two of us."

"Has Ferghus gotten married?" Owyn questioned curiously, a smile tugging the corners of his lips.

I blushed an even deeper shade of red. "*Oh god*! *Oh no*! We're not *married*! We just met in the woods and he helped me. He brought me here to ask for Sloane's assistance. I'm not sure if he's had a chance to speak to him about anything yet..." I broke off, realizing I was rambling.

Owyn frowned. "This is highly unusual. Are you sure you understand Ferghus's intentions?"

"His *intentions*?" I asked in confusion.

Owyn sighed. "He's a bit of a lost sheep. If I can give you some friendly advice – avoid being *alone* with Ferghus. I love him – he's my kin, after all – but he should know better than to – "

"Please don't get the wrong idea," I interrupted, "Ferghus didn't do anything *inappropriate*. He found me after a bit of an ordeal and was kind enough to help me. He actually risked his life getting me here safely."

Owyn stared into my eyes for a few seconds before replying, "okay. I will get the full story from him, I'm sure. Well, welcome, Brigid. I'm not used to seeing such a lovely guest in Sloane's house."

"Thank you," I said.

"Speaking of guests, do you know where everyone is? I just arrived and the sitting room was empty."

"I'm not sure; I was in my bedroom."

"Well, let us go in search of everyone together," Owyn suggested.

"Okay," I agreed and followed him down the hall to the front entrance.

The butler nodded and said, "they're in the Great Hall. Dinner is almost ready."

"The *great* hall?" I questioned.

"I'll show you," Owyn replied.

He was so gentle compared to his other cousins. I wondered what his story was.

Chapter Twelve:

Owyn led me down the long hallway, stopping at the entrance to an expansive room that reminded me of my high school cafeteria. I could hear loud voices inside, so I wasn't exactly excited to cross the threshold, but Owyn smiled at me and said, "it's okay; they won't bite a lady."

I blushed and nodded before we stepped inside together. It was the most awkward situation I had experienced since my own *prom*. Everyone in the room stopped talking and fixed their eyes upon me. It suddenly dawned on me that none of these men, including Ferghus, had seen me fresh from a bath before, wearing their traditional style of dress. There was a loud scraping of chairs as everyone in the room stood as one body. I quickly scanned the room and noticed two new men among them: one was young, probably in his twenties, with dark brown hair and blue eyes, while the other was his twin, but twenty-five years his senior. I was light-headed from nerves, whisky, and travelling with very little food or rest. I needed to sit down. I took a hesitant step into the room, wondering where etiquette demanded I sit. I avoided Ferghus's gaze; I was still angry at having to take a cold bath. He was a selfish man who didn't deserve my attention.

"Over here," I heard Owyn say from behind my left shoulder. He was pointing at one of the long tables.

"Okay," I whispered and started to move towards it when suddenly Nyle strode over, a broad smile upon his face.

"Brigid, ye stole all the light from the room," he gushed, his pale blue eyes twinkling.

"Thank you," I said, keenly aware no one had sat down yet or resumed their conversations. I was beyond embarrassed.

"Let her sit *down*," Owyn told Nyle. He turned to me and gestured to an empty seat between Sloane and the younger of the two new men.

I hesitated, but Sloane smiled and stepped back so I could be seated. It wasn't an easy task to climb onto a bench in an enormous dress with layers of undergarments. Once I'd manoeuvered onto the seat, all the men sat too. I could feel Sloane's muscular thigh pressing against mine and the new man was gazing at me curiously. "Hugh," he said by way of introduction, "and ye must be the lass we've all been hearin' aboot."

"Oh god, you've all been *talking* about me?" I couldn't help but blurt.

"All good things," Hugh assured me, "Ferghus was bringin' us up tae speed on the MacDonalds."

"Okay," I said softly, glancing over Nyle's head, who had sat across from me, to where Ferghus was seated at the other table with Owyn and Hugh's father. They were already deep in conversation. I had a feeling Nyle had switched seats so he could be closer to me. There were empty tankards and glasses strewn across both tables. It appeared the drinking had continued while I'd been bathing. "What did Ferghus tell you?"

"How ye met; what Tristen did tae ye – how he sent his men tae attack the two of ye – "

"Tristen didn't really hurt me *himself*," I began, but Nyle interjected.

"We'll all help ye as soon as mah birthday's over," he told me confidently.

"The *epic* ceilidh," Sloane joked.

Just then, several servants entered the room with trays laden with food. A full plate was set before me, containing roast mutton, sliced pear, and some kind of root vegetable covered in parsley. It was savoury and delicious, and the room grew quiet as everyone began to eat. The servants brought out a local wine made from flowers, as well as plates of oat cakes. Everything tasted so different from my usual fare back home. I ate slowly, savouring each item and appreciating the seasoning; I had been eating nothing but rabbit, nuts, and berries for three days, so the contrast awakened my tastebuds. Soon, the men began to talk again. I listened quietly to their conversations, most of which weren't in English, aware they probably knew more about my predicament than I knew about each of *them*. When there was an opening, I asked Hugh if he was a cousin too. "Aye, on mah mother's side."

When I had finished everything on my plate, I observed the room better. There was dark wood panelling everywhere, which would have made the room exceptionally dim if not for the expansive windows along one wall letting in the sun. There was an unoccupied table along one wall positioned on a raised platform and, instead of benches, it contained ornately-carved chairs with plush velvet backs and seats. I wondered if that was where Sloane's father sat when he wasn't away on business. When everything was cleared away, more whisky was brought out. I shook my head when Hugh offered me a glass. Sloane laughed. "The lass already tried some of mah family recipe."

"It burned my throat!" I confided and Nyle and Hugh laughed too.

Once, when I happened to glance up, I caught Ferghus staring at me, but he quickly averted his eyes and continued his conversation with Hugh's father. Sloane noticed and whispered in my ear, "Ferghus seems quite taken with ye."

I shrugged and responded as casually as I could, "I think he's eager for more bloodshed. He seems happy to have an excuse to seek revenge."

"Nae, lass," Sloane said, shaking his head, "Ferghus doesn't dae anythin' without careful plannin'. He's more battle savvy than any of us, even if he *is* moody…"

Nyle grinned. "Aye, Ah remember our games as a lad; Ah never wanted tae compete against him. He never relents, and gets right pissed off when he loses."

"Which is rare," Sloane commented.

Nyle changed the subject. "Have ye had a chance tae see any of the grounds?"

"No," I answered, "can we do that now?"

"Of course," Sloane interjected, "I'll take ye round."

"Dae ye mind if Ah join ye?" Hugh asked.

"Not at all," I said easily.

The four of us started towards the door, but Ferghus suddenly asked, "caite a bheil thu a'dol?[68]"

"A 'dol timcheall air an togalach,[69]" Sloane replied. Ferghus nodded and stood also, falling in line behind us. His dark hair was freshly washed and I could smell the same glycerin soap scent I had used. I noticed he had changed out of his faded green and blue tartan and was wearing the same bright yellow pattern as I was. "Tha mia 'gealltainn gum bi mi sabhailte,[70]" Sloane added.

"What are you all saying?" I finally interrupted, feeling annoyed with their secret discussions in front of me.

"Just tryin' tae decide where tae take ye," Sloane answered.

---

[68] Where are you going?

[69] Touring the property.

[70] I promise I'll keep her safe.

"And with *whom*," Ferghus added pointedly from behind me.

Hugh was immediately to my left, but Nyle kept trying to catch my eye. "Did the MacDonalds bring ye by Galley then?" he asked conversationally.

"I'm not sure – " I began, but Ferghus interrupted.

"It was a birlinn," he stated evenly.

"A *birlinn*?" I questioned, looking over my shoulder at him.

"Aye, it had twelve oars," Ferghus stated firmly, his blue eyes flashing intensely.

I knew my own expression must have been a combination of confusion and annoyance; I was still angry at him for the bath, but wasn't sure how to handle the line of questioning from Ferghus's over-enthusiastic cousins. Perhaps I should have welcomed his interference, but instead I decided to change the subject. "It's such a lovely day," I commented as Sloane led us around the outer walls and up a grass-covered hill overlooking the water.

"Tis," Sloane agreed, "shall we go down by the shore?"

"Yes, please!"

The hill sloped gently down to the water's edge, which was a mixture of rocky and sandy patches. "It's smoother over there," Sloane told me, pointing down the water to a beautiful golden section. Several wooden docks had been constructed to secure boats. They were situated between three enormous trees that helped create a shady space to rest.

"Are all those boats yours?" I asked, shading my eyes to see them better.

"Nae, that one's mah father's," Hugh said, pointing at the closest one.

"The rest are mine," Sloane said proudly.

"Dae ye like tae swim, Brigid?" Nyle questioned with a grin.

"Yes, very much," I answered as we headed towards the docks.

Ferghus cleared his throat and said, "but not taeday."

"Why *not* taeday?" Nyle questioned enthusiastically, "nae time like the present." He had a mischievous grin upon his face and exchanged a look with Sloane.

Sloane just chuckled, but Ferghus suddenly switched back into his own language so I wouldn't understand. "*Cuir as e!*[71]" he said gruffly.

"She said she likes tae swim," Nyle stated, looking at me for support, "isn't that right, Brigid?" He winked.

I found myself blushing. "I *do*," I replied softly, "but perhaps now isn't the best time."

We had reached the docks. The cries of gulls filled the air as they dove for fish. It was a perfect day: the waves were calm and the sky didn't have a single dark cloud in it. "We should take advantage of this fine day," Nyle pressed. He ventured onto the first dock where Hugh's boat was moored. Sloane and Hugh followed, so I did as well. I heard Ferghus sigh, but he joined everyone at the end of the dock.

"You have a beautiful property," I complimented Sloane.

"Thank ye," he said, a proud smile upon his face, "it just needs feminine touches tae make it more agreeable."

"Carson nach iarr thu a lamh direach an-drasta?[72]" Ferghus exclaimed.

I turned to see what had upset him but, other than a stormy look in his eyes, I could not find a source of his grievance. Sloane laughed. "Tha mi a 'faireachdainn cuid de fhaireachdainnean air ur pairt…[73]"

[71] Knock it off!

[72] Why don't you just ask for her hand right now?

"Nae, just decorum," Ferghus said defensively.

"Ye won't find it from our cousin," Sloane pointed out.

That's when we all observed Nyle had already removed his boots and sporran, and was pulling off his kilt too. *"Oh my god!"* I laughed, clapping my hand over my mouth in shock.

"Tha thu crubach air leanabh![74]" Ferghus yelled, his face turning red.

Hugh laughed. *"Tell us how the water is!"* he exclaimed.

The last of Nyle's clothes fell away, leaving him stark naked in front of us. Thankfully, he was facing the water so all I saw was his rear end. He ran to the edge and, without pausing, leapt into the air before plunging into the water below. He surfaced a few seconds later and tossed his head back and forth a couple times to shake the water from his hair. "Come in, Brigid! It's warm!"

"Let's go back tae the house," Ferghus implored me, an anxious look in his eyes, "ye don't need tae be exposed tae this."

"Nothin' wrong with a swim," Sloane interjected. He pulled off his bonnet and grinned.

"Stad a 'nochdadh![75]" Ferghus scolded.

"Nyle's not competin' fair," Sloane said, dropping his sporran onto the dock and sliding a knife out of the top of his long socks, "but everyone knows Ah have the best assets in the family!"

"Nae," Ferghus disagreed, "the smallest. Perhaps ye should be hidin' em instead!"

---

[73] I sense some feelings on your part.

[74] You crazy child!

[75] Stop showing off!

"Don't listen tae him, Brigid," Sloane said as he dropped his kilt onto the dock. My entire face turned scarlet as I saw all of him bared in front of me. "Ah have somethin' tae keep ye warm when winter comes!" he joked and ran backwards off the dock.

Sloane surfaced beside Nyle and shoved Nyle's head under water for a few seconds. When Nyle broke free, he spit a mouthful at Sloane and they started laughing. Hugh chuckled and began to undress too. "*Ni Dia cron air*!" Ferghus swore, "tha mi cairdeach dha clan![76]" Suddenly, his strong hand was grasping my forearm and dragging me down the dock. I stumbled and regained my balance before I knew what was happening.

"*Ferghus*!" I exclaimed, but he stared straight ahead and hauled me along with him.

"Ah think ye've seen enough of mah cousins fer one day!"

"*Let me go*!" I cried, "*or I'll hurt you*!"

He stopped abruptly and released his hold. "They're a bunch of *bairns*!" he complained, his face still flushed.

"Yes," I giggled.

"It's not *funny*, Brigid," Ferghus chastised lightly, folding his muscular arms across his chest.

"It's *kind* of funny," I teased. I glanced back at the dock just in time to see Hugh jumping off. I giggled again.

Ferghus was silent as he stared at my profile. "Ye look just like one of our *own* lasses," he suddenly said, his voice unexpectedly husky.

I glanced at him quickly and saw his eyes were still smouldering, but no longer with anger. "I *do*?" I asked in a small voice, "is that a good thing?"

---

[76] God damn it! I'm related to a bunch of children!

"Mah cousins seem tae think so," Ferghus replied, watching me closely, "but Ah warned ye about them earlier. What dae ye think of them *now*?"

I looked back at the water, shielding my eyes from the bright sun. "I think they like to have fun," I commented with another giggle.

"Aye, that they dae," he agreed.

I smiled at his serious face. "Why aren't you joining them?" I teased, "don't you like to have fun too?"

"Aye, Rosa, Ah like tae have fun," he answered, his gaze piercing, "but at the right times."

I giggled again. "Will you jump off the dock later then?"

He shook his head grumpily. "Not while yer in mah care."

I laughed loudly. "If I promise to stay *right here*, will you go in the water?"

He stared at me for a full minute before answering, "Ah can act like a bairn another time."

"You were *tempted*!" I teased, "you must be tired after all those days in the wild. If I promise to sit in the garden, will you join your cousins?"

His eyes actually twinkled. "Ah don't think Ah can trust ye tae stay put," he told me, "yer a wild Rosa, not easy tae tame."

"Go have fun," I ordered lightly, "I'll be *fine*, Ferghus. I'll sit in the garden and smell the *roses*."

He finally laughed too. "Promise me."

"I *promise*," I said more seriously, "just like I promised I wouldn't tell Sloane about you seeing me in my – "

He waved his hand dismissively. "Okay, okay – I'll go."

"Good. Go *frolick*."

"It's just a swim," Ferghus said, walking backwards towards the dock.

"I bet you boys get up to more mischief than *that*!" I accused with a smile.

"Aye, Sasannach – that's why Ah don't want ye here for Nyle's party," Ferghus replied, "go get into the garden and *stay* there."

"Yes, my king," I retorted with a laugh and turned to walk around the circular wall to the gardens.

Chapter Thirteen:

"A bheil I beo?"[77]

"A 'cadal, tha mi a smaoineachadh."[78]

"Co i?"[79]

"Chan fhaca mi I a-riamh."[80]

"Seo airson a 'phartaidh?"[81]

"Tha mi'n dochas gu bheil.[82]"

I awoke slowly, the sounds of different voices pulling me out of my dreams. When I opened my eyes, I stared in disbelief at one-two-three-four-*five* male faces hovering curiously over me. Not one was familiar. I blinked and opened my eyes again, wondering if I was dreaming, but the faces were still there. "Where am I?" I asked, lifting my torso to gaze around me. I was in Sloane's garden beneath a shade tree.

"Tha I na Beurla,[83]" a boyish one commented with a grin.

"Is docha gu bheil i na tiodhlac dhuinn,[84]" a muscular blond one stated with a mischievous gleam in his eyes.

---

[77] Is she alive?

[78] Asleep, I think.

[79] Who is she?

[80] Never seen her before.

[81] Here for the party?

[82] I hope so.

[83] She's English.

[84] Maybe she's a present for us.

"I don't understand," I said nervously, but the sound of laughter from the entrance to the garden pulled all of our attention away from one another.

Sloane entered first, wearing nothing but his kilt. Behind him came Ferghus, his dark hair still dripping. Nyle and Hugh were close behind, jostling each other like brothers. Then complete chaos erupted in the garden. Nyle and Ferghus's voices competed with each other as they both called out at the same time.

"*Thainig thu!*[85]" Nyle cried, hurrying towards the five men hovering around me in their kilts.

"*De an ifrinn a tha thu a 'deanamh?*[86]" Ferghus shouted, also rushing across the garden.

I sat straighter, still groggy from sleep. Ferghus knelt beside me, staring angrily up at the strange men, while Nyle smacked each one on the back and even punched the stockiest man in the shoulder. "*What's going on?*" I whispered.

"Ah hoped ye could tell *me*," Ferghus responded testily, "why the hell are ye lyin' on the ground?"

"I don't know," I answered, "I think I fell asleep…"

Ferghus rolled his eyes. "Ye promised me."

I blushed. "I've been in the garden the *whole* time," I said defensively, "I just fell *asleep*, Ferghus…"

He held his hand out to me and hissed, "*get up!*"

I grasped his palm and he helped me stand, dropping my hand immediately. I brushed the grass off the front of my dress and smiled sheepishly at all the men gathered around. They were talking and laughing

[85] You came!

[86] What the hell are you guys doing?

121

so boisterously, I thought they probably didn't even know I was there. I was mistaken.

A hush slowly descended over the garden as one-by-one everyone focused on me. "Brigid, meet mah friends," Nyle said with an enthusiastic smile, "this is Hamish, Ewan, Edan, Cam, and Brodie." He pointed to each one as he introduced their names, but I couldn't tell them apart; he'd gone much too fast.

"Hi," I said shyly.

"Aam Hamish, and yer bonnie," the bulky blond man joked. Ferghus rolled his eyes.

"Easy, Hamish, or she won't come tae mah party," Nyle scolded, giving him a friendly punch on his other shoulder.

"We have tae leave before then anyway," Ferghus told the group.

"Ah, let her stay, Ferghus," Sloane interjected, "she can watch us compete and choose the winners." His large chest rippled; it was highly distracting and I wondered why he hadn't gotten dressed like the rest of them. I noticed he was holding the rest of his clothes, dripping wet, in his large hand.

"Nae, we leave at dawn," Ferghus insisted.

"Who will we dance with if she goes?" the boyish one teased.

"Mah point exactly, Ewan," Nyle agreed, fixing me with a grave look, "please stay, Brigid. The party clearly needs yer presence…"

"Speakin' of parties, dae ye have anythin' tae drink in this place?" a tall, thin man with crooked teeth asked, "we worked up quite a thirst on the road, didn't we jimmies?"

"Ah bet ye did, Cam," Nyle laughed, "Aam sure Sloane can have his man bring ye somethin'."

"Finest whisky on Skye," Sloane boasted for the second time that day, "let's get inside. Mah cousins thought it'd be fun tae throw mah clothes in fer a swim tay."

Hugh and Nyle chortled, and the five newcomers joined in. Ferghus hung back with me as the large group entered the castle for more merrymaking. He ran his hand through his damp hair, a scowl emphasizing the deep scar running down his face. He glanced at me and, when he saw me staring at him, growled, "what are ye starin' at?"

"I wasn't staring," I replied slowly, unsure how to proceed.

"Aye, ye were," he retorted, "enjoyin' the entertainment, are ye?"

"I don't know what you're talking about," I answered quietly, casting my eyes downward to avoid his hostile glare. I inhaled sharply and added, "I did everything you asked, Ferghus. I stayed in the garden; I didn't go in the water; I kept my dress on…"

He rolled his eyes again. "Did ye now? And have ye decided which one will be first?" he inquired, his voice laced with sarcasm.

"First for *what*?" I wondered aloud.

"Are ye goin' tae have them court ye all at once then? Watch em compete fer ye and then trample their hearts into dust one-by-one?"

"*Court*?" I said incredulously, "what are you talking about? I don't even *know* these people!"

"Brigid, Ah warned ye, didn't Ah?"

I gaped at him. "Warned me about *what*? You said this place was going to be our safe haven – that we'd find welcome, and rest, and *help*!"

"Always so damn smart!" he cried, his face red.

"I should never have come here; I should never have listened to *anything* you said!" I shouted back and marched towards the door.

Just then, Owyn stepped into the garden. "Thought I'd check on you, Brigid. When the others returned, I started to worry they left you behind." Owyn suddenly noticed Ferghus fuming by the shade trees. "Oh, hello Ferghus. I didn't see you there."

"Thanks for your concern, Owyn, but I'm fine," I said curtly, "I just want to return to my bedroom and forget any of this ever happened."

Owyn glanced from my flushed face to Ferghus's and nodded slowly. "Okay, I'll leave you in peace. I hope your rest is rejuvenating." He bowed slightly and disappeared down the hallway. I climbed the stairs and was just about to enter my chamber, when Ferghus said, "Ah will let ye know when supper is served." His voice was trembling from suppressed emotion.

I jumped slightly and turned. "You scared me; I didn't know you came upstairs."

"Ye may know yer katas and karate and exercises, Brigid, but Aam *still* the better hunter." He stared at me meaningfully and added, "and Ah can smell another hunter a *mile* away. Trust me. Ye aren't safe here. We leave at dawn…"

***

I awoke to a commotion in the hall. First, a loud crash, then crazy laughter, shouting, and the sound of something, or *someone*, falling against my door. I stood quickly, trying to shake off sleep, and readied myself in case the wooden door was kicked in, or the lock picked. I heard more shouting and banging, but I couldn't understand anything being said. I tiptoed towards the door, listening intently for any snippets of English that might help inform me of the situation. Suddenly, the doorknob rattled and I heard Nyle's boyish voice call out, "ye hidin' in there, Brigid? Ye ready fer me?"

A second voice guffawed and more crashing ensued. "She's hidin' *from* ye, Nyle; doesn't want tae see how little ye have tae offer!" It sounded like his burly friend Hamish.

"Mah bod's as big as *Nessie!*" Nyle boasted before descending into a fit of raucous laughter.

The doorknob jiggled violently as Hamish replied, "maybe as monstrous tay!"

Something heavy smashed against the door, shaking it on its hinges. Fear prickled the back of my neck. I'd thought Nyle was supposed to be one of the men assisting me in escaping from the MacDonalds. He was acting like a drunken school boy trying to get laid.

"Where's mah birthday present, Brigid?" Nyle teased, but was suddenly interrupted by a third voice.

"Faigh air falbh bhon doras![87]" I recognized Ferghus right away, "agus cuir an d n asns agad air falbh![88]" he added in disgust.

"Come on boys – outside or tae bed tae sleep it off!" Sloane stated firmly.

I let my breath out slowly, feeling a weight lift from my shoulders. "It was *yer* idea!" I heard Nyle whine.

Hamish laughed. "Aye, twas, but it wasn't *mah* cock poundin' on her door!"

"Outside before Ah cut yers off tay!" Ferghus exclaimed, his voice filled with wrath.

I covered my mouth to keep from giggling. I could picture him actually following through. These boys had no idea who they were dealing with – mister 'I tie women up and march them through the forest for fun'.

[87] Get away from her door!

[88] And put your damn prick away!

"*Brigid*?" Sloane said after a minute, "*ye okay*?"

"I'm *fine*," I replied through the door.

"Ye can open it now, Sasannach," Ferghus told me. His voice was gentle this time.

I unbolted the heavy door and peered into the hall. Sloane was fully dressed now and Ferghus's hair was dry. "*Oh god*!" I cried when I saw the state of the hallway. Broken glass was strewn about and there was a wooden bench broken in two. "*Look what they did*!"

"Aye," Sloane laughed, "and he's not even *twenty-two* yet!" He didn't sound concerned.

"Watch yer feet," Ferghus instructed, "take mah hand." He held his hand towards me and I grasped it for support. I stepped carefully over the glass and descended the stairs with Ferghus while Sloane found his butler to clean up the mess.

"Ah have a mind tae leave *now* – not stay the night," Ferghus confided as he led me to the sitting room, but kept going when he saw Owyn, Hugh, and Hugh's father talking in there.

"But wouldn't it get dark awfully fast?" I questioned, feeling nauseous at the thought of going back the way we'd come. "They were shooting arrows at us this morning, Ferghus!" I reminded him.

He pushed open the front door and sighed heavily. "Ah know," he agreed, "Ah can't decide what tae dae and it's makin' me *crazy*!"

"I've noticed," I teased, trying to lighten the mood.

Ferghus glanced at me sharply. "Ye should be more careful, Brigid. Truly."

"I can take care of myself," I reminded him.

"Aye, maybe against one or two – but against a whole group? And with weapons?" He shook his head.

"Do you mean with their pants down?"

Ferghus stared at me aghast. "What kind of question is *that*?"

I giggled. "I heard Nyle mention his 'bod'. It's the second time he's used that word today."

Ferghus opened his mouth and then closed it again. He didn't smile. "Enough talkin' about Nyle. That man cannot hold his drink."

"Can *you*?"

"Can Ah *what*?" Ferghus asked peevishly. I loved the way his dark eyebrows lifted and his peacock eyes flashed every time I asked him something that made him uncomfortable.

"*Hold yer drink*?" I asked, imitating his accent and deep voice.

"Go on," Ferghus said dismissively as he led me in the opposite direction of the docks.

I giggled again. "*Can ye hold yer 'bod'*?" I questioned in the same voice.

Ferghus stopped abruptly. "Brigid, *stop*." I clapped my hand over my mouth, my cheeks red from laughing. "Ah said, stop."

"Sorry," I said, but I was still laughing.

"*Brigid…*"

"*Yes*?"

"Yer behaviour is inappropriate and mockin'; it's unladylike." He placed his hand upon his hip and gave me a sulky expression.

"It *is*?"

"Aye."

"Even though I look like one of your *lasses*?" I asked, imitating his statement from earlier in the day.

His sulky expression deepened. "Ye need a good whippin'," he told me, but his tone was annoyed rather than angry.

"*Never!*" I cried and took off running up the grassy hill. It ascended gradually, so wasn't as difficult to climb as some of the hills on our way to Sloane's. When I got about halfway up, I turned to look over my shoulder. Ferghus was only an arm's length away. I shrieked and ran as fast as I could, but he managed to grasp me around my waist. We tumbled to the ground, out of breath. I had landed on my hands and knees with his hand still grasping the side of my gown. I felt euphoric as I quickly spun my hands in a circle to force Ferghus to let go. I rolled to the left and pushed my palms hard against the ground above my head; in one motion I was standing upon my feet, gazing down at him. He looked surprised.

"*Ye win!*" he told me, but the next thing I knew, he had swiped my feet out from under me. I fell back onto the hill and Ferghus pinned both my wrists above my head before I could react.

I could hardly draw breath, but I managed to say, "*you cheated!*"

"Nae, Rosa," he panted, "ye lost fair and square."

"I let you win," I retorted, grinning.

Ferghus's lips twitched. "Did ye now?"

I giggled and nodded. I could feel the heat from his torso searing into the top of my blouse and I suddenly felt a strange sensation in my stomach as I stared into Ferghus's eyes. My smile slowly faded and my lips felt as if they were frozen and wouldn't work properly. I wondered if he felt odd too, or if it was just something I'd eaten earlier. "*Mmmhmm,*" I murmured, wanting him to stay on top of me like that forever, but also wishing he'd free me so I could breathe normally again.

Ferghus swallowed and smiled, glancing suddenly at my hair. "*Rosa,*" he breathed, touching the pieces that had strayed from the strange head band I was wearing.

Suddenly, the sound of male voices nearby brought us both to our senses. Ferghus was on his feet and offering me his hand in a blink of an eye. As soon as I was standing, he dropped my palm. He had a guilty look upon his face as he brushed grass from the front of his kilt. I followed suit, running my hands over my dress to remove grass and dirt, and reaching around to check my hair for pieces. In another few seconds, the source of the voices became plain and two of Nyle's friends appeared on the hill above us. Cam, the one with the crooked teeth, was drinking straight from a bottle of whisky. His companion had light brown hair and dark eyes, but I couldn't remember his name. They seemed surprised to see us. "What are ye two up tae, eh?" Cam asked, eyeing me curiously.

"Showin' the quine Sloane's property," Ferghus answered, his voice firm.

"Ah hope tae have the pleasure tomorrow night," Cam slurred, wiping his chin and grinning.

"Ye should come," the other man suggested with a wink, "ye can watch the games." He held his hand out for the bottle and Cam reluctantly passed it to him.

"Unfortunately, we have tae leave in the morn," Ferghus told them with mock remorse.

"*Pity*," Cam said.

"Aye, pity," the other man said after taking a long swallow from the bottle, "mah name's Brodie, lass. Nice tae meet ye."

"You too," I whispered, feeling the hairs on the back of my neck prickle as the two men turned and started walking down the hill towards the house. Neither of us spoke until Cam and Brodie had disappeared from sight. I touched my stomach with my palm. "Why do I feel so creeped out?"

Ferghus turned to look at me. "'Bout time, Rosa," he commented softly. I looked at him quickly and blushed. His use of the nickname for my hair reminded me of what he'd been doing when the men had interrupted us. I felt suddenly shy. "Ah should take ye back tae the house," Ferghus said, but his voice contained no urgency.

"To the drinking and fighting," I mumbled.

We were silent for a couple minutes. "Or we can walk a little longer," he suggested hopefully.

I nodded, but didn't look at him directly. "That sounds nice."

Chapter Fourteen:

Ferghus walked with me along the bluffs until the sun had partially sunk below the surface of the water. I noticed there was an even wider physical gap between us than ever before. We made small talk mostly, or commented on the wildlife and weather, or what we might have to eat when we returned to the house. When we stepped into the Great Hall, everyone else was already seated. Sloane stood and came over to us. "Where have the two of ye *been*?" he asked, giving Ferghus a funny look.

"Brigid wanted tae see the rest of yer property," Ferghus explained.

"Ah see," Sloane said with a nod, "and what did ye think?" Before I even had a chance to respond, Ferghus left my side and went to sit at the furthest table. Out of the corner of my eye, I could see him pour himself a glass of whisky and down it. I don't know why, but I felt a strange, achy feeling in the pit of my stomach as I sat with Sloane at the table closest to us.

"It was all lovely," I answered absent-mindedly.

"Mah cousin has somethin' tae say tae ye," Sloane told me, glancing pointedly at Nyle.

Nyle's face flushed. "Aam sorry about earlier, Brigid. Ah had some of Sloane's famous whisky."

"Not *some*," Sloane corrected with a grin, "Ah think he had a whole bottle!"

My eyes opened wide. "Oh, Nyle – I had *one* glass and it was enough for me!"

Everyone at the table chuckled. I looked up to see Ferghus watching me. He raised another glass of whisky in the air as if proposing a toast, and drank it in one swallow. "You must go through a lot of alcohol," I commented aloud.

"Aye, lass, we dae," Sloane agreed, tipping back a shot of whisky himself.

I chose a glass of the Heather wine instead; it was sweeter and didn't burn my throat. It was strong though; two glasses in without supper and I already felt tipsy. I waved away a third when a servant offered to refill my glass. I glanced around my table: I was seated with Sloane, Nyle, Hamish, Ewan, and Edan, and they proved to be a boisterous group when they'd gotten more drink into them. Just as the servants started to serve bowls of steaming lentil and barley soup, Nyle stood and tapped a knife against his glass. "Before we eat, Eh'd like tae thank everyone fer comin' tae mah birthday, especially the bonnie Brigid." I lowered my eyes in embarrassment.

"Yer birthday's *tomorrow*!" Hugh's father called from the other table. Everyone laughed.

Nyle wasn't dissuaded from his cause. "Thank ye tae Sloane fer havin' us," he said, "and now fer some wee entertainment before ye eat…"

"He fancies heemself a singer," Ewan teased as Nyle started to sing *Auld Lang Syne*. I lifted my head to watch him, but I felt embarrassed the entire time.

He sat proudly when he'd finished. "Eat yer damn food now, Nyle!" Cam cried across the room.

"*Shut yer gantin gob!*" Nyle shot back. When he turned to face our table, he smiled as if he hadn't said anything rude at all. "How's the soup?"

I was still staring at him with wide eyes. Sloane interjected. "If ye ever wish tae get married, Nyle, ye might want tae work on yer speakin' skills…"

Ewan and Hamish chuckled, but Edan just smiled at me. "Ye'll have tae excuse mah friend; he's not used tae bein' in the presence of a *real* quine…"

"And ye *are*?" Nyle tossed back.

"The soup's very good," I said, trying to change the subject, but it had no effect.

"Aye, Aam a natural with the ladies; they enjoy listenin' tae mah stories."

Hamish laughed. "Give us one then," he urged, "is it the story of how Nyle tried tae break into Brigid's chamber?"

"*Hamish!*" Sloane warned. Hamish grinned, but fell silent.

"Nae, it's a tale of mah mukker Ewan," Edan announced dramatically.

I took a sip of my soup while Ewan joked, "I've inspired many a story. Let's hear it then…"

"There once was a man named – *Ewan*," Edan began, "he was a disagreeable sort of man-bairn – always arguin' with his friends and family…"

"That sounds more like *Cam!*" Hamish interrupted.

"*Shhh*," Ewan hissed, "Ah want tae hear mah tale."

"More whisky," Sloane asked a servant.

"One day, this disagreeable Ewan set a date tae meet a man he'd pissed off. We'll call him Brodie."

"Ye should be tellin' this later – when everyone can hear it," Nyle suggested as the servants brought out sausage rolls, smoked salmon, and potato scones.

"Stop interruptin' mah tale!" Edan said in frustration, "so the disagreeable man, *Ewan*, consulted the Devil as tae how his visit with Brodie would turn out. The Devil told Ewan that if his wife offered Brodie food without being asked, Ewan would win the fight. If not, he'd probably die a painful death…"

I nibbled a potato pancake while I listened attentively to Edan's story. "What happened next?" I asked curiously.

He grinned, pleased by my enthusiasm. "The day of the meetin' arrived. Ewan's ugly wife, we'll call her *Hamish* – "

"*Screw you!*" Hamish exclaimed.

Edan laughed. "Hamish was *so* lazy, he didn't prepare any scran fer the meetin'. Ewan got as nervous as a lass on her weddin' night, and begged his wife fer somethin' tae eat. Hamish, being a selfish kind of wife, brought out bowls of the runniest porridge Ewan had ever laid eyes on."

"*Ith mo choileach!*[89]" Hamish said, but he was grinning too.

"Ye served runny *porridge*, not yer *prick*!" Edan chortled.

"Hey," Sloane interrupted, "not in front of the lass." He drank another glass of whisky and smiled at me sympathetically.

"Sorry, Brigid," Edan apologized, "where was Ah?"

"The runny porridge," I informed him.

"Aye. The ugly wife brought it out without any spoons. Ewan asked her how they should eat it, and she said like a Gannet. So Brodie,

---

[89] Eat my cock!

134

being a greedy little bastard, scooped the runny porridge up in his hands…"

"Sounds about right," Nyle commented, glancing across at Brodie, who was shoving enormous quantities of food into his mouth. I looked over to see what he was talking about and saw Ferghus staring at me, another glass of whisky in his hand. I blushed and tried to focus on Edan again.

Edan chuckled and threw back a shot before continuing, "Ewan didn't eat *any* of the disgustin' food prepared by his gantin wife, Hamish."

"*Piss off!*" Hamish said, smiling widely.

"In the violent battle afterwards, Ewan was carved up, left scarred and bleedin'. But, because he hadn't eaten anythin', he died fastin' and was saved. He's now a ghost who haunts all the ugliest people in Scootland."

"Aam not as ugly as *Ferghus*!" Hamish said, "no scars on *mah* face!"

Nyle and Ewan laughed, but Sloane said, "that was unkind. The marks of battle are honourable and ye ought tae be ashamed of mockin' a family member as brave as he…"

"It's just a *story*," Nyle responded, winking at me as the servants brought in roast mutton and carrots.

I picked at my food, feeling a sudden desire to switch seats. The other table was much more subdued, even *if* Cam wasn't my favourite one of Nyle's friends. "Ye gettin' full lass?" Sloane asked sympathetically.

"Yes," I said quietly, "everything was so good. Thank you for inviting me."

"The pleasure is all mine," Sloane said meaningfully.

Suddenly, Nyle stood again. He tapped his glass loudly, swaying slightly on his feet. "Yer drunk agin, ye wee bairn!" Hugh's father yelled.

Everyone laughed. "Ah have a little tune Eh'd like tae perform before we move the party elsewhere…"

"It's past your bedtime, Nyle!" Owyn piped up.

Nyle cleared his throat and looked at me though heavy eyes, a lopsided grin spread upon his lips. "*Oh god,*" I breathed, wringing my hands in my lap.

And suddenly, he was singing the most embarrassing song I'd ever had directed at me:

"Ah loove a lassie, a bonnie red-haired lassie,
If ye saw her ye would fancy her as well:
Ah met her in September, popped the question in November,
So I'll soon be havin' her a' to ma-sel'.
Her faither has consented, so Aam feelin' quite contented,
'Cause I've been and sealed the bargain wi' a kiss.
Ah sit and weary weary, when Ah think aboot ma deary,
An' ye'll always hear me singin' this..."[90]

My cheeks were on fire even before he'd finished the first line. I wanted to flee, but everyone was laughing. I finally managed to lift my eyes and saw, with a sinking feeling, Ferghus slamming his whisky glass down before exiting the Great Hall. When Nyle had finished, he gave a half bow to the room and everyone clapped. "Ah don't think Ferghus was a fan of yer awful singin', Nyle," Sloane joked.

I desperately wanted to escape, but the servants were serving plum muffins and pudding. I tasted each, and then told Sloane I was exhausted

---

[90] Original lyrics by Harry Lauder (1909)

and wanted to retire to my chamber. "I'll see everyone in the morning," I said to the table.

"Sleep well, fair Brigid!" Nyle said, trying to stand. He almost toppled backwards, but Hamish grasped the back of his kilt and tossed him onto his seat. Everyone chortled loudly.

"Good night, Brigid," Sloane and Ewan said together. Edan just smiled drunkenly.

"Good night." I hurried from the room, making a wrong turn before I realized the circular walls did not extend to the entire house. I passed the Great Hall again and made my way to the front door, then past the sitting room to the staircase. I hesitated. Should I search outside for Ferghus? He had seemed angry at the end of dinner, but perhaps he just wanted to be alone. Finally, I decided to go up to bed and bolt my door before the revellers got into any more trouble.

I climbed the stairs in the dark; I had no idea where to find a candle and had completely forgotten to ask a servant to help me. When I got to the second floor, some moonlight pooled upon the hall from an open window at the end. I missed being able to turn the lights on with a flip of a switch. I inched towards my bedroom, but a sudden swishing sound nearby gave me pause. I heard it again, followed by the scraping of glass upon a table. "*Hello*?" I called into the darkness. I heard low laughter and a gurgling sound of liquid. "*Who's there*?" I questioned, peering inside my chamber.

From the light of the moon, I could just barely make out the outline of a person reclined upon my bed. He was holding a half-empty bottle of whisky, which he tipped to his lips when I moved further inside. "*Ferghus*? Please tell me that's you..." I moved towards the bed and tripped unexpectedly on something strewn upon the floor. "What *the* – " I managed to stop myself from falling and when I knelt to see what I'd tripped on, I gasped. "Ferghus, are you *naked*?" I was holding his bonnet and kilt in my arms.

He laughed low in his throat, sliding the bottle onto the nearby bench. "Nae, I've got mah chib in mah stockin' in case ye need mah help…"

"Oh my god, you're *drunk*!" I breathed, pressing my palm against my forehead, trying to decide what the hell to do.

"It's how ye like em," Ferghus slurred, "drunk and fun, right?" He laughed again, a nonsensical sound of someone not in control of his own faculties.

"You need to go to bed," I said, hovering by the door, "someone might come up the stairs and see you."

"Come see mah knife, Rosa," Ferghus said in a husky voice. I could see him trying to lift his torso off the mattress. He laughed again and the sound reminded me of a school boy half his age, not someone who had cut the hand off a MacDonald.

"*You can't even sit up*!" I complained. He started laughing again, and the sound of it went on and on. "Ferghus, let me help you…" I took a hesitant step towards my bed.

"Aye, ye can help me," he joked, "tha mo sgian mu thrath geur!⁹¹"

"I don't know what that means," I scolded gently, moving a foot away from where he was lying across my mattress. I avoided looking directly at him, but I could see the glow of his stockings in the dim light. "Ferghus, why'd you come in here? You should have gone to bed if you were tired…"

---

⁹¹ My knife's already sharp!

"Aam not tired," he laughed, trying to push himself onto his side. I could see the muscles in his bicep flexing. I forced myself not to trace his entire body with my eyes.

"We should find a candle, so you don't hurt yourself," I told him, turning to scan the room.

"Nae, lass; Ah don't want ye tae see me," he said quickly. The next thing I knew, Ferghus had leaned forward and wrapped a strong arm around my waist, pulling me back against him on the bed.

"*Oh god, no!*" I cried, but he was already placing a muscular leg around my side to try to climb on top of me, "*Ferghus, please!*"

He entwined his fingers through my own in slow motion, as if all he desired was to experience the sensation of our skin making contact. I wanted to scream: my body had suddenly burst into flames of desire, while my brain was shouting run. He was holding my hands above my head, and slowly lowered himself down until he was lying on top of me with his head pressed against the crook of my shoulder. He laid still, not speaking. I was frozen from fear, my hands trembling inside his, but suddenly he whispered against the bottom of my chin, "Ah won't hurt ye, Rosa."

"You need to put some clothes on," I whispered, "and go back to your own room…"

He sighed and I could feel him nodding against my shoulder. "Aye, ye might be on tae somethin', Sasannach." I waited a couple minutes, but he was still lying across me, unmoving.

"Ferghus, did you fall *asleep*?" I hissed into his ear. He started.

"*Brigid?*"

"Yes, it's me. You need to get off me."

"Aye," he agreed. A moment passed and he asked, "didn't this already happen?"

I couldn't help but giggle. "Yes, you're drunk and tired and need to get to your room before anyone comes *upstairs!*" He finally rolled off me towards the wall so I could slide off the bed. I smoothed my dress and held his kilt out. "You need to put this on," I said, trying not to stare.

He laughed. "Na, Ah sleep naked."

I actually blushed and was thankful for the darkness. "I don't care *how* you sleep; you just can't do it *here*. And you need to get back to your own *room!*"

"Just shove me onto yer floor," he told me.

"I can't *do* that," I said, "someone might find you *in* here!"

"*Cha dean iad sin nas fhearr no cha mharbh mi iad*![92]" he said, a note of anger in his voice, although his head was still resting upon my pillow.

"You're a total pain in the ass, you know that?" I sighed deeply and crossed my room so I could bolt the door.

I stood in the centre, wondering where I should sleep. Suddenly, Ferghus said softly, "Ah promise Ah won't hurt ye, Brigid."

"But that doesn't help me find a place to sleep! Should I go to your room?"

"Nae. I'll sleep on the floor," he told me. He pushed himself off the wall with great effort and rolled twice across the mattress until he fell off the edge with a crash.

"*Oh my god, are you hurt?*" I asked, rushing to his side. He had landed on his stomach, so at least he was sort of covered now.

"Tired," he mumbled.

---

[92] They better not or I'll kill em!

I grabbed an extra blanket off the end of my bed and knelt beside him. *"Pain in the ass!"* I whispered as I lifted his head and placed the blanket beneath it, using his kilt to cover the rest of him.

"Mmmhmm," he murmured sleepily.

"Good night, Ferghus."

"Oidhche[93], Rosa."

---

[93] Night

Chapter Fifteen:

I woke at dawn as the light made its way inside my chamber and the sounds of gulls and oystercatchers became too loud to sleep any longer. Suddenly, the memories of the previous evening came flooding back. I sat quickly and looked around the empty room. The folded blanket was still lying upon my floor, but Ferghus was gone. I stretched and climbed out of bed, careful not to trip on the stairs. I glanced outside; it looked like another clear day – perfect for a party. As I was smoothing my hair, my gaze chanced upon Ferghus's sporran resting beside the half-empty bottle of whisky. My cheeks coloured as I remembered his behaviour; he'd been a different sort of drunk from Nyle – so gentle in the bed with me – almost reverential. I wondered if he was already readying Selma so we could leave. It made me sad to contemplate so arduous a journey after finally being able to sleep in a real room again, but I had learned to trust his instincts – at least most of the time.

I finished primping and grasped his sporran, hiding it in the voluminous folds of my gown. As I neared the Great Hall, I could already hear a few voices conversing. Sloane was standing just inside the doorway talking to Ferghus, and Hugh, his father, Owyn, and Brodie were already seated at one of the tables. "Where's yer sporran?" I heard Sloane ask Ferghus, "yer room was empty last night..."

"Ah slept outside," Ferghus replied smoothly.

Sloane's eyebrows rose. "Ye've never been one to dally with the servants, but why would ye want tae sleep on the ground when ye have a feather mattress ye can use?"

My cheeks coloured as I reached them; they both stopped talking when they saw me. I suddenly felt tongue-tied and nervous for reasons I couldn't explain. "Good morning, Brigid," Sloane said cheerfully, "up at the crack of dawn, eh?"

"Yes," I answered, forcing a smile, "the birds woke me…"

"Loud buggers," Sloane agreed, gesturing to an empty table. I took a seat and Sloane sat beside me; Ferghus hesitated and then slid onto the bench across from us. "Are ye hungry?" Sloane questioned as the servants filled cups with tea.

"A little," I answered.

"Eat up while ye can," Sloane told me, "soon we'll be fightin' over conies and squirrels…"

I glanced up at Ferghus, hoping for some information about our departure, but he was staring into his tea. His eyes were stormy and I wondered if he was angry at me, or just hungover. "Will we be leaving after the party?" I questioned.

"Aye, Ah think I've finally convinced Ferghus not tae risk it without his cousins…"

Ferghus snorted, finally lifting his head. His blue eyes blazed as he retorted, "aye, one of whom is *still* passed out like a wee bairn!" He paused and then added, "Eh'd rather take Owyn than Nyle!"

"Owyn's nice," I ventured, but I stopped talking as soon as I saw the incredulous look upon Ferghus's handsome face.

"He's a *scholar* lass, not a fighter," Sloane explained as the servant set down a plate of scones, muffins, and tea bread.

I took a piece of bread and inquired, "is he? Does he like to read?"

Ferghus scoffed. "Dae ye want someone who can defend ye, or read Chaucer?"

I blushed. "I've never heard someone recite the original Chaucer before; it's always been translated…"

Ferghus's expression darkened even more. "Yer still thinkin' about Owyn readin' tae ye?"

"No, of course not," I protested, "I was simply intrigued – "

"Aam not hungry," Ferghus said, pushing his plate away as he stood, "let me know when all ye bairns are ready tae set out. Til then, I'll be hidin' mah head in embarrassment that mah cousins are a bunch of kimmers…"

My eyes widened at his insult, but I didn't say anything as he rushed from the room. "Don't pay him any mind, lass," Sloane advised, "he never learned tae read; said the words lifted off the page and gave him a headache."

"Maybe he just needs glasses," I commented.

Sloane gave me a curious look. "Mebbe, but he said he could see the letters, just not stories. He's not meant tae be a scholar. He needs tae settle down, get a farm, and stop tryin' tae win everyone's battles fer them…"

"Does he do that a lot?" I questioned.

"Aye, all the time. Ever since he was almost killed, left scarred, he doesn't seem tae care about anythin' but fightin' and wanderin'."

"He said he has brothers; what are they like?"

"Ye'll see fer yerself; Ferghus wants us tae get ye tae Dunvegan," Sloane answered between bites.

I nodded and finished eating. "Thank you," I said politely.

"Dae ye want some company? Ah can walk with ye if ye wish…"

"Actually, if you don't mind, I'm going to spend some time alone; sounds like it's going to be a busy night."

Sloane chuckled. "Aye, get yer rest while ye can, lass."

"I will."

I took an extra muffin and wandered into the sunshine of a beautiful summer morning, making my way towards the water. When I heard splashes coming from the docks, I shielded my eyes to see who was down there. I could spot Edan's bright red hair, and the other man looked like Ewan. I shook my head and gazed around the property. I didn't notice him immediately, but upon my second perusal I spotted Ferghus reclining beneath a large tree halfway up the hill overlooking the water. I took a deep breath and started the gentle climb. When I got closer, I could see he was watching the jumpers also. He pretended not to see or hear me until I was standing by his side. He gave me a brooding glance, but didn't say anything to break the ice. "Here," I said, forcing a smile and handing him the muffin.

Ferghus glanced stonily at it and responded, "Ah told ye Ah wasn't hungry."

My insides lurched from the harshness of his rejection, but I kept the smile pasted upon my lips and switched the muffin for the sporran. "You forgot this," I said softly, dangling it by his shoulder.

He glanced back, clearly annoyed at being disturbed, but when he saw what I was holding his look became guilty. He grasped the sporran and set it upon the grass beside him, quickly turning to stare at the water. His indifference was somehow worse than the anger he had displayed at breakfast; I spun on my heel and fled across the grassy slope until I was breathless. I stood for a while with my palm across my chest, feeling the thundering of each beat until it finally slowed enough for me to continue. I chose to ascend the hill, desiring to go as far to the top as possible so I could view Sloane's property from such a vantage point. The slope was scattered with deciduous trees, most with slender trunks. I pushed myself harder, willing my tired legs to go as high as I could. When I turned to gaze at the water, it was breathtaking; the docks looked like something from a painting – not quite real anymore. The water was monochromatic from this height, and not the basic navy one saw from the ground.

I was just about to begin the descent when I heard giggling and rustling from a stand of trees a few feet away. I took a tentative step closer, but then wished I hadn't; Hamish was rooting around on top of a young woman with her skirts up to her knees. His face was buried in her cleavage and she was gripping the back of his head. I began to run down the hill, faster than I ought given my clothing wasn't designed for physical pursuits. I ducked under branches and avoided getting my shoes tangled in the grass. I was breathing hard when suddenly I came upon Ferghus climbing the hill. I wanted to ignore him, but he addressed me before I had the chance to slip past. *"Brigid?"*

"What?" I questioned, breathing hard.

"Are ye alright?"

I gestured to the top of the slope. "Hamish is having sex with a *servant*! I don't know why you ever brought me to this place!"

Ferghus didn't appear surprised at all. He looked at me sympathetically. "Aam sorry ye came upon that," he said earnestly, "but it wasn't a servant; it was Sloane's sister…"

I gaped at him. "His *sister*? How do you know that?"

He sighed. "Because she's in loove with Hamish."

"Aila's in love with Hamish?" I repeated incredulously.

"Aye. And her father doesn't approve, so she refuses tae meet with the men he arranges fer her tae see. She locks herself in her room."

"That's awful!"

Ferghus shrugged. "'S docha," he responded with the beginning of a smile.

"'*S docha*?" I said in disbelief, "how can you be so indifferent?" I questioned angrily.

"Because Aam not her father," he replied easily.

"But what if *you* were in love with Aila?" I pressed.

Ferghus actually laughed. "Aam *not* in loove with Aila, Sasannach…"

"I know, but what if you were – imagine you were," I told him.

"Ah can't imagine mahself in loove with Aila," he answered, "it's impossible."

I rolled my eyes and tried again, "it's *hypothetical*, Ferghus. You pretend something inside your mind in order to feel what someone else feels, so you can empathize with them."

"*Philosophy*?" he asked, a gleam in his eye.

"No, not *philosophy*," I corrected, "empathy. Knowing it's *awful* to come between two people who love one another."

Ferghus shook his head. "Not if ye know it's a bad match," he disagreed, "it's her father's *job* tae see her married *well*, Brigid."

"Why doesn't he approve of Hamish?" I inquired, my hand upon my hip.

Ferghus grinned. "Maybe he thinks he lacks moral character."

"*Moral character*? And why would he think that?"

"Because he's havin' a scuttle with his daughter without marryin' her!"

"*Oh my god*!" I burst out, "her dad won't *let* him marry her! So how can he have sex with her within wedlock?"

"He *can't*, Sasannach," Ferghus responded with a wink, "and that's why Hamish should stay away from Aila."

"God, it's so easy for *you* to say!" I cried, feeling exasperated.

"And why is that?"

"Because you're not in *love* with anybody!" I exclaimed angrily, "you just want to *wander* around the woods, fighting with MacDonalds, and insulting every single person you meet!"

Ferghus's eyes looked like they were going to pop out of his head. "Ye think ye have me all figured out, dae ye?" he retorted, the stormy edge back in his voice.

"Yes, I *do*!" I replied, "you're an angry asshole who enjoys hurting people who try to do nice things for you." I folded my arms across my chest and glared at him.

Ferghus laughed sardonically. "Ye think Ah enjoy hurtin' others? *Really*?"

"*Yes*! You're selfish and hateful. You can't even accept a *muffin* without being rude!"

"A *muffin*? Yer standing here yellin' at me because Ah didn't take yer *muffin*?"

My cheeks flamed. "*No*! *Yes*! Of *course* not!" I stomped my foot and yelled, "'*S docha*!" and ran down the hill wishing Ferghus would go drown himself in the lake.

Chapter Sixteen:

I flew inside the house feeling spiteful. I immediately found the housekeeper and asked her if I could borrow a different dress from Aila for the party. She went to fetch Aila, but told me shortly after she couldn't find her. I didn't confide having any knowledge of Aila's sexual liaisons with Hamish; instead, I asked permission to borrow an outfit and, if Aila didn't want me to have it, she could ask for it back before the party started. The housekeeper thought that sounded reasonable.

She selected an attractive royal blue gown in a European design: fitted bodice and sleeves with a more elaborate skirt and small train. There was ruffled lace at the neckline and the housekeeper found me another one of those headbands for fastening my hair, but it was thinner and showed off more of my bright red locks. When I had dressed, she took me into the garden to braid and pin my hair. When she had finished, she stood back and smiled. She was missing most of her teeth. "*Gu breagha!*[94]" she exclaimed, clapping her hands. I took that as a good sign. I thanked her and then sat beneath the shade trees at the back of the garden. It did not take long before one of the many guests also wandered out there.

First came Owyn with a beautiful edition of *Sir Gawain and the Green Knight*. "Good morning, Brigid," he greeted me with a smile, "I see you are enjoying the outdoors also."

"Yes," I replied, "it's a beautiful day. Perfect for a party."

"Yes," he agreed, observing the altered style of my dress, "you look lovely; blue suits you very well…"

"Thank you."

Owyn stood gazing down at me for a few awkward seconds before he asked, "would you mind if I join you? I was going to spend some time

[94] Lovely!

with a favourite book of mine, but your company would be most agreeable."

"This space doesn't belong to me," I reminded him, "it's your cousin's."

"True, but I do not want to impose my company where it is not wanted."

"To be honest, I'm in need of a friend. I have nothing to do."

Owyn sat beside me on the grass. "Do you enjoy reading?" he asked.

"Yes, when I have time." I wanted to tell him about my year in university before I ran out of money, but I thought it best to keep that a secret. I wasn't sure if women were allowed to attend university in his part of the world.

Just then, Hugh stepped into the yard and smiled when he saw us. "There ye are," he said to Owyn, "Sloane needs us tae help carry some chairs outside; we're goin' tae eat under the stars taenight."

"That sounds like fun," I commented.

"I am sorry to leave you; we just got talking," Owyn stated as he stood, "perhaps tonight we can converse again."

"I'd like that," I responded.

"Would you like to borrow my book this afternoon?"

"I'd love to," I answered, "it will keep me busy until the party starts."

"Knowing Nyle, it will begin as soon as he gets his arse out of bed, and end when he's passed out!" Hugh joked as the two of them disappeared inside.

Silence descended once again. I eventually picked up Owyn's book and flipped absent-mindedly through the pages. After a time, movement out of my peripheral vision caught my attention. It was Ferghus entering the garden. When he saw me, he ambled slowly over and paused a few steps away. He stared at me in silence for a few seconds, a crease slowly appearing upon his forehead. "Ye changed."

"*Mmmhmm*," I replied, flipping a couple pages of my book and then lifting my head again.

He swallowed. "Ye already looked bonnie," he offered awkwardly.

"I'm glad you approved," I said icily.

"*Brigid…*"

"*What?*"

"Ye don't have tae dress so fancy," he told me, "what ye were wearin' this morn was fine."

"Would you prefer I wear the ripped wedding dress to the party?" I questioned, my eyebrows raised.

Ferghus's eyes opened wide. "Nae, the every-day one would be suitable," he stated.

"I see," I responded, "so I'm not allowed to wear something special to Nyle's celebration?"

Ferghus's cheeks flushed. "Why dae ye care so much about this *glaikit* party?" he questioned, his blue eyes flashing, "it's not why we came!"

"I *know* that!" I retorted, "but all the people you said were going to help us are occupied with this event. We can't exactly stop it from happening just because you want to take me to some place called *Dunvegan*!"

"Some *place*?"

"*Yes*! I've heard *you* mention it, and Sloane said the same name this morning too."

"Aye, because it's mah *home*," Ferghus said, his voice quieter, "Ah wanted tae take ye somewhere Ah thought ye'd be safe."

I stared at his earnest face, my anger beginning to dissipate. "Oh."

He shifted his weight to his other foot and asked, "can Ah sit with ye fer a minute?"

"Yes."

He eased onto the grass and rested his back against the tree. "Yer showin' off yer hair," he commented, but he was staring at the ground.

I rolled my eyes. "*Oh my god*!"

He glanced at me quickly. "Na, Ah meant it in a *good* way. Yer hairstyle – the way its pinned with the bonnet – it shows it off…"

I took a deep breath to calm myself. "I thought you were criticizing me again," I admitted when I could speak.

"Nae, Rosa," Ferghus said vehemently, shaking his head, "Ah meant tae tell ye how bonnie ye look…"

I blushed. "Thank you."

"Ye'll be hearin' it a lot taenight," he stated, "but maybe it counts fer something' that Aam the first."

"I won't be hearing it a lot, but thank you."

Ferghus laughed ruefully. "Yer tay modest," he said, "ye'll be busy taenight with all the compliments and dances…"

"*Dances*?" I questioned.

"Aye, they'll all want an excuse tae hold ye. When Ah heard Nyle start singin' tae ye last night, Ah knew it was all over."

"What do you mean?"

"He'll be askin' ye tae marry him soon enough. He's fallin' all over heemself, Sasannach, tryin' tae impress ye..."

"A *song*? *Ferghus*, be *serious*. He embarrassed me in front of *everyone*!"

He stretched his long legs out and folded his hands in his lap. "He *did*?"

"*Yes*! I felt *so* foolish! Everyone laughing – it was *awful*!"

"Ah thought ye'd like the attention," Ferghus ventured curiously.

"Not *that* kind of attention," I responded.

"What kind of attention *would* ye like?"

I paused, considering his question. "I honestly don't know, but not something *embarrassing*."

"So if he did somethin' more private?" he inquired.

I shook my head. "I'm not interested in any *private* attention from Nyle. He's not my type."

Ferghus watched my face intently while I spoke. "And what *is* yer type, Rosa?"

I felt myself blushing again. "I misspoke. Of course I don't have one – a *type*. I just know Nyle's not *it*." I glanced back at the pages of my book to avoid his gaze.

"Where did ye get the book?" he suddenly asked.

"Owyn lent it to me," I replied, turning it over so Ferghus could see the cover, "so I wouldn't get bored."

He didn't seem interested in the specific book, however. "When was that?"

"Mmm, a few minutes before you got here," I said, "Owyn came outside to read, but Hugh needed him to set up chairs."

When he didn't say anything, I lifted my eyes to meet his. "Ye must have had a lot in common," Ferghus pointed out, but his voice sounded hurt.

"I don't really know him that well; we didn't get a chance to discuss the story."

Ferghus nodded, but his blue eyes were less clear. "Ah guess Ah should go help set up," he said, but he sounded completely indifferent.

"Do you have to?" I questioned.

"Ah have nothin' else tae dae; should make mahself useful."

"Of course, I didn't mean to hold you back," I said quickly, realizing my voice was suddenly trembling.

"Ye okay, Brigid?" Ferghus asked, his expression shifting to concern.

"Of course," I laughed, "why wouldn't I be?"

He hesitated. "A feelin'."

Tears stung my eyes and I blinked them away. "I'm *fine*, Ferghus. If you need to go, *go*."

He continued to lean against the tree. "How about Owyn?"

"What about him?"

"Is *he* yer type, Rosa?"

"Why do you want to know my type?" I asked, "are you trying to set me up with one of your cousins?"

Ferghus actually laughed. "Nae, Sasannach. Just curious. Aam surprised yer not already married. One look at ye and a man's done fer."

"*Really*?" I asked in shock.

"Aye, Aam not sure if it's the ripped frock, or the way ye can throw a grown man tae the ground, or the wild hair – "

My eyes flashed. "Oh, *I* get it! You're *teasing* me! Yes, yes, I'm *too* masculine in my behaviour, and my hair is ugly. I understand. You don't have to tease me anymore. I promise I won't be crushed when the *only* one at the party to ask me to dance is Cam…" I pretended to pout.

Ferghus became attentive again. "*Cam*? Ye think he's *gantin*?" he wondered.

"Is it awful for me to say so?" I asked, "I'm sorry. I should have kept that to myself. It was rude…"

Ferghus's shoulders relaxed and he laughed good-naturedly. "Na, it's okay. Ah won't tell anyone." He paused and then asked, "what dae ye think of Sloane?"

I looked at him in surprise. "*Sloane*? He's been kind to me."

"Aye, but dae ye think he'd make a good husband?"

I giggled. "*Ferghus*, I'm not here to find a husband. I told you that before!"

"But dae ye? If he asked ye, what would ye say?" he pressed.

"Oh god, I hope he doesn't. I don't want to hurt his feelings. He's a nice guy," I responded honestly.

"Ye wouldn't marry Sloane? He's taken with ye…"

"I don't know about *that*, but no, I wouldn't marry Sloane."

"Why not?"

I shrugged. "I'm not attracted to him in that way. He's like a kind brother. Not *husband* material."

Ferghus was thoughtful for a minute. "So, ye need tae be attracted tae yer husband?"

I giggled again. "Of *course*! Otherwise, what's the point?"

He looked surprised. "*Security*? Someone tae protect ye and take care of ye. Provide fer ye."

"I can protect *myself*, for the most part, and I *have* a job. No, a marriage should be a partnership. And you should think your husband is hot."

"*Hot*?" Ferghus's forehead wrinkled again, "what dae ye mean by *that*?"

"Attractive. Cute. Sexy. I don't know. Just good *looking*. You should *feel* something for him you don't feel for other guys. Like a funny feeling when he looks at you or when you're about to be intimate. It's hard to explain."

Ferghus nodded slowly, as if processing everything I had just said. "What kind of funny feelin'?"

I sighed. "It's too hard to explain. It's like you suddenly feel sick, but in a *good* way. You're nervous and excited all at the same time. It's magical."

"*Magical*?"

"*Yes*. And no amount of money can *buy* that feeling. It's not about the *big* things; it's all the small, everyday things that build over *time*. And that's what makes a man *really* special. When he does all the *small* things and you have that feeling and you just *know* – "

"Ah thought ye said ye didn't want tae get married?"

"I *don't*," I said, and then sighed, "'s docha."

Chapter Seventeen:

The party *did* begin when Nyle finally dragged himself out of bed. His friends pushed him off the docks to energize him for the night's festivities, but everything *actually* started in the middle of the afternoon. When he had finished helping set up tables and chairs in the grassy area between the docks and hill, Owyn returned to the garden to find me. "Hello again Brigid – Ferghus," he said when he saw us together beneath the trees.

"Owyn," Ferghus responded with a slight nod.

"Did you get everything set up?" I inquired with a smile.

"Yes, Nyle wants to start the competitions in a few minutes," Owyn told us.

"Don't know why he even bothers," Ferghus joked and Owyn shrugged.

"How'd you like the book?" Owyn asked.

"*Oh,*" I laughed, realizing it was still open in my lap, "I didn't get very far, but it's always been one of my favourites."

"You've already read it?"

"Yes, I didn't have a chance to tell you before you left," I told him with a smile.

"What's your favourite part?" Owyn asked.

"Eh'd best be goin'," Ferghus interrupted, standing abruptly, "probably want tae shoot mah own brains out before supper, but I'll put in an appearance anyway…"

"Why don't we come with you?" I said, still seated upon the ground.

Both Ferghus and Owyn held their hands out to help me up at the same time. I looked from one hand to the other, but finally decided to place the book into Owyn's hand and grasp Ferghus's. He steadied me and then quickly dropped it again. "Let's go see how the wee bairn's doin'…"

I giggled. "Does Nyle know you call him that?" I asked as the three of us made our way through the yard to where the tables and chairs had been placed.

He shrugged. "Mah cousin's self-centred, but loyal. Sometimes ye have tae take the good with the bad…"

"He handles whisky about as good as I do," I joked.

Owyn laughed. "I'm not a fan myself," he commiserated, "I prefer tea and wine."

Ferghus shook his head. "Ye've spent tay much time kissin' the king's arse."

"*Ferghus*," I scolded lightly.

"I enjoy my travels," Owyn responded neutrally.

Ferghus laughed sardonically. "If ye pulled yer nose out of yer books more often, ye'd see what's happenin' tae yer own people."

"Is everything okay?" I questioned, sensing an argument brewing.

Owyn nodded. "We should focus on Nyle; it's *his* celebration. Put aside our differences for one day, and discuss politics another."

Ferghus scoffed. "I'll leave the two of ye tae discuss yer story books. I'll have a whisky fer each of ye while Ah contemplate *real* life…"

He strode towards a long table where food and drink had been spread. It was mostly bread – scones, and fresh loaves of soda, rye, and barley – in addition to countless bottles of whisky, gin, and heather wine. I predicted a lot of hungover men in the morning. Owyn glanced at me sympathetically. "Can I fetch you something to drink?"

I shook my head. "No, I think I'm okay right now."

"The birthday boy has arrived." Owyn gestured to a dampened Nyle approaching from the docks with Hamish and Ewan.

"It looks like they tossed him in with his clothes on," I commented. Nyle was soaked from head-to-foot.

"Yes," Owyn agreed, "why do we not have a seat?"

We sat at an empty table by the base of the hill overlooking the meadow. "What is all that stuff?" I asked, noticing an assortment of hewn logs, large boulders, hammers, and rope gathered in the centre of the field.

"That's what they'll be using for the competitions," Owyn explained.

I shook my head. "It seems like a lot of work. Will you be competing too?"

"No, I prefer to watch."

I glanced at the food table. Nyle and his friends were pouring themselves drinks. Ferghus was standing nearby talking to Hugh's father. I watched him finish his glass of whisky and laugh at something Hugh's father had just said. He was a very attractive man; tall and muscular, with a strong jaw, and dark hair and brows. His beautiful eyes contrasted with his serious bearing, but I couldn't see their colour from this angle. Suddenly, a deep voice broke into my daydream. "Can Ah join ye?" It was Sloane, smiling down at me with a glass of whisky in his large hand.

"Of course," I answered. Sloane grabbed the back of a nearby chair and sat down.

"What are ye most excited tae see?" he asked.

"I'm not sure," I admitted, "I've never watched any competitions like these before…"

"I thought Ferghus said you're Scottish?" Owyn said curiously.

"I *am*," I replied, trying desperately to think of a reason why I never would have viewed something they seemed to think was common place. Fortunately, Nyle saved me by heading over at just the right time.

"*Brigid*!" he called loudly, his entire face lit up, "can Ah count on ye tae cheer me on taeday?"

"Of course, Nyle," I answered with a smile, "and *happy birthday*!"

"Thank ye," he beamed, "we're going tae start with a little warm up..."

Nyle turned and joined his friends in the centre of the meadow. I saw him shake his head back-and-forth a couple times to get some of the water out of it. Hamish was stretching the backs of his arms, and Hugh's father was chatting with all of them. "What are they going to do first?" I questioned.

"They're goin' tae throw stones at one another," a familiar voice said from behind me. I turned in the direction of the voice and saw Ferghus carrying a plate of bread, a bottle of wine, and two glasses. "Switch seats with me," he said matter-of-factly to Owyn.

"There are lots of places to sit, Ferghus," Owyn protested, sounding slightly peeved for the first time since I'd met him.

Ferghus laughed. "Aye, but Ah need tae explain the rules tae Brigid, and everyone knows ye don't know a *thing* about athleticism..."

Owyn's face flushed and Sloane chuckled. "God gives us different gifts; I'm happy with mine." Owyn stood and sat one more chair over so Ferghus could sit beside me.

Ferghus rolled his eyes and plunked into the seat. He held the plate out to me. "Ye should eat somethin'; it's going tae be a *long* night..."

I took the dish and eyed him warily. "I won't have to compete in anything, *will* I?"

He grinned. "Ye never know, Sasannach. Eat up." He set the bottle and glasses on the table in front of us and started to pour the wine.

I took a piece of tea bread and set the plate on the table. "Are they *really* going to throw stones at each other?"

"No, Ferghus is just trying to scare you, Brigid," Owyn piped up.

I looked across Ferghus's broad chest at Owyn. "He should know by now, I don't scare so easily..."

Sloane laughed. "Mebbe ye should be competin' yerself, Brigid." He winked at me and I blushed. The amount of attention I was receiving was overwhelming.

I bit into the bread to avoid a reply. When I'd finished, Ferghus passed me a glass. "Thank you," I said quietly.

"S e do bheatha," he responded very slowly, his eyes intense.

"S e do bheatha?" I repeated.

"Very good," he stated softly as he lifted his wine glass to his lips.

"Does it mean you're welcome?" I questioned.

"Aye."

I finished my bread and drank some of my wine as well. I watched curiously as Nyle lifted one of the enormous stones and everyone else backed away. He stared across the meadow for a second and then started to run with the stone balanced over his shoulder. When he reached Hugh's father, he launched the stone as far as he could across the grass. Everyone clapped, and Hugh's father and Brodie went to measure how far he'd made it. "Was that *good*?" I wondered.

Sloane and Ferghus exchanged amused glances. "The wee bairn did a *fine* job," Ferghus joked, draining his glass and leaning back in his chair.

"Are you being *sarcastic*?" I asked.

"Nyle's enthusiastic, lass, but he cannot compete with a *real* man," Sloane replied, flexing his bicep and grinning.

"*Oh my god*," I said, "I suppose everyone watching thinks he can always do better. Is that how these parties go?"

"You're exactly right, Brigid," Owyn said, "and that's why I don't participate. My cousins make fools of themselves, boasting and behaving recklessly!"

Ferghus clapped his hand onto Owyn's back. "That's all right, cousin; we wouldn't want tae embarrass ye in front of the bonnie lass..."

"I don't see *you* up there!" I said, as Hamish let the stone go.

Ferghus grinned. "Is that a challenge, Brigid?"

I shook my head. "Looks like Hamish did all right. Is he the one to beat?"

"Fer now," Sloane answered as Ferghus headed onto the field.

"Is he really that good?"

"Aye, but not as good as *me*," Sloane boasted.

"Are you going to throw?"

Sloane shook his head. "Aam savin' mah energy fer later..."

I shielded my eyes and stared at the men on the field. Edan had just thrown the stone, but it didn't come anywhere close to where Hamish had gotten his. Ferghus was up next, but just as he was about to begin, Nyle ambled over and stood in my line of view. "Not as far as Eh'd hoped, but ye'll be mah good luck charm fer the hammer..."

"Sure," I said quickly, and stood so I could see the field. Nyle was too tall. I sidestepped, but Ferghus was halfway to the food table. *"Did he throw?"*

Sloane shook his head. "Nae, he must be savin' his energy like me..."

"Hamish will win this event then," Nyle stated.

"Excuse me for a moment," I interrupted and headed towards Ferghus but, when I reached the meadow, Ewan and Edan addressed me.

"Brigid, ye fancy a try?" Ewan teased.

"No, I don't think I could even *lift* the thing," I said, trying to see around Edan to the food tables.

"We'll help ye," Edan said with a wink.

"No, that's okay. It's fun just to watch."

Ewan was lifting the stone onto his shoulder. "We can dae it taegether," he suggested with a mischievous grin.

"Is Brigid enterin'?" Cam called from his spot on the field.

I felt my face growing hot. "No, just watching," I replied, turning to see if Ferghus was still close by. He was drinking a glass of whisky, his back to the field. Just the sight of him made my stomach turn over. I couldn't seem to get away from these men. "Excuse me, everyone, I'm going to get something to drink," I stated, but Nyle had followed me and interjected.

"What dae ye need?" he asked, "Aam thirsty mahself..."

Hamish guffawed. "Ye just recovered from yer *last* bout!"

Nyle smiled sheepishly. "That was Ewan's fault," he said, "his stories go well with liquor..."

Everyone laughed. "Come on, Brigid," Ewan said, "watch me throw..." He stepped away from us to the middle of the field.

When Brodie and Hugh's father called out the results, Hamish was currently in the lead, followed by Hugh and Nyle. The distraction finally gave me a chance to slip away but, when I got to the food table, Ferghus was gone. I couldn't explain it, but I felt deeply disappointed. I scanned the property and finally saw him sitting by himself on the opposite side of the meadow, a bottle of something in his hand. I trailed through the tall grasses until I was standing in front of him. "You didn't throw," I said, trying to keep my voice neutral.

He took a long swallow from the whisky bottle and met my gaze; his blue eyes were tired. "Changed mah mind," he said simply.

"*Why?*"

He shrugged and stared intensely at me. "Nae reason, Sasannach. Ah guess Aam not in the mood."

I swallowed, working up the courage to talk to him when he was behaving so indifferently. "But I thought you wanted to beat Nyle and Hamish?" I stated quietly.

"Not much fun if ye have no one tae cheer ye on now is it?" he asked pointedly.

I blushed and stared at the tip of my shoe. "You have lots of people to cheer you," I argued lightly.

Ferghus laughed ruefully. "Is that so, Rosa? Like *who*?" His eyebrows were raised in amusement.

I laughed nervously. "All your cousins; all Nyle's friends…"

"Aye, they seem *real* keen," he joked, pointing across the field. I turned to observe what he was gesturing at and saw Hamish with his head tilted back, mouth wide open, while Nyle poured whisky down his throat.

"Why are they doing that?" I questioned.

"Hamish must have thrown the farthest," Ferghus commented indifferently.

"It's a *drinking* game?"

Ferghus chuckled. "One way of lookin' at it." He paused, his lips twitching again. "Ye came a long way tae ask yer questions. Aam sure Owyn or Nyle could have answered them fer ye…"

I blushed again. "I was curious how you would do," I admitted.

"Ye didn't seem very curious, Brigid," he contradicted with a frown.

I twisted my hands in my lap. "I was; I tried to see you, but Nyle stood in front of me. When I walked over to where you were throwing, you had already left."

Ferghus watched my face quietly for a few seconds, as if processing my earnest explanation. "Ah saw ye with Nyle; Ah didn't think ye was very concerned if Ah threw or not…"

"I was," I said in a rush, "Sloane said you might win…"

Ferghus laughed. "Not *might*," he boasted with a grin. I returned his smile. "Fer a minute there, it looked like *ye* might enter tay," he teased.

"*Ewan*," I said and rolled my eyes.

"Can't decide whose worse – mah cousins, or mah cousins' *friends*…"

"They have some good qualities too, don't they?" I inquired.

"Aye, but they get on mah nerves tay," he replied.

"Owyn seems the calmest," I commented.

Ferghus frowned. "Yer not still thinkin' about his book, are ye?"

"No, but it isn't *bad*, Ferghus. I think you'd enjoy it."

Ferghus smirked. "Maybe if Ah was a wee *bairn*."

"Stories aren't just for little *kids*," I argued, sitting beside him on the grass.

He shook his head. "Aam tay busy tae read," he stated dismissively.

"I think you'd really like Sir Gawain," I told him, "it's a romance."

Ferghus smirked. "Ah see why Owyn's so taken with it."

I felt suddenly embarrassed. "I didn't mean a *love* story; I meant a tale of adventure and bravery," I said defensively.

"Ye think bravery is *romantic*?" he questioned, suddenly curious.

"It's more about a story's *components*," I said and then sighed. It was difficult to put my thoughts into words. "The knight in the story is brave, but also flawed. He makes mistakes and yet receives redemption by the end. It teaches us that we can be tempted, but it doesn't mean we're a bad person if we have moments of weakness..." I stopped suddenly when I realized how quiet Ferghus had gotten. He was sitting still, listening intently to me speak.

When I finished, he nodded slowly. "Ye get all that from one book?"

I smiled at him. "*Yes.*" I paused and then added shyly, "I could read it to you sometime..."

He looked at me incredulously. "Ah can read it *mahself*, Brigid..."

"Mmmhmm," I said, "but it's okay if you *can't*. I don't mind helping..."

Instead of contradicting me this time, he said something unexpected, "Aam not an *imbecile*."

I blushed. "*Oh my god*, I never said you *were*! Why would you say that?"

"Because ye suggested readin' tae a grown man."

"Ferghus, I didn't mean it in that way," I told him.

He laughed ruefully. "Bonniest lass I've ever seen and she wants tae read tae me like a bairn."

Tears stung my eyes. "That's not what I meant – "

"Aam goin' tae get drunk," he told me, standing with the bottle in his hand. He towered above me, his eyes blazing with indignation.

"Ferghus, you misunderstood me – "

"Nae, Ah don't think Ah did," he stated firmly, "enjoy the party. We leave at dawn." He started to walk away, but I grasped his muscular forearm before I realized what I was doing.

He looked startled. *"Please don't go,"* I pleaded, my voice frantic, "I honestly didn't mean it the way you think!"

His lips were pressed into a firm line, but the urgency in my voice held him there. "Ye said ye could read the book tae me. There's nae other way tae take it, Brigid…"

My face was flushed when I hurried to explain, "I wondered if you might need glasses…"

He scowled. *"Ah see just fine!"*

"Okay, okay," I responded, "then maybe you have a learning disability…"

"Ni Dia cron air![95]" he exclaimed, and shook my hand off his arm before marching towards the hillside.

I raced to keep up with him. *"Ferghus!"* He didn't slow. *"Please!"*

I managed to catch up with him, but he kept going. His long legs made it difficult to stay beside him. I kept falling behind and was soon out of breath despite my physical conditioning. *"Ferghus, please!"* I called,

[95] God damn it!

but he soon reached the top of a slope and disappeared from view. I sat dejectedly on the grass and cupped my head in my hands in frustration. For a few minutes, my body was too full of adrenaline to cry, but eventually I shed a few tears until I was numb. I didn't know what to do. Everything felt all mixed up and hopeless, but I couldn't return to the party without talking to Ferghus first.

I inhaled, brushed the dirt off my gown, and started to climb further up the grassy slope. I found him a few feet up, lying beneath a tree with his arms folded behind his head and his eyes closed. I hesitated, not wanting to wake him, when he suddenly opened one eye and asked, "go enjoy the ceilidh, Brigid."

I took a few steps closer to him. "I thought you were sleeping."

He laughed sardonically. "Ah *can't* sleep – Ah keep thinkin' of all the reasons not tae go with ye taemorrow…"

I felt as if someone had knocked the wind out of me. "*Oh,*" I managed to whisper, turning my gaze to the ground.

"Why didn't ye go back tae the party? They'll be bringin' the food out soon…"

"I wanted to find you first," I told him nervously, still not meeting his gaze, "I wanted to apologize for making you angry. I'm really sorry, Ferghus…"

"So ye find me stupid as well as ugly?" he questioned unexpectedly.

I lifted my head, my mouth gaping in shock. "*What?*"

Ferghus rolled his eyes and stared at the leaves above his head. "Go back tae the party. I'll see if Sloane will keep ye here instead of makin' everyone go out of their way tae Dunvegan; I'll get there faster on mah own…"

I could feel the tears already starting to roll down my cheeks and I choked back a sob, embarrassed at falling apart in front of him. The rejection seared through me, causing my vision to blur. I turned my back and took several deep breaths. I wanted to reply before rushing down the hill to my chamber, but I couldn't get any words out. I felt more ashamed than I'd felt in years. Finally, I blurted, "I've never thought you were stupid *or* ugly. I hope you get to Dunvegan safely…"

I fled down the hill. When I reached the bottom, I could see the men engaged in a new game, but I had no interest in watching any more competitions. It was only mid-afternoon; I had several hours of merrymaking to get through before I could sleep and then slip off quietly in the morning without troubling anyone. I was certain I could find my way back to the spot where Ferghus and I had encountered the MacDonalds; after that, I would have more decisions to make about what to do, but for now I simply wanted to feel calmer – more like myself.

The first thing that entered my head when I thought about finding my centre again was performing a kata; I knew it would ground me and help me focus on my breathing and self-confidence. I entered the house and bolted the door to my chamber. As I moved into the middle of the room, I felt a sense of peace wash over me. I closed my eyes, took several deep breaths, and then began Kata Heian Yondan. I went through the moves three times before switching to Kata Empi. I loved its combination of sharp, quick hand and foot movements, blended with its elegant flow. When I finished, I stood at the window for a few minutes, breathing in the fresh air to clear my mind even more. I was resolved that I had done nothing malevolent towards Ferghus; in fact, my attention had been nothing but friendly and helpful. He owed *me* an apology for the way he had spoken – *not* the other way around. I would sit outside with his cousins and their friends, and eat and drink until the sun set on Nyle's birthday.

***

When I returned to the meadow, more food had already been added to the table. This time there was cheese and fresh fruit, as well as wild salmon and neeps in a whisky sauce. I took a sampling of everything and was just about to pour myself a glass of wine when Hugh's father offered to assist me. I smiled at him and asked if he was having a good time. "It got me out of the house," he joked, "makes me feel young agin."

"I bet you're just letting them win," I teased and he laughed.

"Aye, they wouldn't know what hit em if Ah tried mah hardest…"

"Sloane said he's waiting until later to compete. I hope you do too."

He smiled at me. "Aam strong as an ox; Ah might try a toss of the caber…"

"Is that the huge log I saw?" I questioned, my eyes wide.

"Aye, lass. Tis me favourite…"

"Well, I can't wait to watch."

I moved away to find a seat by the base of the hill; almost everyone was relaxing now, enjoying some supper. Nyle stood when he saw me. "Come join us, Brigid." He had a fist wrapped around a bottle of whisky. I sat in an empty seat beside him and took a sip of wine.

"Ye missed the hammer; Ah came in first," Hugh told me.

"Congratulations! Your dad said he's going to enter the caber later."

"Ye talked him into it then?" Hugh said good-naturedly, "he was always top notch…"

"Ah remember him when we were kids," Nyle agreed, "but now I'll probably get the most points…"

Sloane laughed. "It's yer birthday; we can't give ye a greater gift than that…" Hamish almost spit out his beer.

"I'll win fair and square," Nyle boasted, grinning at me between drinks and giving Hamish a withering look.

Sloane shook his head. "Ye might want tae slow down on the drink, Nyle; we have an early start in the morn…" He looked meaningfully at him.

"You still mean to leave for Dunvegan?" Owyn asked.

I hesitated, heat rising in my face. "Um, you'll have to check with Ferghus about that; he keeps changing his mind…"

"Ah know he wanted tae leave today, lass; he's just anxious tae keep ye safe is all," Sloane told me. I knew he was wrong, but I didn't want to spoil the mood.

"Mebbe Brodie and Ah should come tay," Cam suggested with a crooked smile, "Aam always up fer a little bone breakin'…"

Sloane shook his head. "Yer more likely tae get yer *own* bones broken; leave the MacDonalds tae us."

"Ah don't know why yer takin' Nyle," Cam retorted, "he's not much bigger than Ah or Ewan…"

"We've fought together before and we're first cousins," Sloane explained, "he may like tae party, but in the wild Eh'd trust him with mah life."

"Is that the last bottle?" Edan complained, eyeing the whisky disappearing down Nyle's throat.

"Nae, I'll have the servants bring out more," Sloane said, glancing around for the closest servant.

Suddenly, Ferghus stepped up to the table and placed his half-empty bottle of whisky into Edan's hand. "Ye can have the rest of this," he said. I could feel my body heat rise just from the sound of his voice. He fixed his blue eyes upon me; his dark eyebrows were brooding and intense, but he didn't address me.

"Ye been nappin'?" Sloane joked.

"Aye," Ferghus answered without further explanation.

"You should eat something," Owyn suggested, "or else you won't be able to stand by the time the pipes start." Ferghus levelled him with a scornful gaze, but didn't reply.

"Have ye ever seen Ferghus drunk, Owyn?" Sloane questioned, his lips curled in a smile.

"I don't recall..."

"That's because he can *hold* his drink," Sloane teased, "unlike *some* of our kin." He smacked the back of Nyle's head.

"*Hey!*" Nyle protested, "Ah need mah strength fer the *caber!*"

"Ah did see him fallin' down blooter'd *once*," Sloane continued, pausing to recall the memory, "it was just after the incident."

"Did ye take down a bunch of yer cousins?" Hamish asked, a twinkle in his eye.

Ferghus sat in a chair beside Hugh and gazed out at the field as if completely indifferent to what was being discussed. "Funniest drunk *I've* ever seen; gigglin' like a lass," Sloane joked.

"Screw off," Ferghus retorted, but he looked like he wanted to smile too.

"Sounds like me," Nyle stated.

Several of his friends laughed. "Except *ye* try tae break into young quines' chambers," Hamish pointed out. Nyle glared at him and hit him hard across the chest. Hamish put him into a headlock, but let him go a few seconds after.

I lifted my eyes and found Ferghus watching me. Sloane's description of him drunk was pretty accurate from what I'd seen the night before, but I didn't betray his secret. A servant restocked the alcohol at our table and left sweets as well. I looked away from Ferghus, aware he was probably still thinking how much he loathed me. "Try the Cranachan," Sloane said, "mah cook makes a perfect one..."

"Need another swim," Edan said, "it's gettin' hot."

"Only if Brigid comes in this time," Nyle replied with a mischievous grin.

"You're not getting me to jump off a dock," I said, shaking my head.

"Mebbe ye'll change yer mind taenight," Nyle said hopefully.

"Come on men, let's have a little more competition," Sloane suggested to change the subject. I smiled at him gratefully. Everyone stood except for Ferghus and Owyn. "Come *on* Ferghus – time tae bury our competition," Sloane joked. Ferghus stood slowly and followed everyone onto the field where Hugh's father and Brodie were preparing the next game. At first, I thought they were going to do some strange limbo dance, but after Hamish picked up an enormous boulder and heaved it over a wooden pole, I realized it was a test of strength to see how high they could throw.

"So far everyone has gotten it over," I said aloud after Nyle and Edan threw the boulder.

"Yes, but the next round the bar will be *lifted*. Eventually, it will come down to just the strongest."

"Oh, that makes sense," I stated, watching closely as Sloane and Ferghus easily made the throw, "who do you think will win?"

Owyn thought for a minute. "I'll pick Sloane," he decided, "since he hasn't had as much to drink as Nyle and his friends."

"What about Ferghus?" I asked, trying to keep my voice indifferent.

Owyn glanced at me. "He has a good chance; Hamish too," he answered, "but Ferghus doesn't just have brute strength, like Hamish; he's skilled too…"

I nodded in agreement. "I saw him fight," I told Owyn, "he's definitely experienced." I didn't tell him that Ferghus had also attacked *me* when we'd first met, so I'd felt his skill firsthand.

During the second round, Edan and Cam were eliminated, and Ewan just barely made it over. "Third round," Owyn commented.

I watched as Hamish, Sloane, Ferghus, and Hugh all managed to get the boulder over the much higher pole. "Wow, it's got to be over *fifty pounds* they're throwing," I mused.

"Down to four," Owyn stated, "want to get closer to see better?"

"Sure," I agreed. Everyone was gathered around the competitors, guessing who they thought would win.

"Anyone want tae wager?" Cam questioned eagerly.

"Aam in," Nyle said.

"Me tay," Brodie called.

"Ye can't bet," Sloane told him, "yer judgin' the match!"

The friends discussed their wagers while Brodie lifted the pole higher. Hugh threw first, but knocked the pole off. "*So close!*" he cried, shaking his head.

Hamish threw next and got it successfully over. "Get ready tae name me champion!" he boasted.

"Not yet, ye arrogant fool!" Ferghus exclaimed and lifted the boulder into his arms. He bent his legs and heaved it into the air. It went over! As soon as he made the throw, he turned around and glanced my way. I felt as if I was back in high school, watching a boyfriend's sporting event. Sloane prepared to throw, pausing for a long while before tossing the enormous rock. He knew as soon as he let go it wasn't going to be enough.

"*Ifrinn Fhuilteach!*[96]" he cried, but laughed immediately after.

Brodie elevated the pole again. Hamish was first up. He stretched his shoulders and biceps before bending to pick up the boulder. "Come on, Hamish!" Cam said, "I've got bunsens ridin' on ye!"

"Ye wasted yer precious money," Sloane told him.

Hamish launched the rock as hard as he could, but it wasn't enough; it crashed into the pole and almost crushed Brodie's foot. "*Watch it!*" he joked.

"Ye owe me, ye bastard!" Cam hollered.

Ferghus was quiet as he stepped up to the pole. He didn't do a bunch of stretching as Hamish had; he simply stared down at the rock for a few seconds and then hoisted it onto his shoulder. He paused again, lifting his eyes to judge how hard to heave it into the air. I watched him let go, my insides queasy as I waited with everyone else for the result.

It soared just past the pole and landed with a loud thump on the other side. "*He did it!*" Sloane cheered.

Everyone except Hamish and Cam either punched Ferghus in the arm, shoulder, or chest. I thought it was a rough way to say

96 Bloody Hell!

congratulations. I watched with Owyn from just outside their circle, until they began to drift over to the food table or to find drinks at our other seats. Ferghus finally looked at me, his blue eyes bright from exertion and triumph. I couldn't manage any words. "Would you like a drink?" Owyn asked.

I started, having forgotten he was still standing beside me too. "Okay," I replied, still staring into Ferghus's eyes.

"Congratulations, Ferghus," Owyn said as the three of us headed back to our table.

"Thank ye," Ferghus responded quietly. He didn't speak to me, and I didn't speak to him, but somehow I knew he wasn't angry at me anymore.

Chapter Eighteen:

Hugh's father won the caber toss; I wondered whether the other men let him win. They also did a test of endurance whereby they had to start at the base of the hill and race up the slope to the very top. Nyle asked me to wait at the bottom as a token of good luck; he was certain he would be the victor of the race, because he said he had the greatest stamina of the group. Owyn and I chatted while everyone else raced up the grassy hill. The sun had changed direction so the trees near the bottom provided almost full shade. After a time, Owyn and I heard shouting as the men started to emerge at the top of the closest ridge; Ferghus had a significant lead, but I could just make out two tiny specks resembling Nyle and Hugh following. I bit my lip, watching Ferghus descend. He was the most attractive man I had ever met, and he had no idea.

When he reached me, he leaned forwards, his palms upon his muscular thighs, while he worked to catch his breath. I wanted to congratulate him, or tell him how proud I was of him, but I felt consumed by shyness. When he finally lifted his head, his eyes locked with mine; my heart was beating so fast I felt as if *I* had just run a race. I blushed deeply, and tried to work up the nerve to speak to him, when suddenly an object whizzed past my arm and smashed into Owyn's wrist; the sounds of shattering bone and agonized cries filled the air. *"Intae the trees, Brigid!"* Ferghus yelled as he grasped Owyn around the waist and hauled him backwards into the cover of the leaves.

Ferghus helped Owyn lean against a trunk. "Get yer sgian-dubh out and give one tae Brigid!" he commanded.

"I don't carry any," Owyn managed to say, cupping his bleeding hand in his other one.

Ferghus's eyes widened, but he didn't say anything; instead, he pulled two daggers out of his stockings and pressed a hilt into my shaking palm. *"Stay under cover!"* he ordered before rushing through the sparse trees to call to Nyle and Hugh, who were the only two visible so far. *"Luch!"* he cried, *"a-steach do na craobhan!*[97]*"* and then continued up the hill until he disappeared over the first slope.

Nyle and Hugh burst into our cover, breathing hard as they each pulled a knife free. *"What happened?"* Nyle questioned between gasps.

"We were on the field and Owyn got shot by an arrow," I answered, my voice shaking.

In a split second, Nyle placed himself in front of me, peering down the hill in the direction I'd stated. *"Get ontae the ground,"* he whispered. I helped Owyn slide down the trunk into a seated position.

"Do you have anything we can use as a bandage?" I asked. Owyn's eyes were glassy, but he nodded silently. "Is it in your sporran?" He nodded again.

"They must be hidin' behind that stand of trees," Nyle observed as I started to wrap a handkerchief around Owyn's wrist. He sucked in his breath, but otherwise didn't make a sound.

"We *have* tae get tae the castle," Hugh said, "we don't know how many there are."

"Aye, we need more weapons," Nyle agreed as Ewan, Edan, and Sloane flew under the canopy.

"Ferghus is gatherin' everyone from the hill," Sloane told us, inhaling deeply.

"We need tae get into the castle," Nyle repeated.

---

97 Ambush! Into the trees!

"Aye, but not until everyone's back; we'll break into groups," Sloane insisted knowledgeably. Clearly, he'd been through similar situations before. I was shocked by how calmly everyone was taking this.

"Aila's in the house," I reminded them, "with all your staff. They'll be vulnerable if they're attacked; there's no one to protect them…"

Nyle exchanged a look with Sloane. "Tha i ceart,[98]" Nyle stated, glancing at me with respect.

"*Daingead*!" Sloane hissed, "*marbhaidh mi gach fear mu dheireadh ma ghoirticheas iad mo phiuthar*![99]"

"Should you send the fastest to the house?" I questioned, "leave the strongest for the field?"

"It's folly to go down the hill," Owyn said through gritted teeth.

"Aye, we need a surprise attack," Sloane agreed.

"We can hide along the slopes," Nyle said to Sloane, "take the docks tae the garden…"

"We can't leave Brigid and Owyn here," Sloane argued, his brow creasing.

"Ferghus will be down soon," Nyle insisted vehemently.

"And he's one of the fastest and strongest," I interrupted, "he gave me a knife; I'll be fine. Get a head start; we'll tell him to follow as soon as he gets back…"

Nyle was nodding as I spoke. "Let's go, Sloane, before it's tay late…"

Sloane stared at me for a few seconds, as if trying to decide what to do, but then he turned to Ewan and Edan and commanded, "watch out fer Brigid and Owyn; Nyle – Hugh – let's go…"

[98] She's right.

[99] Damn it! I'll kill every last one if they hurt my sister!

The three crept through the trees and disappeared above us; it was eerily quiet again as Owyn and I watched Ewan and Edan peering through the branches to the meadow below. "Can you see anything?" I asked.

"Nothin'," Edan replied quietly.

Hamish and Cam arrived next, followed closely by Brodie, Hugh's father, and Ferghus. Everyone was breathing hard. "Sloane took Nyle and Hugh tae the house; they're followin' the hills tae the docks, and enterin' through the garden," Ewan explained to Ferghus.

He nodded. "I'll take Hamish and join them," he decided, preparing to leave immediately.

"Ye need more in case they brought an army," Cam argued, "what if ye get there and are outnumbered? Irven and Ah can stay with Brigid and Owyn."

Ferghus and I locked eyes and I nodded. "I'll be *fine*," I assured him, "you need *numbers*. Aila's in there and all the staff..."

"Aye," he agreed quickly, "let's go. Hamish, ye head tae the third floor as soon as we get inside. Ewan, ye and Edan get all the staff outside tae the garden. Brodie, ye and Ah will find Sloane, Nyle, and Hugh and gather weapons so we can reinforce the front."

Everyone nodded their understanding and crept silently away through the trees, but Ferghus leaned down to whisper in my ear, "this is *nae* time fer defense; *kill them*..." He grasped the knife in my hand and shook it before rushing after his kin.

Chapter Nineteen:

Hugh's father was peering through the trees when Ferghus left. Cam crept behind him and whispered, "see anythin' yet?"

Just as Irven was about to speak, Cam wrapped his arm around his neck and quickly jerked it at an odd angle. There was a sickening snap from the intensity of the force, and Irven's body went limp in Cam's arms. I cried out in horror as Cam slid his sgian-dubh from his kilt hose. *"Toss me yer knife!"* he commanded.

"Get behind the tree!" Owyn exclaimed at the same time. He pushed himself into a kneeling position and tried to slide up the trunk to stand.

"Give me yer knife!" Cam repeated, his face turning purple.

"Brigid, run!" Owyn yelled.

I stood slowly, never looking away from the sgian-dubh in Cam's outstretched hand. "Why are you doing this?" I asked, clutching the knife Ferghus had given me. My hand was shaking, so I pressed it tightly against my side.

"Brigid, get behind me!" Owyn called, but I ignored him.

"Ah only get mah money if Ah return ye tae them *alive*," Cam blurted angrily, "so don't dae anythin' stupid, lass. *Drop the knife!*"

"You would betray your own friends just to make some *cash*?" I commented, pretending to be interested in his reasons.

"Ye know *nothin'*," Cam snarled, his crooked teeth rendering him even more menacing. I took a step closer, tying to keep my hand from trembling.

"I know your friends would help you – if you asked them," I stated, forcing my voice to sound sympathetic, "Nyle is kind and loyal; go to him…"

Cam's brown eyes narrowed. "Ah have debts tae pay," he retorted, "people comin' fer me; ye don't understand." He shook his head, as if trying to clear my words from his mind. "They said ye ran away – humiliated Tristen and his kin…" I inched closer, keeping my blade lowered and my head up.

"I didn't agree to the wedding," I told him honestly, "and none of my family did either!" I took one more step before Cam finally noticed.

"Get back or Ah *swear* I'll kill ye!" he yelled, "*drop yer knife!*"

But I was close enough to thrust my blade against Cam's, and then quickly sidestep, which allowed me to wrap my arm around the hilt of his knife. Before Cam had time to react, I had already pressed the blade of my weapon against the back of his forearm, administering so much pressure on his wrist he had no choice but to drop his knife. It didn't stop him, however; he was so fueled by rage, he hurled himself at me. In the chaos, my knife plunged into his side. I'm not sure who was more shocked, but Cam dropped to his knees, clutching at the hilt still sticking out of him. I picked up the blade resting upon the ground and rushed to Owyn's side. "We need to take to go," I pleaded.

Owyn nodded and followed me up the grassy slope, still cupping his bandaged hand. When we were out of sight of the trees and ground, he finally spoke. "I don't know how you did it; I feel as if I just woke from a dream…"

My entire body was shaking. "I might have just killed a man," I said.

"He murdered Hugh's father, Brigid," Owyn reminded me. I didn't stop to look at him.

When we neared the water, I finally paused. "What do we do now?" I asked.

"I'm no good to you," Owyn apologized, "I can try to fight one handed, but I won't be able to balance properly..."

"I know," I agreed, "but we can't risk being caught by ourselves, especially if Cam told the MacDonalds to use the cover of the hills. I'd rather try to get to the house where your cousins are..."

Owyn nodded. "Yes, but if we run into any trouble, you have to promise to save yourself. Don't worry about me..."

"We're in this together, Owyn," I told him earnestly, "I'm not leaving you..." He looked unexpectedly grateful. "Let's go," I said, more for myself than Owyn. I felt nauseous and wanted to get into one of the boats at the end of Sloane's dock and sail away rather than put myself in any more danger, but my thoughts kept straying to Ferghus; he hadn't thought twice about risking his life. How did someone grow into such a man?

From the dock area we could discern movement towards the back of the castle, but it was impossible to tell whether it was friend or foe. I knew we should head there regardless, because that was where Ferghus had told Ewan and Edan to take the staff. We crept along the rocky shore; it was slow going because of Owyn's injury. I could see blood seeping through the bandage I had helped him tie, but not once did he complain. When we drew closer, it was a ghastly sight that met our eyes. "*Oh god!*" I cried, unable to stop myself.

Just inside the garden, I could see the lifeless bodies of Brodie and the butler, but that was nothing compared to the inquisition taking place on the grassy area before us. Ferghus, Sloane, Hamish, Nyle, and Ewan were all kneeling upon the ground, their hands wrapped around the backs of their necks, a MacDonald holding a weapon to each throat. Even worse was the sight of Aila being held by a fistful of her hair for the five men to watch. "*An e seo i?*[100]" a tall Highlander shouted.

"What's he saying?" I hissed.

"He wants to know if Aila is you; he must not know what you look like," Owyn answered, "or is too stupid to remember…"

"He looks familiar," I murmured, "I think he was one of the men chasing me on the night of the wedding…"

"It's Turi," Owyn stated, "Tristen's brother."

"We have to do something or they'll all be dead," I whispered.

"I'll do whatever I can to help."

I shook my head. "You should stay here; don't let them see you."

"*Brigid*…"

"I'm *serious*! *Don't move!*" He sighed. "I just wish I had more weapons. One knife isn't going to do much…"

"You should get into one of the boats and sail away," Owyn said in frustration.

"I'm *not* leaving them," I said firmly and crept along the shoal towards the group. As I neared, I could see more dead bodies at the edge of the garden; it looked like the housekeeper had fallen as well as Edan. I was thankful I couldn't see their faces. I was wondering how such strong men had fared so poorly in battle when several more strange men emerged from the castle garden. We must have been considerably outnumbered, not to mention they had surprised us in the middle of Nyle's party. Cam's betrayal had ended in more tragedy than my mind could process at the moment.

I couldn't decide what to do. To attack with a knife meant I had to be close, but if all those men saw me, what chance did any of us have of

[100] Is this her?

---

coming out of this alive? I had to trust I could make a difference – at least surprise them and create enough of a distraction for the men of my clan to take a few down with them. My breath caught in my throat when I realized what I had just thought: my *clan*. But I was a MacDonald. Why had I been sent here to fight on the opposite side of my surname?

I was so close I could see Aila's tears glistening on her pale cheeks. She was beautiful in a waifish sort of way, but she looked as if she had been dragged downstairs; her dress was torn and muddy. I could see Hamish gritting his teeth in fury, but he was helpless, as were the other four men.

I inhaled deeply and then charged from the shore, straight at Aila's assailant. Just before I reached her, I threw the knife as hard as I could at the man pressing his blade to Ferghus's neck.

Chaos quickly ensued; Ferghus ripped the knife from his attacker's throat and slit the men's necks on both sides of him in a half second, allowing Nyle to kill Hamish's combatant. I kicked Aila's hostage taker hard in the elbow; he dropped her and came at me. He managed to punch me once in my chest; a shocking pain seared through me but, instead of backing away, I leaned in as close to him as I could and executed the Do Mawashi Kaiten Geri. He was on the ground before he knew what had happened. I had no weapon, but it didn't matter; before I had time to stand, Hamish had already knelt beside the man and snapped his neck. I stood shakily and swivelled in a circle, falling right into Ferghus's arms. "*Are ye alright?*" he implored me, his handsome face panicked.

Tears stung my eyes; I tried to inhale, but my chest throbbed. "I think he hit me," I managed to say.

"Ye *think?*" Ferghus said, his voice incredulous, "Brigid, he might have broken yer ribs!"

I gazed around me, feeling dazed. I could hardly process the horror of it all; I had never seen anything of its equal in real life. And there was none of the emotional disconnect I'd had while viewing violence in movies. This was a new feeling that my karate training had not adequately prepared me for. I broke free of his grasp and ran to the rocky shore, doubling over as I began to throw up everything in my stomach. Even with my eyes closed, I could see Hugh's father, staring blankly up at me after Cam murdered him. I could see Ferghus slitting two men's throats, Hamish breaking a man's neck, and Nyle stabbing a man in the chest. I squeezed my eyes shut, willing the images to disappear, but they didn't. Brodie – the butler – the housekeeper. Edan. Cam. MacDonalds. They were *all* dead. They had all been murdered. I had killed Cam. I was a murderer too. "*Brigid*?" Ferghus said from behind me.

"I killed him," I whispered to the water, "I'm a murderer…"

Ferghus moved closer so he could hear me above the waves. "What happened? Who'd ye kill?"

I straightened, blinking back tears. When I met his gaze, my vision was blurred. "Cam. He's dead."

Ferghus's eyes narrowed. "Where's Cam? And Irven? Where's Owyn?"

"I'm here," a voice said.

Ferghus and I both whirled around and saw Owyn making his way towards us, his bandage more red than white now. "What the hell happened up there?" Ferghus demanded, stepping in front of me as if to protect me from Owyn.

"He's okay," I said, "it was Cam; he turned on us. He killed Hugh's father and then tried to take me to the MacDonalds. Said they offered him money…"

"She was unbelievable," Owyn interjected, a note of awe evident in his voice, "he tried to take her sgian-dubh, but Brigid somehow knocked his out of his hand!"

"Ye said ye killed him," Ferghus said, turning to face me, "is he dead?" He was suddenly curt.

I wiped away my tears and shook my head. "I don't know. Owyn and I ran as soon as we could..."

"He was on the ground when we left," Owyn said.

"Ye should have made *sure*, Owyn," Ferghus accused him.

"It was my fault," I apologized, aware I'd made an immense mistake, "I was frightened – "

"Twas *Owyn's* responsibility," Ferghus interrupted. He quickly turned back to the scene behind us. "*Bhrath Cam sinn!*" he shouted to his cousins, "*tiugainn!*[101]"

Sloane and Nyle hurried over. "What happened?" Sloane questioned, wiping sweat from his brow. Nyle had blood running down his forearm.

"*Mharbh Cam athair Uisdean,*[102]" Ferghus explained, glancing quickly at me, "Brigid stabbed him, but he might still be alive."

Sloane and Nyle both nodded. "*Fuirich comhla ri Aila!*[103]" Sloane called to Hamish.

"Yer comin' with us," Ferghus commanded, a scowl upon his face.

I felt my entire stomach bottom out from disappointing him so badly. "Okay," I responded quietly.

---

[101] Cam betrayed us! Let's go!

[102] Cam killed Hugh's father.

[103] Stay with Aila!

"Owyn, stay with Hamish," Ferghus said without looking at him. He set out down the shore and I hurried to keep up with his long legs. Nyle and Sloane fell in behind me. Their unspoken arrangement belied how well they knew one another, and how many times they'd been in tense situations together. All traces of Nyle's school-boy partying were gone.

"Where did yer blade hit him?" Ferghus asked as we moved past the docks.

I wished he would turn and look at me. "In his right side – stomach I think…"

"With how much force?"

"He was running at me, so a fair bit," I replied nervously. I felt as if my answers might elicit the same type of censure he'd shown Owyn.

"Leon, ach is docha nach eil marbh," Ferghus stated grimly.

"*Docha*? Perhaps *what*?" I questioned, feeling my skin growing hot from embarrassment. How could he speak to his cousins in his own language in front of me? He was clearly trying to shut me out.

Ferghus sighed and said over his shoulder, "probably not dead."

"*I'm sorry I failed all of you!*" Tears threatened to spill from my eyes again, "I did my best; I *swear* I did my best!"

"Aye, lass, we know," Sloane's smooth voice came from behind me. He wasn't the man I wanted to hear from, however.

"I tried to reason with him," I said, my voice quavering, "I told him he didn't have to hurt anyone else, but he wouldn't listen…"

"Tha e na gambler. Feumaidh a bhith ann am fiachan,[104]" Nyle said in frustration.

Ferghus scoffed. "*He never should have been invited here!*"

"Tha mi duilich,[105]" Nyle said sadly.

---

[104] He's a gambler. Must be in debt.

When we reached the slope, the pain in my chest began to throb more noticeably. My pace slowed until finally Ferghus turned around and barked, "*hurry*!"

I clutched my chest and nodded, trying to keep up with him. Each breath I took burned, but I pushed myself until we neared the grove of trees where we'd taken cover from the arrow fire. Ferghus's hand flew up, signalling us to stop walking. I glanced around, but didn't see any signs that a large group of people had come this way. We crept slowly through the tall grasses until we were just a few feet away. Ferghus told Sloane to wait with me while he and Nyle examined the scene. Nyle motioned us to follow shortly after. Hugh's father was still crumpled upon the ground where Cam had dropped him, but Cam's body was gone. The grass was covered in blood. "Ye hit him *hard*, Brigid," Ferghus commented, following the blood trail outside the cover of trees. We spotted Cam lying face down upon the slope. Ferghus used his boot to turn Cam's body over. "Aye, he's dead. Ye did well."

I should have felt elated by his praise, so desired earlier in the day, but suddenly the absolute travesty of everything overwhelmed me. I stared blankly at his face, his scar pale in the sunlight. I was lightheaded and nauseous, and could hardly draw a full breath. One minute I was staring into his peacock-blue eyes, and the next I was feeling a strange sort of weightlessness as my body finally capitulated to pain and anguish. Perhaps I'm too embarrassed to admit I fainted. 'S docha!

---

[105] I'm sorry.

Chapter Twenty:

I've watched a lot of historical movies. In real life, they didn't use smelling salts; when I came to, Ferghus was carrying me in his strong arms. I glanced around in shame, realizing he'd already traversed half of the hilly slope. *"Oh my god,"* I moaned, "I'm *so* sorry. Put me down; I can walk."

He stopped moving and stared down at me. "Are ye *sure*?" he questioned skeptically, his brow furrowed.

I nodded slowly. "I *think* so," I answered uncertainly. His brows lifted even more. "I won't know until I've *tried*!" I added defensively.

His lips actually looked like they were going to curl into a smile, but movement ahead caught the attention of everyone. "Wish Ah had an arrow; Eh'd stick him mahself," Ferghus stated. Sloane and Nyle chuckled.

I squinted hard. "It's just *Owyn*!"

"Ah *know*," Ferghus responded with a smirk, "he's followin' ye around like a bairn. Are ye sure ye didn't lose one?"

My cheeks flushed. "Put me down! *Now*!"

"As ye wish." Ferghus gently slid me out of his arms until my feet were resting upon the grass.

I felt angry instead of appreciative, and it was all his fault. "Why are you being so mean to him?" I questioned, tilting my chin in the air.

Ferghus laughed. "Because he should have protected ye; he should have made sure Cam was dead."

"He *tried*!" I retorted angrily, my green eyes flashing, "he told me *more* than once to run. He was going to face Cam alone!"

"But ye wouldn't listen?" Ferghus questioned, his eyes amused, "ye needed to save yer bairn first?"

"His wrist is probably broken!" I cried, "yet he never complained. He's stronger than you think, but for *some* reason you taunt him – make him feel inadequate. Well, *fuck you!*"

By this time, Owyn was within earshot. He glanced furtively from Ferghus to me. I was so angry, I could feel heat reaching my ears and finger tips. "Let's go, Owyn. Your cousin is a *jackass!*"

"*Aam* not a jackass," Nyle said quickly, "Ah haven't properly thanked ye fer saving mah *actual* ass." He flashed me a brilliant smile.

"Aye, lass, that was brave," Sloane agreed, wiping sweat from his brow, "we all owe ye our gratitude."

Ferghus levelled a withering glare at his cousins. "We have dead tae bury; help me lift Irven." Sloane and Nyle turned to assist. I stood beside Owyn, hating Ferghus more than I'd ever hated anyone. Why did he have to act like a prick all the time?

"Why'd you come all this way?" I whispered to Owyn.

He looked embarrassed. "I was worried something might happen to you," he explained quietly, "after you saved my life, I didn't want to let you go off by yourself…"

"She wasn't by *herself,* ye incompetent *fool!* She was well protected. Ye should have stayed at the house and read a book!" Ferghus called over his shoulder.

"*Let's go!*" I exclaimed in exasperation and grasped Owyn's good arm.

The other three followed, carrying Hugh's father between them. "Feumaidh mi a posadh![106]" Nyle said enthusiastically.

"Tha i cus dhut. Feumaidh I cuideigin mar mise san leabaidh![107]" Sloane boasted.

---

[106] I need to marry her!

"What are they saying?" I asked Owyn.

"You don't want to know," he replied, giving me a sympathetic smile.

"Am biodh a h-uile duine a 'dunadh?[108]" Ferghus growled.

"Bu mhath leam a bhith ag eigheachd![109]" Nyle joked. Sloane laughed.

"What are they saying?" I repeated, my ire growing, "*tell me!*"

"*Brigid* – " Owyn hedged.

"Cha do stad thu a 'smaoineachadh mun choileach agad airson aon diog![110]" Ferghus barked in disgust.

"Nae, tis too formidable an organ," Nyle replied arrogantly.

"If ye don't shut up, I'll slice it off!" Ferghus shouted.

"*Oh my god!*" I cried, looking sideways at Owyn, "are they *seriously* comparing the size of their – "

"I think it's best if we change the subject, Brigid. My cousins lack any sense of propriety around a lady!" Owyn remarked.

"Ye can shut yer gob *tay*, Owyn!" Ferghus exclaimed, "Ah had *nae* part of this!"

"That *is* true," Owyn confided in a whisper, "it was just Sloane and Nyle – "

"*Shut up, Owyn!*" Nyle said from behind us," ye shouldn't betray yer cousins or ye'll end up like Cam!"

---

[107] She's too much for you. She needs someone like me in bed!

[108] Would everyone just shut up?

[109] I'd like to make her shout!

[110] You haven't stopped thinking about your cock for one second.

Silence finally descended, much to my relief. When we got back to the castle, I sat with Aila and Owyn in the garden while those who had survived the attack carried the bodies to a small grave site to the west of Sloane's property to be buried. The sun was beginning to set when they finished. Ferghus approached us and said, "we should leave fer Dunvegan *now*, Brigid."

I looked at him incredulously, but it was Owyn who responded. "She's unwell, Ferghus. She needs rest."

Ferghus's face contorted with suppressed rage. "Ah can't protect her here! There's not enough of us left! We *have* tae get tae Dunvegan."

"Eh'd like tae help ye, Ferghus, but Ah can't leave mah home now until mah father returns," Sloane said regretfully.

Ferghus sighed. "Ah know. Ah didn't expect anyone else tae come. Yer all needed here." He swallowed hard and turned back to me. "I'll ready Selma. We leave within the hour." He stalked out of the garden.

"I don't envy you the journey to Dunvegan," Owyn said quietly.

Aila giggled. "Ah don't envy ye havin' tae see that awful *scar*!"

I was surprised to hear her speak, since she'd been in a daze since the attack. "I've grown used to the scar; it's his temper I don't understand…"

Nyle glanced at me quickly. "I'll meet up with ye as soon as Ah can, Brigid."

I smiled at him. "I'm sorry your birthday ended this way," I said sympathetically.

"Aye, twenty-two came in monstrous," Nyle agreed.

"Dae ye need any more frocks?" Aila asked.

"No, if I can borrow the ones you already lent me, I should be okay. There's nowhere to do laundry in the forest," I joked, trying to liven my spirits before setting out on another arduous journey.

"Ah don't know how ye dae it, lass," Aila admitted, "Ah need a feather pillow tae fall asleep!"

***

Aila gave me a leather bag to store my gown in; I changed into the everyday dress, but skipped the petticoat this time. It was too bulky and if we were attacked, I would hardly be able to move in it. Sloane gave us some food to start us off. We said our good byes and then Ferghus led Selma along the edge of the hill. He said he thought it would be safer than taking the shorter path we'd come in on, because the greater views would prevent another ambush.

We travelled in an awkward silence for the first half hour or so. Ferghus had changed back into his faded blue and green tartan. "What's the difference between the dark and yellow colours?" I asked curiously, finally breaking the quiet.

Ferghus looked up at me from where he was walking beside Selma. I noticed for the first time that he *always* chose the side that hid his scar. "Both are mah clan colours," he said, "but the yellow is mah dress kilt."

"As in *dressy*?" I questioned.

Ferghus actually smiled. "Ah guess," he responded, "we wear it fer special celebrations. Nyle's birthday seemed an appropriate occasion; Ah didn't know it would be a funeral tay…" His smiled disappeared and he looked straight ahead at the road.

"I'm sorry," I murmured, "you lost so many…"

He didn't respond, so we travelled in silence once again. My anger dissipated and my feelings for him became more neutral. The last of the light faded and the melody of night insects filled the air. "How are ye feelin'?" Ferghus asked unexpectedly.

"I'm okay," I responded quickly.

"Ye sure?" he pressed, glancing up at me shrewdly.

I shrugged. "It aches," I admitted, "all the time..."

"Did ye check fer broken ribs?" Ferghus questioned.

I looked at him guiltily. "No, I changed quickly so we could leave. It's bruised. I'll be okay..."

Ferghus stared at me in the gloom as we plodded along. "I've never met another quine like ye," he finally said.

"That's because there's only *one* Brigid MacDonald."

Ferghus smiled. "Ah meant yer personality, not yer name."

"Thank you, I guess," I mumbled self-consciously.

"Think about it: Cam betrayed our *whole* clan – threatened ye with deadly force – yet ye managed tae kill him *and* escape," he said with reverence.

"It happened so fast – I didn't really *do* anything. He ran at me; the knife just sort of stuck into him."

"Then how'd ye take away his *own* knife? Owyn said ye disarmed Cam. Then ye risked yer life coming back tae the castle. Ye freed me and mah cousins so we could end the fight," Ferghus pointed out.

"Owyn told me to sail away," I admitted.

Ferghus glanced at me sharply. "Why didn't ye?"

I met his gaze. "I'm not sure," I began, not wanting to reveal too many of my own personal feelings, "it just didn't seem right to walk away and leave everyone to die..."

Ferghus looked back at the road. "Ah get that feelin' a lot," he said.

"Why do you think everything's your responsibility? Like helping *me* – you just met me in the forest by chance. You shouldn't have to go out of your way or risk your life for me."

"Aam not a very good sailor," he said ruefully, "Eh'd feel guilty tae flee like a coward."

"I understand helping your *cousins*," I said, "but I'm just some random girl you accidentally crossed paths with. You should just let me go and help Sloane instead."

"'S docha," Ferghus teased.

"You're an ass," I retorted and he laughed.

"Ah don't believe in accidents, Brigid. If our lives are just one big chaotic mess – then Ah should have run mahself through with mah own sword ages ago!"

I didn't exactly know how to respond to that, so I bit my tongue. It was near midnight when we crossed the narrow channel where we'd been attacked the day before. "Ah suspect those are the same men we fought taeday," Ferghus commented as we continued along the road for a few minutes.

Eventually, the woods on either side grew thicker and Ferghus led Selma off the path so we couldn't be seen. This slowed our pace, however; the moon was full in the inky sky and I kept nodding off on Selma's back. Ferghus was worried I'd accidentally slide off, so he searched for a suitable location for us to make camp. Instead of a clearing, he chose a more secluded section of the trees. I felt decidedly claustrophobic, especially considering my breathing was much shallower than normal. It didn't feel too cold for sleeping, but Ferghus reminded me I would become chilled once we stopped moving, and the dew settled over us. He tied Selma to a tree and made a hurried shelter for us to sleep within. I helped place the bed roll on the ground and we sat together under the criss-crossed branches to share some of the food Sloane had given us. I hadn't realized how hungry I was until the food touched my lips. Ferghus passed me the water container and I took a sip. "Thank you," I said.

Ferghus waited for me to lie down and then he spread his great kilt over us. Once again, I felt as if I shouldn't move for fear of taking up more than my half of the shelter. I laid on my back, staring up at the branches. Ferghus was still as well for a time. Suddenly, he broke the quiet by saying, "Ah heard Nyle say he was goin' tae come tae Dunvegan…"

I wasn't sure if it was a question, so I simply responded with a "yes".

"Did he say when?" he continued.

"No."

"*Ah.*" It was quiet again for a few minutes. An owl hooted and a small animal scurried through the leaves. "*Brigid?*"

"*Yes?*"

"Ah was just checkin' if ye were still awake."

"*Mmmhmm,*" I murmured, my stomach all a flutter.

Suddenly, Ferghus rolled onto his side and propped his head up to gaze at me in the darkness. He wasn't looking directly *down* at me, but he'd never tried to converse once we'd gone to bed before. "*Brigid?*"

"*Yes?*" I turned my head slightly to acknowledge him. He didn't say anything. I started to feel extremely nervous. "*Yes?*" I breathed.

He cleared his throat. "Ah was just goin' tae say Ah think ye should get married…"

I giggled. "You've already told me that before, remember?"

"It's not funny," he said indignantly, "Aam serious."

"I know you are," I responded, "but I told you I'm not here to get married. I don't know anything about it. I'm too young!"

He made a sort of huffing sound and then continued, "yer not tay young; plus, ye have tae consider how ye'd be helpin' yer *husband*…"

I stared at him blankly. "*Helping* him?" I asked incredulously.

"Aye."

"You're not making any sense. I think you're tired."

"It's not fair tae make yer husband think sinful thoughts," Ferghus managed to say. The awkward feeling in the shelter intensified.

"Why would I make him think sinful thoughts?" I questioned, unsure whether I wanted to even *know* the answer.

Ferghus was quiet again and I thought he might have actually fallen asleep with his arm propped up when he finally replied, "ye make him think about kissin' ye."

My cheeks immediately flushed. "You mean I *would* make, *right*? Not I *make*. I'm not married yet."

"Aye, ye *would* make."

"But if I *was* married, wouldn't it be okay for him to kiss me?" I asked, my brow furrowed, "please don't tell me this is another one of your rules I don't know about!"

"Aye, that's why ye have tae get married."

I shook my head to clear it. "I don't get it. Go to sleep, Ferghus. You're tired."

He sighed and tried again. "Ye would make him think about touchin' ye. He'd want tae see ye the way God made ye…"

"In my birthday suit?" I giggled.

"*Brigid*!" I could almost picture steam coming out of his ears.

"*Yes?*" I was still laughing.

"*This is what Ah mean!*" he said angrily, "ye'll make him sin and ye don't even care. Ye don't try tae see what yer doin' tae him!"

"Okay, okay," I said, inhaling to try to calm myself, "I promise I won't make my husband sin when the time comes."

"And ye'll consider gettin' married soon?"

"*Ferghus!* I agreed *not* to sin. Isn't that enough?"

He grunted and flopped onto his back, his arms folded over his chest. "Yer makin' *him* sin, not *ye!* If ye got married, he wouldn't have tae feel *guilty!*"

I giggled again. "I thought you were only interested in *facts*? This is all hypothetical…"

"*Daingead!*[111]" he exclaimed and rolled over so his back was facing me.

"What does *that* mean?" I asked, "did you just tell me to fuck off?"

"Nae, Ah said why are ye so blasted stubborn and feisty? Why can't ye just listen and dae what Ah say?"

"I don't think you said all that. It was *one word!*"

Ferghus suddenly sat bolt upright and glared at me. "Fer fuck's sake, did ye want tae make me angry? Dae ye like makin' me *so* furious Ah want tae pin ye tae the ground and teach ye tae behave like a woman?"

I stared at him in shock, but after a few seconds the mirth bubbled up inside me again. "You want to pin me to the *ground*?" I questioned slowly, "and teach me to *behave*?"

"Are ye *still* laughin' at me?" he growled incredulously, "*Ah give up! Death tae all hens!*" He jumped up and crashed into the branches in

---

[111] Damn it!

the pitch darkness. I could hear him cursing in his own language, but then total silence fell.

I sat on the bed roll and listened intently, but I couldn't hear anything for a while. Eventually, I thought I could hear someone breathing not too far away. "*Ferghus?*" I whispered, but he didn't respond. The sound grew louder, but resembled suppressed crying. I wondered if he'd hurt himself when he'd left our shelter. "*Ferghus?*" I tried again, "are you *hurt?*" I stood and peered into the darkness. "Ferghus, where *are* you?" I took a few steps forward, stretching my hands in front of my face so I wouldn't scratch myself. "*Ferghus?*"

"*Go tae sleep!*" he finally blurted. His voice was strangled with emotion, but I could tell he wasn't too far away. I took a few more tentative steps in the direction of his voice

"*Ferghus?*" I said at the exact moment I tripped over his boot and landed sprawled on top of him. "*Ouch!*" I exclaimed, clasping my hand to my chest as the pain seared through me, "*oh god!*"

"Oh, *fer fuck's sake*, what are ye doin' tramplin' through the woods in the dark *anyway!*" Ferghus shouted.

I pushed myself off the ground into a kneeling position over top of his lap. "It *hurts*," I whispered, unable to catch my breath, "really bad…"

He sighed deeply and grasped me by my waist. "Come on ye menace of a woman!" he said, "yer a *temptress* is what ye are!"

He helped me walk slowly back to our shelter. "How am I a *temptress?*" I balked, "I tripped on your *feet!* I didn't try to make you take *drugs* or something!" I took a shaky breath, but the pain was so intense I thought I might vomit.

He looked at me as if I'd lost my mind. "What are ye ramblin' on about *now?*"

His tone made me want to laugh again but, when I started to, the pain grew worse. "*Oh god*, don't make me *laugh!*"

"It isn't *God*, and it isn't *me!*" he retorted angrily, "ye just can't take anythin' seriously, Sasannach! This injury is God's punishment!"

We were sitting beside one another again, my hand clutching my chest. "You think my sore ribs is punishment for killing *Cam*?"

Ferghus almost snorted. "Nae, Rosa, killin' Cam was yer *duty*! Nae! Yer bein' punished fer *laughin'* at me when Ah tried tae talk tae ye about somethin' very serious!"

I stared at him wide eyed. "*Oh god*, you're not back to *that* again, are you?"

"Yer tay bonnie fer yer own good, Rosa. It's made yae reckless with men's feelins…"

"I'm not reckless at *all*! I'm very cautious. I thought *everything* through today. I tried not to hurt Cam. I tried not to involve Owyn. I even considered sailing *away*! I debated about how to help Aila, and about which one of *you* to save first. I wasn't reckless. I'm *not* reckless!" I was breathless when I finished speaking.

We stared at each other for a minute, my laboured breathing the only sound. Finally, Ferghus spoke, "why did ye pick *me*?"

"*What?*"

"Why did ye free *me* first?"

I paused, thinking back to that moment. "I thought I had the best chance of surviving, and saving everyone else, if I picked you."

He nodded in the darkness. "Ah have no idea how ye did that kick of yers, but ye saved us all…"

I smiled. "I'm like a modern-day Mulan," I teased.

"Who's *Mulan*?"

I bit my lip to keep from laughing. "Someone from back home," I replied.

"Go tae sleep now. Ah want tae make it tae Dunvegan by nightfall tomorrow."

"Okay. Good night, Ferghus."

Chapter Twenty-One:

I was walking up the grassy slope; the sky was a perfect shade of baby blue directly above me, but to the west dark clouds were rolling in. I heard the distant rumble of thunder.

"What are ye up tae, eh?" Cam asked, eyeing me curiously.

"Exploring Sloane's property," I answered.

"Ah hope tae have the pleasure tomorrow night," Cam slurred, wiping his chin and grinning. When he lowered his hand, I saw a knife sticking out of his side. "Dae ye see what ye did, Brigid?" he questioned, still leering, "how does it feel tae have killed a man?"

I jolted awake, my heart pounding. I blinked, but it was still dark. I was lying on my side upon the ground, but I couldn't move freely. I glanced at my stomach and saw a hand resting there. I tried not to freak out. I replayed the events of the past couple days in my head: I had killed Cam – he was dead – we had fought the MacDonalds – I had left with Ferghus. I squinted, but it was so dark. The arm was definitely masculine. I shimmied backwards slightly and felt his hard chest brush my dress. I turned my head in slow motion to peer at the ground. The person lying beside me was wearing a kilt; it was one-hundred percent Ferghus. The relief I felt from knowing it was Ferghus was momentary; how could I move away from him without waking him? And if I tried and he woke, what would he think I was doing? Just sitting with someone in the wrong spot, or barely touching their hand, was considered sinful in this world.

I was still holding my breath, trying to decide what to do, when I felt Ferghus stir behind me. I laid perfectly still, pretending to sleep. I watched him flex his hand, as if it had fallen asleep. He slid his arm gently across my waist until he was no longer touching me. He was still curled on his side, his chest warming my back. I expected him to move away, but he didn't. I squeezed my eyes shut, afraid he would somehow discover I was awake, when he did something unexpected. The arm he'd slid off me reappeared, but above me, without resting against the curve of my hip; instead, Ferghus took his fingertips and ran them along the fabric of my dress. His touch was so gentle I could barely feel it, but my awareness of his action sent heat coursing through me. I tried to exhale normally, but it came out shaky. He was going to figure out I was faking; I had to do something. I pretended to murmur in my sleep, stretching my back slightly to mimic a dream. His hand disappeared so quickly I almost wondered if I'd imagined his fingers brushing against my dress. Ferghus rolled onto his back and I exhaled slowly to clear away all traces of anxiety, and heat, and curiosity from my being.

***

The next morning, Ferghus seemed unusually quiet, even for him. I tried to keep my questions and responses neutral, and my voice even. Inside, all I could think about was him touching me. How could such a strong man display such sensitivity? I had assumed his behaviour on the first night at Sloane's was caused by his excessive consumption of whisky, but now I had seen him repeat the gesture. Did he have feelings for me, or was he curious to see what a woman *felt* like? I couldn't tell, but every time he looked at me I had to force myself to act as if I wasn't psychoanalyzing him.

After breakfast, we set out again. I knew some silence was normal, but I desperately wanted to try to make the vibe natural and comfortable. The only topic I could think of was Ferghus's childhood; he'd told me very little. I looked down at him in the pale morning light. "How did you learn to hunt?" I asked.

Ferghus stared straight ahead. "Mah father taught us," he replied.

"That's *it*? There's nothing more to say?" I urged with a smile.

He looked bashful. "Not really; he took me and mah brothers out when we were young. We would sleep outside and set traps. Ah learned how tae survive by mahself." He shrugged. "It's not that hard..." I giggled and he glanced at me sharply.

"*What*?"

His cheeks were flushed. "Nothin' – just that sound..."

"You don't like my laugh?" I inquired, a fluttery sensation beginning in my stomach while I waited for his answer.

His blue eyes were intense when he replied, "Ah like it fine."

"Okkaayy," I said, drawing out the word to show I didn't believe him.

He shook his head and sighed. "Ah like it *fine*, Brigid. Ah was tired last night."

"I don't think I've heard you laugh very often, except for our first night at Sloane's," I pointed out.

Once again, his cheeks flushed and he clenched his free hand. "Eh'd rather not talk about that," he said imploringly.

"Why not?" I questioned.

"Leave it, *okay*?" he pleaded.

"Okay, okay," I responded, feeling hurt by his rough tone. I looked down at my hands and bit my lip.

A few minutes passed in silence. "Aam sorry Ah was cross," Ferghus suddenly said, "Ah acted like an arse that night and Eh'd rather not be reminded of it..."

I met his eyes. "Okay," I said softly, surprised by his apology; he rarely admitted he was wrong. "Can I tell you something?" I asked.

He stared at me without speaking, as if trying to ascertain from my expression what decision he should make. "Aye, go ahead…"

"I didn't think you acted like an '*arse*'," I told him, imitating his pronunciation of the word ass.

"Ye agreed tae drop it, Brigid," Ferghus reminded me.

"I know, but I just wanted you to know I thought you were really sweet that night."

He stared at me dumbfounded as if I'd said the most ludicrous thing he'd ever heard. "Ah wasn't sweet. Ah was an *arse*. Ah can't even *remember* half the stupid things Ah said tae ye, but Ah know Ah was an imbecile…"

"I thought you were cute," I admitted, a smile inadvertently spreading across my lips.

"That's because ye think everythin's funny," Ferghus criticized.

I shook my head. "No, I don't find most drunk men funny *or* cute," I corrected him, "back home, they hit on you or say disrespectful things; sometimes they even grab your body." I rolled my eyes. "It's *so* annoying!"

Ferghus's brow had creased as soon as I started describing the bar scene. "They *hit* ye?" he fumed, his tone becoming angry immediately, "and they're allowed tae get away with that? Don't the other men defend ye?"

I realized the misunderstanding. "No, not *hit* – hit *on*. They hit on me. It means they flirt and try to pick me up. They want to take me home with them. They use the alcohol as an excuse, but they're really not great guys to begin with…"

Ferghus's entire countenance grew angry. "Is this how ye ended up here? The men hit on ye and gave ye tae the MacDonalds when they took ye? The drunk men kidnapped ye?"

"No, no, *no*," I said, holding up a hand, "no one kidnapped me – at least not that I know of. I was at work, *remember*? I went into the closet to get supplies and when I came out, I was in Tristen's castle and his sister was putting a wedding dress over my head."

Ferghus looked as if he didn't believe a word I'd just said. "Ah think these men had somethin' tae do with it, Brigid. They sound like scoundrels. If we meet them, Ah shall kill every last one fer ye…"

My eyes opened wide. "You can't *kill* them!" I said appalled, "it's against the *law*!"

Ferghus scoffed. "Nae, hittin' a woman fer no reason is against the law of the land. It's between ye and yer husband how ye settle yer disputes. Nae other man has the right tae lay a hand on ye, Brigid!"

"They didn't *hit* me, *remember*?" I reminded him, "just hit *on*." I felt frustrated with the conversation. "Perhaps we shouldn't talk about this, okay?"

"As ye wish," he agreed reluctantly.

We picked our way through the forest for another hour before the land began to steadily ascend. It was slow going, but Ferghus told me there was a beautiful waterfall where we could refill our bottle and gather berries. It sounded lovely, so I tried not to fall asleep as Selma bumped along. It grew quite rocky and eventually the trees thinned and ended. Exposed once again, Ferghus warned me to keep my wits about me. Soon, we saw what appeared to be a hill but, as we neared, I noticed the waterfall at its base. The pool was a beautiful turquoise. "It's so pretty," I breathed, "I wish we had more time to stay."

"These are the Fairy Pools," Ferghus told me as he splashed water on his face. He refilled his container and passed it to me.

I took a long drink and almost coughed. "It's so cold!" I said in surprise.

"Aye, ye wouldn't want tae bathe here," he teased, "even if ye *did* remember tae keep yer frock on…"

"*Ha, ha* – very funny!" I took another drink, slower this time, and then refilled the bottle so it would be full for the last part of our journey.

Ferghus took the time to show me the smaller pools at the top of the slope. The water looked like someone had swirled blue and green paint together, but it hadn't properly blended. "If I lived here, I'd build a house," I stated, a wistful smile upon my lips.

Ferghus looked at me with interest. "Ye *would*?"

I laughed. "Yes, right *here*, so I could drink the cold water and sleep close to the fairies every night. And I'd become a painter and draw the waterfalls and hills. It's the prettiest place I've ever seen…"

Ferghus seemed surprised by my enthusiasm. A sudden frown appeared on his handsome forehead. "Ah would worry about how close it is tae Dunscaith and Armadale though," he mused, as if taking what I had said literally.

I giggled and he glanced at me sharply. "I was *teasing*, Ferghus. I know I can't build a house here. I don't have any money."

His cheeks coloured. "Ye don't need currency tae build a *home*, Brigid. If ye got married, yer husband would take care of all that…"

"He'd just start felling logs from that forest back there and drag them up this hill?" I knew I was teasing him more than I ought, but I was in a good mood. The fresh air and chance to stretch my legs had done wonders.

Ferghus ran his palm across the top of his head and down the back of his hair. "A man would do whatever ye asked him tae," he said quietly, "if he looved ye." His eyes met mine for a few seconds and then he cleared his throat and began to ready Selma.

"What's Dunscaith and Armadale?" I questioned as Ferghus helped me into the saddle.

"Two MacDonald strongholds just south," he told me, "buildin' a home here would be invitin' disaster…"

We skirted the pools and climbed to the top of the hill where the land levelled off again. "How long is it to Dunvegan?" I asked after a time.

"About ten hours walkin'; if we were both ridin' stallions we could do it in eight."

"I'm slowing you down, aren't I?" I lamented.

Ferghus shrugged. "Sometimes it's nice not tae rush," he answered diplomatically.

I giggled again and he sighed. "*What*? I thought you *liked* the sound of my laugh," I accused gently.

He glanced over at me and his eyes were almost shy. "Ah *do*," he admitted, "it's musical – and free. Ah wish it didn't have tae end…"

"Why do you think it has to end?"

He was quiet for a moment and then replied, "what ye've been through the past three days is mah *life*, Brigid. It's been mah *whole* life."

My chest suddenly ached when I heard the pain in his voice. "I'm sorry," I breathed.

"Don't blame yerself, Sasannach. Things were complicated before ye came; ye didn't cause this."

"But I feel responsible for *adding* to it," I confided, "I'm sorry for that…"

He laughed sardonically. "Don't be; ye did more tae help than some of mah cousins…"

"Not everyone is born strong, Ferghus," I ventured, not wanting to make him angry.

He snorted. "Aye, some men are bairns in disguise. Put them in the middle of battle and they start tae cry fer a teat."

I gaped at him. "I hope you're not talking about Owyn," I said with trepidation.

"Aye, he fits the description; Brodie wasn't much better, although he isn't blood kin," he responded.

"Brodie is *dead*," I reminded him, "you shouldn't criticize him."

Ferghus shook his head. "When Ah have sons, they'll learn how tae defend themselves. They'll learn how tae be strong and courageous. Otherwise, they might as well wander around the Fairy Pools in a frock…"

"What about *compassion*?" I questioned, "or emotional intelligence?"

Ferghus actually stopped walking. "What are ye on about now?" he balked, "a man has tae protect his home and family, Brigid."

"But shouldn't he also be able to talk to them – hold them – *cry* with them?"

His eyes opened wide in shock. "Aye, he'll be cryin' with em when they've all got arrows stuck through their wee hearts and he's left alone!"

"It's okay for a man to *cry*, Ferghus. There's no shame in it…"

"We'll have tae disagree on *that*, Brigid. There's nothin' *but* shame in it. If Ah cried as a lad Ah got a hard smack on the back of mah head. Ah don't make the mistake anymore."

"That's *awful!*" I cried, aghast, "a man should be allowed to grieve or vent. Sometimes crying makes you feel better. You get it all out and can focus again."

Ferghus's lips actually curled into a smirk. "Ye sound like a hen, Rosa," he teased.

"I *am* a woman," I muttered, feeling frustrated again.

"Aye, I've noticed," he said, "and so did all mah cousins." He winked to end the conversation and started walking again.

My face flushed with anger, but I couldn't form my thoughts into coherent words. I sulked for the next leg of the journey, but Ferghus seemed in a fine mood. His cheerfulness only added to my ire. I glared down at him from time-to-time, hating how close-minded he was about almost everything. I would never want to marry a man like that, least of all bring children into the world with him. He'd have all the lasses tied up in the kitchen while the boys were off killing rabbits. He was a sexist prick. I hoped he'd die alone.

Chapter Twenty-Two:

We came to a large stream an hour later. Ferghus led Selma to the water's edge to drink and passed me some of the berries he'd collected at the Fairy Pools. I hadn't spoken to him the entire ride, but I was so hungry I took the berries and sat on a large rock to eat them. He stood to eat his. I wondered how long it took him to get *really* tired, since he seemed to have never-ending stamina. When Ferghus wandered a few feet away from me to look out over the stream, I stole furtive glances at his body. If I *had* to admit it, he was very handsome, even if he had warped views of how to raise a family. Suddenly, he glanced my way and saw me staring. I blushed and looked down at my lap, expecting him to assume I was behaving like a school girl crushing on a boy in her class, but his reaction was hostile and startled me. "Why dae ye always *stare* at me?" he cried in frustration, "if it bothers ye so much, *just don't look*!" He stalked further down the water's edge and threw the rest of his berries into the gentle waves.

"*Oh my god*, I wasn't *staring* at you!" I exclaimed, standing quickly and folding my arms across my chest in anger.

Ferghus couldn't hear me over the rush of the water, however, so we both stood facing away from one another until finally he came to ready Selma for more walking. His shoulders were tense and he wouldn't make eye contact. "You're such a jerk, you know that?" I cried, unable to suppress my feelings.

"*Get in the saddle!*" he growled, grasping Selma's lead and waiting with fury in front of her.

"*No!*" I shot back defiantly, "I'm not your slave. You can't order me around all the time! And you can't accuse me of doing things I wasn't doing!"

Ferghus's eyes were stormy when he turned to look at me. "Get in the saddle, Brigid. Don't add lyin' tae yer actions tay!"

"*Lying*?" I said disbelievingly, "you pompous *ass*! I'm not *lying*! I wasn't staring at you, you *fucking asshole*!"

Suddenly, Ferghus dropped Selma's lead and ran around her side, restraining my wrists before I'd even blinked. "*Don't speak tae me like that*!" he warned, his face red, "ye might never loove me, but ye should at *least* respect me!"

My eyes opened wide and I could feel my shoulders start to tremble. "*What did you just say*?" I asked in a whisper.

Ferghus's own eyes registered shock as well. He dropped my hands in horror and covered his face as if trying to clear his head. "*Tha thu mar phuinnsean nam fhuil*!" he lamented in a husky voice, "tha thu a 'toirt orm diochuimhneachadh mifhin![112]"

"I don't understand what you're saying. Why won't you *look* at me?" I questioned, my heart pounding wildly. Ferghus just shook his head slowly, his hands still covering his face. "I'm *sorry*! I didn't mean to yell at you; I just don't like being accused of things I didn't *do*…"

Ferghus suddenly whirled in a circle and grasped Selma's lead firmly in his hand. I still couldn't see his expression, but the tension between us was thick. I moved silently to Selma's side and climbed into the saddle. Ferghus gave the lead a tug and we started moving. My chest ached with unresolved feelings, but I knew better than to try to communicate them. We were from two different worlds – two different *times* – and nothing could bridge that divide no matter what words we uttered.

---

[112] You're like a poison in my veins! You make me forget myself!

***

We continued along the beaten path for what felt like hours. It never grew much warmer and the sky had grown grey and sombre. In reality, we had probably travelled for *two* hours, but the silence made it extremely dull. Finally, Ferghus tied Selma to a stray tree and suggested we take some of the food Sloane had given us. We sat side-by-side upon the grass and shared the dried meat and bread. After a while, I tried to make things right between us. "Ferghus, I wasn't staring at you before…"

He sighed loudly. "Ah don't want tae talk about it, Brigid," he responded firmly.

Tears stung my eyes. "*Okay,*" I whispered.

He glanced over at my dejected countenance. "*Okay,*" he said, as if calling a truce.

I met his gaze and his eyes were sad. I quickly wiped my tears away and sighed. "I'm tired."

"Me tay, Rosa. Ah wish Ah could get ye there faster."

"Do you think we'll make it there by dark?" I questioned.

"Aye," he replied, "and in a couple more hours, we'll be out of danger…"

"Why's that?"

"They'd be crazy tae attack us anywhere *near* mah home," he stated confidently, "unless they want a full-scale war between every member of our clan."

"What they did at Sloane's – that won't cause any more fighting?" I asked.

Ferghus grinned. "Oh, we'll pay them back fer those we lost. But not right away. Have tae weigh the decisions carefully and attack when it means somethin' tae them."

I shook my head. "Makes no sense. If *you* stopped, they would stop. Then everyone could just live their lives!"

"Dae ye think Hugh wants revenge? Or Edan's and Brodie's families?" he argued.

"Yes, but – "

"And they *deserve* it!" Ferghus fumed, "absolutely deserve it! Edan and Brodie were *young*; they've lost all their dreams, Brigid. Ye can't get that back and someone has tae pay!"

"But if you kill the ones who murdered them, their families will send someone else to kill *you*! How would your brothers and sister feel?"

Ferghus stood and held his hand out for me. "It's time tae go," he said, "ye just don't understand."

I climbed onto Selma, feeling numb. I understood everything Ferghus had said on an emotional level. There had been countless people in my life who had wronged me – people I had wanted to hurt back. But once I'd become so involved with karate and found acceptance from my Dojo, the need for revenge had lessened a little more each day. Now I was glad I'd never sought to harm anyone. I would have had that on my conscience every single day for the rest of my life – the way I'd now have *Cam's* death on my hands. Murder didn't solve anything; it simply created new problems that would eventually grow into larger ones. Total destruction of a way of life seemed inevitable.

Chapter Twenty-Three:

A few more hours of riding upon Selma passed in emotional agony. The silence and isolation were beginning to drive me mad. The landscape was hilly and covered in long grasses. The sun was beginning to set and if I'd been less tired, I would have appreciated the way the colours spread through an unpolluted sky and reflected off the lake I could observe to the east of our path. Even when Dunvegan Castle made itself known, I thought of selfish needs like sleeping in a warm bed, eating a hot meal, and perhaps taking a bath. Its perfect defensive position nestled in a forest overlooking a pristine beach never occurred to me. I could already tell from this distance that Dunvegan dwarfed Sloane's home. Ferghus had never boasted, however, and it made me wonder if it was due to humility or jealousy: he wasn't set to inherit the castle, after all.

We passed numerous sheep grazing upon the land. Their repetitive bleating made me feel calm and sleepy. I felt as if I had nodded off a couple of times and was just sitting straighter in the saddle to clear my head when the thundering of hooves startled me. "And *here* he comes," Ferghus muttered under his breath.

"*Who*?" I wondered aloud.

The hooves grew ever louder until I could see three stallions galloping towards us. Ferghus whispered, "whoa" into Selma's ear and she slowed.

"What's going on?" I pleaded, but the stallions were already upon us.

Their riders brought them to a quick halt, and I could see breath escaping from their nostrils. The enormous stallions were not what frightened me, however. A giant of a man had dismounted from the middle horse. He was dressed identically to Ferghus in a kilt of green and blue. He wasn't as tall, shorter by a couple of inches, but he was bulkier across the chest and arms. He had thick, dirty-blond hair and a full beard; his blue eyes were the same shape as Ferghus's, although paler in colour. He instantly reminded me of Thor and, when he spoke, the power in his voice confirmed my impression. "Mura h-e mo bhrathair a th 'ann, da latha fadalach![113]"

"*Dail*, gun a bhith fadalach![114]" Ferghus responded defensively.

The blond man laughed deeply in his chest and turned his gaze upon me. "Agus co a 'bhan-dia a thug thu leat?[115]" he questioned, his eyes dancing over my hair and face as if Ferghus had brought home a prize.

"She speaks *English*," Ferghus stated, glancing quickly up at me and then back to the man.

"Mah apologies," the man said smoothly, bowing his head slightly. When he straightened, his eyes were even more curious than before. "What is the identity of the Goddess of Fire?"

I blushed and stumbled over my words as I tried to reply, "*oh my god*, do you mean *me*?"

"Of course, lass," the man stated, coming to my side and reaching for my hand. I placed it into his enormous one and he helped me to the ground. I'd been riding for so long my legs felt like rubber, but the man continued to hold my hand while he smiled down at me. "I've never seen hair so bonnie," he told me, "it's like a ruby. Is that yer name?"

"No," I said in embarrassment, "Brigid."

---

[113] If it isn't my brother, two days late!

[114] Delayed, not late!

[115] And who is the goddess you've brought with you?

"Just as lovely," the man intoned, grinning at Ferghus, "and who are ye, Brigid?"

"I'm – I'm visiting," I stammered, "from far away…"

Ferghus sighed audibly. "It's been a long journey, Doughal. Let's take Brigid inside and ye'll get yer answers, okay?"

"Are ye hungry, Brigid?" Doughal questioned, a wide smile upon his face.

"I'm okay," I said, not wanting to be rude.

"Of course she's guttin'," Ferghus said peevishly, "come *on*, Brigid, let's go." He glared at his brother and added, "ye can release her *hand* now."

"Of course," Doughal said, dropping my hand slowly, "why don't ye ride upon *mah* cuddie? It's faster than yer mare…" He winked, and I couldn't help blushing again.

"She's used tae Selma," Ferghus interrupted, staring at me meaningfully, "get into the saddle, Brigid, and I'll lead ye the rest of the way…"

Doughal grinned. "Ah can see Ferghus is in *fine* spirits, as *usual*." He turned and mounted his stallion. "I'll have the servants set two extra plates." He manoeuvered his horse in a half circle and kicked him in the side. The other two riders quickly followed and I was left alone with Ferghus.

"So that's your *brother*?" I asked breathlessly as I managed to get back into the saddle despite feeling suddenly lightheaded.

"Ah don't want tae talk about it!" Ferghus growled as he yanked on Selma's lead to get us moving again.

"You haven't brought me here so you guys can sacrifice me in some weird ceremony, have you?" I inquired.

"Of course not!" he barked, "ciamar a thig thu suas le rudan cho seolta?[116]"

"I don't know what that means," I reminded him.

"It means if ye don't stop askin' questions, Aam goin' tae tell mah brother tae sacrifice ye fer dinner!" He glared at me over his shoulder and then stomped down the path towards Dunvegan, his hands clenched into fists the entire way.

***

"Ah can give ye a tour tomorrow when it's light," Ferghus told me as he led Selma into the stables located on the western side of the grounds.

"Okay," I agreed. Ferghus handed Selma's lead to an older man and gestured for me to follow him. He was walking incredibly fast, as if lost in his own thoughts.

I was out of breath when we crossed a stone moat to reach the main entrance to the castle. Before mounting the stairs, Ferghus suddenly turned to me and said, "Ah know yer pretty and everythin', Brigid, but try not tae say tay much. Ye need tae use yer brains as well. Some of the things ye told me – others might not understand..."

My face flushed. "I'm not an *idiot* you know!" I said defensively.

"Aye, Sasannach, but just because *I've* concluded yer not in league with the Devil doesn't mean others will side with me so easily," he explained as two servants opened the front doors to let us inside.

"Thank you," I said and they nodded. I was fuming over what Ferghus had just said, but my anger quickly evaporated as Doughal came striding towards us across a large, open courtyard.

"Ah thought ye'd gotten lost agin', Ferghus," Doughal joked, "dinner's almost ready."

[116] How do you come up with such crazy things?

"Um, is there time for me to change?" I asked timidly, "I had to sleep in this outside."

Doughal glanced at Ferghus for a fraction of a second and then smiled. "Of course. I'll have Gilda sent tae yer room. Let me show ye where it is…"

"Ah can take her," Ferghus offered, but Doughal interjected.

"Na, from the smell of ye, ye'll need freshenin' up, Ferg…" he teased.

"Ah competed in games and fought in a *battle*," Ferghus growled, "Ah didn't have *time*!"

The tension in the courtyard was palpable. "Sounds like ye'll have lots tae tell us at supper," Doughal finally said, holding out his arm to me.

I placed my trembling palm onto his forearm and he whisked me away from Ferghus up a few more stone steps and inside a whole other area of the castle. It seemed as if the chambers off the courtyard were for storage and servants' quarters, whereas the part he was leading me through *now* was the main lodging. Doughal led me up a set of steep stone steps onto the second floor. This hallway wound around until we came to a smaller set of stairs, which led to a split-level. On this floor there were just three bedrooms. He entered the first room and lit several candles for me. "Ah hope this will be suitable fer yer stay. I'll send Gilda tae help ye change. She can fill yer basin and air out the chamber. Ah look forward tae dinin' with ye." He smiled and bowed before exiting.

By the light of the flickering candles, I could make out the shapes of the various furniture. The bed was a four-poster similar to the one I'd slept in at Sloane's, except this one contained more elaborate curtains surrounding it. There were also paintings on the walls, although I couldn't see well enough to make out their designs. I went to the window, grasped the heavy drapes, and threw them open to let in some moonlight. I sneezed as dust fluttered in a cloud, gently settling upon the floor. This room must have been vacant for some time. The extra light helped some. Beside the bed was a small wooden chest of drawers upon which sat an empty basin. On the wall above was a charcoal drawing of a rocky shoreline. It was signed M.M. in the bottom, right-hand corner. On the other side of the bed was a small dressing table and chair, with a looking glass resting upon it. On the far wall there was a large wardrobe like the kind in C.S. Lewis's famous story. After what had happened to *me*, I was terrified to open it. The chamber was larger than the one I'd slept in at Sloane's, and the lack of furniture made it feel even more so. Upon the wall across from the door was another painting, but this one was enormous and took up most of the space. It was also an M.M. design, but this one had been done in thick paint. It captured the Fairy Pools I had just visited that morning with their green and blue water swirled together. As I was studying it, a young woman wearing a bonnet and apron came bouncing in. She grinned and said, "is mise Gilda."

"Is mise Brigid," I responded, returning her friendly smile, "I speak English," I added.

She just shrugged and motioned for me to turn around. I spun in a slow semi circle and she began to unbutton my heavy dress. In her arms she carried a new gown, which I assumed must belong to Mirna. This outfit still included the white undergarment, but it had puffed sleeves that were visible when the green velvet, tank-style dress was laid over top. It was heavy and reached all the way to the floor. I hoped I wouldn't trip on my way to dinner. "Bidh Doughal a 'smaoineachadh gu bheil thug u math," Gilda remarked when she'd helped tidy my hair, "is toigh leis dearg.[117]"

"I'm sorry – I don't understand. I speak English," I told her again. She just smiled and gestured to the door as she pulled it open for me. "Can I have some water to wash?" I asked. I rubbed my hands together and her eyes lit up. She held one finger in the air and nodded, then bustled from the room. I waited uncertainly, but she soon returned with a full pitcher and placed it upon my bedside table. I poured some into the basin and splashed it onto my face. After I had cleaned my hands, I followed her into the hall and back down two flights of stairs lined with flickering torches.

Ferghus and Doughal were waiting at the bottom, absorbed in a conversation in their own language. Ferghus had changed into his yellow kilt and combed his hair. I thought he looked very handsome, but my attention was captured by Doughal who addressed me first. "Ah had forgotten how long it takes a lass tae dress fer supper," he teased.

Ferghus rolled his eyes. "Nae, ye didn't; ye live with our *sister*!"

"Don't listen tae him, Brigid; he'll make a liar out of me," Doughal whispered conspiratorially, "and ye can take as long as ye like; ye look very bonnie in green. It makes yer hair stand out even more…"

"*Oh god*!" I said, glancing at Ferghus with a panicked look in my eyes, "how do I hide it?" I hissed.

Ferghus was about to reply when Doughal interjected, "why would ye want tae hide it, lass? It's the bonniest hair I've seen in mah life!"

"It *is*?" I questioned.

I followed Doughal down a long hallway until we entered a Great Hall like the one at Sloane's, except this one felt more intimate. I soon realized it was because it had more decorations and was even carpeted in places. I wondered if this had something to do with wealth, or it being the home of the Chief. As soon as we crossed the threshold, a young woman

[117] Doughal will think you're pretty. He likes red.

about my height hurried over to greet us. She had blonde hair the same shade as Doughal's, but her eyes were green and guileless. *"Brigid,"* she said, kissing me on one cheek and then the other, "Aam glad we finally get tae meet each other!"

I stared at her dumbfounded. "Ah might have told mah sister there was a lass here tae dine with us," Doughal laughed.

"Oh, of *course!*" I said, my cheeks flushing in embarrassment.

"Ah asked a servant tae put ye beside *me*," Mirna told me, grasping my hand and pulling me towards a long table at the head of the room. I looked wide-eyed at Ferghus over my shoulder and saw his lips were curling into a smile. "Right here," Mirna said, pointing to a high-backed chair that gleamed in the torchlight. She pulled it out for me and even pushed me in when I'd sat.

"Thank you," I said, staring around me anxiously. There was so much to take in, from the paintings and armour hanging on the walls, to the people conversing at rows of tables in the middle, to an older gentleman seated two chairs down from me.

He nodded and said, "good evenin', Brigid. Welcome to Dunvegan." His hair was as dark as Ferghus's, but his eyes were brown. He had a fur pelt hanging around his shoulders, but I could see the yellow tartan beneath.

"Thank you for having me on such short notice," I said as Doughal pulled out the chair on my other side and sat down.

"That's mah father," Mirna explained, "Murtagh MacLeod…mah mother has a cold and isn't comin' down fer dinner."

"And he's the Chief?" I whispered.

"Aye," she answered as Ferghus sat beside her.

A servant walked along the front of the table and poured everyone a glass of heather wine. I overheard Ferghus asking for whisky too. It was interesting how he never brought any alcohol on his long journeys. He must relish in the comforts of home when he had the chance. He looked noble in his dress kilt and fresh tunic. Even Mirna was wearing a dress that combined the yellow tartan in its skirts. "Thank you for sharing your dress with me," I said to Mirna.

"Yer welcome," she said, her eyes bright, "Ah was excited tae have someone mah own age tae talk tae!"

Her enthusiasm made me laugh and suddenly Ferghus was staring at me. I wondered if he was about to say something, but Doughal leaned down and whispered in my ear, "tell me how ye met Ferghus; it couldn't have been easy spendin' so much time alone with him." He was so close to my skin I felt goosebumps break out on my neck and forearms. I shivered and tried to compose my thoughts into a coherent sentence.

"What are ye whisperin' about, Doughal?" Mirna chastised, "let the lass drink and eat. There'll be time fer stories later!"

I smiled at her gratefully and saw Ferghus's eyes were still fixed upon me. His pale scar was facing me for a change, and I observed how it disappeared beneath his tunic. I wondered how far it stretched. When my eyes flickered back to his face, he was scowling. A servant placed a glass of whisky in front of him and he slammed it back and stared at his empty dinner plate.

"Sorry, Brigid," Doughal apologized, "I'll let ye enjoy our wine before we get tae know one another better."

"Okay," I agreed softly, and lifted my glass to my lips and took a long swallow. "Who are all these people?" I questioned.

"Kin," Doughal said.

"Aye, mah cousins, aunts, and uncles," Mirna added as the servants began pouring a creamy stew into bowls already set in front of each of us. Mirna clapped her hands and enthused, "mah favourite!"

"What is it?" I inquired.

"Pheasant," Mirna answered, taking a small bite.

I lifted my own spoon and tasted the liquid. To my surprise, it was delicious. I sampled about half of it, determining that in addition to pheasant, the stew contained root vegetables and some kind of cream. "It's very good," I stated.

We ate in silence for a few more minutes. The servants added loaves of bread to the tables, as well as smoked salmon. I spread honey onto my bread and took a bite. I almost wanted to cry it tasted so good. I had grown tired of the rabbit and berries Ferghus and I had subsisted on in the wild.

"Where are ye from?" Doughal asked as he swallowed a piece of fish.

"Um, it's a small town called Huntsville," I said, hoping he wouldn't ask too many follow up questions.

Doughal frowned. "In the countryside?"

"Sort of," I hedged, "it's a town, not very big, but there are farms not too far away."

"Never heard of it," Doughal commented, "in Scootlund?"

"No," I replied, my insides beginning to churn.

Doughal turned to stare at my profile in the torchlight. "What country? *Englain*?"

I knew my pauses were going to be interpreted as lies, but I didn't know what to say. I glanced down the row at Ferghus, but he was into his second glass of whisky, his cheeks still red. "No, it's not in England," I replied. I turned to look into Doughal's pale blue eyes and smiled. "Everything is really good," I said shyly, "I was getting tired of rabbit."

Doughal paused, as if trying to remember what he'd been asking. He smiled slowly and leaned closer to me. "Ah bet ye were gettin' tired of sleepin' on the ground tay. That's nae place fer a lass. Ye need a soft bed with lots of furs tae keep ye warm."

"Will it be like that tonight?"

Doughal's eyes caught the torchlight and danced as he replied, "aye, lass, nice and warm..." My skin was burning underneath my dress, but I didn't dare break eye contact; I was too scared he would ask more questions about Huntsville.

"What are ye two talkin' about?" Mirna questioned, her eyebrows raised, "yer keepin' Brigid all tae yerself, Doughal! *Aam* the one who needs a friend. Tay many men in this house!" She grasped my bicep and pulled me closer. "Let's talk about *fashion*, Brigid; what's yer favourite colour?"

Doughal leaned back slowly in his chair, but I could still feel his eyes on me. "*Red,*" Doughal guessed.

I laughed, trying to erase the tension that had developed between us. "No, I actually love blue. The Fairy Pools were so pretty," I said.

Brigid squealed. "Ah love them tay! Did ye see mah paintin' in yer chamber?" she inquired excitedly.

Suddenly, Ferghus glanced over at the two of us. "What chamber did ye put her in?" he asked, his tone irate.

"The big one," Mirna replied, "with the nice view of the lodge *and* beach."

Ferghus looked as if he was going to kill someone. "Doughal, may Ah have a word outside?" I could sense the supressed rage in his voice, but Doughal didn't seem to notice or care.

"Nae, Aam *hungry*, little brother. We can exchange news after we've eaten, as Mirna suggested."

"Ah want Brigid moved tae a different chamber," Ferghus hissed.

My eyes opened wide in surprise. "What's wrong with the one I have?" I asked, "is it haunted or something?"

"He's just upset it's on the same floor as *mine*," Doughal laughed, "but it doesn't matter; we're all *excellent* hosts. Ferghus just seems tae think he's above the rest of us, isn't that right, Ferg?"

"Does your father know which room I'm in?" I asked Mirna.

"He won't care; it's the nicest guest chamber," Mirna said, "so Ah think ye should keep it. She has the most *beautiful* view, Ferghus."

When I glanced at Ferghus again, he was staring at his half-eaten fish in defeat. He didn't respond to her comment, or say another word throughout supper. I never saw him drink any more whisky, or even eat dessert. And when we adjourned to the drawing room at the end of the meal, he excused himself, saying he was exhausted and wanted to go to bed early.

Chapter Twenty-Four:

The drawing room was stunning; when we entered, there was a fire blazing in the hearth beneath an ornately-carved fireplace. The room was cozy with fur pelts draped across the backs of chairs and upon the floor. Wood panelling covered all four walls and large oil portraits of the immediate members of the household were displayed proudly. I quickly found Ferghus's likeness hanging above a table containing several bottles of alcohol and glasses. "That was before the incident," Mirna said quietly.

I turned and saw her watching me from the edge of a sofa. "*Oh*," I responded, "I wasn't sure how long ago it happened."

"Three years; he looks a lot better now than he did," she confided, coming to stand by my side, "it's faded a lot…"

"Enough about mah little brother," Doughal joked, "let's sit a while." He gestured to an arrangement of sofas and chairs.

Mirna grasped my arm and pulled me over to a long sofa covered in tan fabric. "How old are ye, Brigid?" she asked.

Doughal sat opposite us and listened for my answer. "Twenty-one," I replied, "my birthday was in May."

"Oh, we're almost the same age. I'll be twenty-one in October."

"And married if all goes well," Doughal commented pointedly.

Mirna blushed and released my arm. "Father introduced us; his name's Robert. He's a second cousin on mah mum's side. Ah wanted tae marry Owyn, but dad and Doughal didn't approve. Not *sturdy* enough," she lamented.

"*Owyn MacLeod?*" I questioned, "Ferghus's *cousin?*"

"Aye," Mirna said, "mah cousin; ye've met him then?"

"Yes, he was at Sloane's," I explained, "at least I think it's the same man. Very well spoken and likes to read?"

"That'd be the one," Doughal interjected, "Ah mean, can ye really blame father, Mirna?"

Mirna sighed. "Ah guess not, but we had some nice conversations."

"What does not sturdy enough mean?" I inquired.

"Ye saw him, lass," Doughal laughed, "he couldn't compete in *anythin'*. Ah doubt he could even lift a *sword*. The wind would blow him away."

Mirna laughed too. "Ah guess, but he's handsome and kind."

"Yer tay romantic," Doughal criticized.

She sighed again, but didn't reply. A servant entered the room and asked if we wanted drinks. "Of course," Doughal answered, flashing his grin, "some of our best gin." He winked at the young girl before she went to the serving table to pour the drinks. After she handed us each a glass, Doughal winked at her again and she left the room.

I took a sip of the gin; it wasn't as strong as the whisky I'd had at Sloane's, but it was still stronger than the heather wine. "How dae ye like tae wear yer hair tae a banquet, Brigid?" Mirna asked while she sipped her own drink.

"Um, I usually wear it natural," I stated, unsure what the going hair style was for this time period.

"Ye don't like feathers or combs?" Mirna wondered.

"I'm afraid I don't have anything like that with me," I admitted.

Mirna's eyes lit up. "Ah have lots; ye can borrow some of mine tomorrow. Gilda can help us. We'll be the bonniest lassies in Scootlund!"

"Yer already the bonniest lassies I've ever seen," Doughal commented, staring at me unabashedly.

Mirna giggled. "Oh, yer mah brother; ye have tae say that!"

Doughal grinned. "Aye, tis true."

"Dae ye like this frock Ah picked out fer ye?" Mirna questioned, running her hand along my thigh.

"It's lovely – thank you."

"Ah like how soft it is," she mused, "not like those scratchy wool ones mah mum used tae make me wear when Ah was a bairn." She laughed softly, but I could sense nostalgia in her voice.

Doughal set his glass on the edge of a side table. "So, Brigid, Ferghus told me about the battle at Sloane's. Aam sorry ye were there when it happened."

"Thank you," I said softly, "it was terrible. There were many lost..."

He nodded slowly. "How did ye come tae meet Ferghus? He didn't say how ye ended up at Sloane's together..." His eyes were curious, but I sensed an edge of some other emotion burning in their depths as well. Was this what Ferghus had tried to warn me about?

"I wish he was here to tell you himself," I managed to get out. Once again, my stomach was churning as if there were a hundred rhinos stampeding inside it. "I met Ferghus after a journey across the Atlantic," I explained, trying to think up details that would be okay to share.

Doughal's eyes widened in surprise. "Ye live on an island then – came by galley?"

"Mmmhmm," I murmured vaguely.

"How excitin', Brigid," Mirna enthused as she took another sip of gin, "how far away is it?"

"Very far," I responded, "Ferghus was nice enough to help me find shelter."

"Why would ye leave yer home, lass?" Doughal questioned, his brow furrowing as he picked up his glass and swallowed the remainder.

"Was there a great battle?" Mirna asked, her voice dreamy.

"Yes, my people were involved in many wars over the years," I said, feeling like a fraud, "but always on the side of righteousness."

"Oh, of course!" Mirna agreed.

"Who controls the land?" Doughal inquired. He was much too astute to be taken in so easily by my responses. I glanced across at him quickly and saw he was intent on gaining answers.

"I'm not sure," I replied, "I just knew I had to get out quickly, but when I arrived here things got even *worse…*"

Doughal frowned. "Why didn't Ferghus stay up fer this? Ah have questions tae ask him!" His voice was laced with suppressed hostility.

"Oh, calm down, Doughal…Ferghus was tired after his long journey. Ye sent him on it in the *first* place," she reminded him bluntly.

Doughal sighed and sat back against the sofa with his hands clasped on the back of his neck. "Ah guess we can discuss it in the morn." He had just finished speaking when Ferghus entered the room with a young man in his early teens with hair the colour of pumpkin juice.

"*Anghus!*" Mirna exclaimed, "*ye missed supper*! Come meet our guest!" She grasped my arm and pulled me to my feet.

Ferghus wandered over to the drink table while Mirna introduced me to Anghus. His boyish face was covered in freckles and he had the same eyes as Mirna. "Anghus, say hello tae Brigid," Mirna instructed, as if he was five instead of thirteen.

Anghus flushed. "Hello," he stammered. Out of the corner of my eye, I could see Doughal refilling his glass beside Ferghus. Soon, he would know everything.

"Nice to meet you, Anghus," I responded.

"Where did Ferghus find ye?" Mirna teased.

"Ah was huntin'," Anghus said defensively, "Ah had tae set mah traps…" He realized his tone wasn't the friendliest and turned sheepish eyes to me. "Aam sorry Ah missed supper; Ah didn't know Ferghus was bringin' a guest…"

"He brought her fer *me*," Mirna said enthusiastically, "he knew how lonesome I've been fer a friend…"

"It had nothin' tae dae with *ye*," Ferghus contradicted. I started at the sound of his voice and saw he hadn't remained with Doughal.

I felt suddenly self-conscious in his presence – somehow worried he would discover what I had told Doughal and fault me for it. I stole a furtive glance at him at the exact moment he made eye contact with me. He was holding a glass of gin, but his face transformed into a scowl. He swallowed the liquid quickly and then said tersely, "Brigid, may Ah have a word outside?"

"Of course," I answered, trying not to blush. Ferghus set his glass on the sofa table and proceeded to the door ahead of me.

Mirna dropped my arm and giggled. "Don't be alarmed; he's almost never able tae relax and make merry. He's much tay serious – about *everythin'* – these days!" She gave me a sympathetic look as I followed Ferghus to the door.

"Leavin' so soon?" Doughal questioned from the drink table, flashing me a brilliant smile, "Eh'd hoped tae get tae know ye better, Brigid – Goddess of Fire…"

Ferghus made a huffing sound in the back of his throat. "I'll just be a *moment*, Doughal, and then she's all yers."

That was enough to make my cheeks flame. The hallway was darker than the sitting room had been, despite the torches flickering upon the walls. He walked about halfway before stopping. I felt angry, but I waited with my arms folded across my chest to hear what Ferghus had to say. "Eh'd appreciate if ye would show me some basic respect; ye may not like me, but at least ye can treat me with decency." His neck was red and he was staring at the stone walls instead of my face.

"*What?*" I said in shock, "I have no idea what you're talking about!"

"*Like Hell ye don't!*" Ferghus blurted, finally looking at me with tormented eyes, "every time Ah see ye, yer starin' at me as if the very *sight* of me makes ye recoil. Ah have sacrificed more than mah own life these past few days. Could ye not repay me by keepin' the scorn out of yer every glance?" I could smell the gin on his breath and wondered how much alcohol he'd consumed since we'd arrived.

"Ferghus, the drink has made it difficult for you to see reality. I've been very appreciative of your help..."

Ferghus stared at me incredulously. He started to reply, but a servant exiting a room two doors down stopped him short. He clamped his mouth shut and waited impatiently. When the man had disappeared around a corner, Ferghus glared at me. "How dare ye blame the whisky!"

"And the *gin*," I reminded him quickly.

"*Boireannach diabhal!*[118]" Ferghus exclaimed, "Aam not drunk!"

I snorted. "I believe you *are*," I retorted saucily.

"And Ah believe if yer not careful, yer goin' tae wind up in Doughal's bed!"

---

[118] Devil woman!

My mouth dropped open in shock. We stood glaring at one another in silence for a few seconds. "How dare you speak to me of *respect*! Screw you for suggesting I'd sleep with your brother! I just met him for fuck's sake!"

It looked as if Ferghus's head was going to explode. "Just *met* him?" His hands were curled into fists. "Just *met* him?"

"*Yes*!" I cried, stomping my foot upon the floor and instantly regretting it, "I'm not a fucking *whore*!" I turned on my heel and ran towards the staircase that led to the bedrooms, my toes throbbing.

Ferghus chased after me. "But if ye knew him *longer*?" he hissed as I mounted the stairs. I could hear his angry breath as he ascended behind me.

When I reached the floor with the smaller set of steps, I whirled around to confront him and he ran right into me. I almost toppled over, but he grasped my arms to prevent it. We were face-to-face, out of breath, and filled with the strongest dislike possible for another person. I didn't know what possessed me, but I suddenly slapped him hard across his face. He actually looked stunned, releasing my arms instantly. "Ah beg yer pardon," he said, sounding as if he didn't quite believe what was happening either.

I was dumbfounded. "What the hell are you talking about *now*?"

"Ah shouldn't have put mah hands on ye, Brigid," he said, "Ah – "

"*Oh my god*!" I cried in frustration, "you think I hit you because you *touched* me?"

He looked confused. "Aye."

"But you were trying not to let me *fall*, weren't you?"

"Aye, but Ah still touched ye." His expression changed to condescension, as if I was too slow to understand anything.

I finally held up my hands in exasperation and shrieked, "I *hate* this place! You're all fucking *crazy*!"

I turned to hurry up the stairs, but I still heard Ferghus call out, "bolt yer *door*, Brigid. Fer God's sake, just bolt the damn door!"

I rushed inside my chamber, wanting to scream from pent up frustration; instead, I slammed the heavy wooden door and slid the bolt into place. I paced the room for a few minutes until my pulse slowed. I splashed water on my face and started to undress. Just as I was about to untie the strings on my corset, a soft rap sounded upon my door. I stared at the lock with hostility, ready to shout at Ferghus again.

"It's Doughal. Just checkin' if ye need anythin'."

"No, I'm fine," I replied quickly.

I saw the doorknob turn, but the bolt stopped it from opening. "Are ye findin' everythin' okay?" Doughal asked.

"I'm sorry – I'm already in bed," I called, "I'll see you in the morning."

There was a short pause and then Doughal said, "Sleep well, Brigid."

I slid into bed with my corset still on, my hands shaking. I thought Ferghus had said Dunvegan would be the *one* place he could protect me from the MacDonalds, but he hadn't said *anything* about needing to protect me from his own kin.

Chapter Twenty-Five:

I woke before dawn, but was unable to fall back to sleep. I lit a candle and pulled on a dress Gilda had left for me. It reminded me of the every-day dress Aila had lent me, but this one was forest green and pale yellow. I tiptoed down both sets of stone steps. At this early hour, there were already numerous servants up and about. When I reached the inner courtyard where the servants' quarters and kitchen were located, the number increased. One woman was fetching water from the well, while two others were carrying baskets of laundry outside. I hurried to catch up with them and asked, "would it be okay if I took a walk along the beach?"

The younger of the two shrugged and answered, "it's not up tae me how Doughal's guests behave."

"Oh, I'm not *Doughal's* guest; Ferghus brought me to Dunvegan," I tried to explain as we walked over the moat.

The two women exchanged amused glances and the older one smiled at me sympathetically. "Bonnie thing like ye doesn't stand a chance. Looks like a fine morn, dear; enjoy yer walk."

They began chatting in their own tongue and left to finish their chores. The sky looked as if it was on fire now as the sun crept over the hills and dazzled my eyes. I began walking around the castle, but soon realized the trees prevented easy access to the beach by this means. I had to follow a narrow path through immense conifers until finally they thinned and I could discern a rocky shore leading to clear water. When I emerged from the forest, I gasped. The entire eastern view took my breath away. Miles of pristine beaches wound around the base of the hills until my eyes could no longer perceive what came next. This was not like the docks at Sloane's; this view was better than the best private resorts back home. No wonder Ferghus was bitter he would inherit nothing. I stood for several minutes just taking it all in, but eventually the beauty of the water tugged at me. I hesitated, glancing around at the deserted shore, before I slipped off my shoes and moved closer so I could dig my toes into the softest golden sand I had ever felt. I closed my eyes and inhaled, feeling a sense of peace finally envelop me. Suddenly, two male servants came through an entrance at the back of the castle completely hidden in the wall of charcoal stone. The men nodded as they passed and took their axes into the trees. I was left with the gannets and oystercatchers.

I moved to the sand's edge, squealing as the cold water covered my toes before it receded again. Each time it repeated its gentle ebb and flow, I cried out. My feet never got used to the frigid temperature, and I began to make a sort of game out of it while I waited for the rest of the castle to wake. Eventually, I grew bolder, forcing myself to go a few steps further out each time before racing back as quickly as I could to avoid the waves. Let's just say I'm fast, but not as fast as Ferghus; eventually, I misjudged a surprise wave and, being caught out too far, found my feet swept from under me. I landed face-first in the water, completely submerging my gown, before surfacing again. I sputtered, coughing up a mouthful of water as I plodded dismally back to shore. I began wringing out small sections of fabric, but it wasn't much use; I was completely drenched.

I bent over to twist my hem, continuing my fruitless efforts for a few more minutes. *"For crying out loud!"* I exclaimed and, when I straightened, I came face-to-face with Ferghus and Doughal. They were both staring at me wide-eyed, but their expressions were very different: Ferghus's mouth was gaping and his hands were balled into fists, while Doughal's pale blue eyes were full of mirth and his lips were curving into a grin. It was he who spoke first. "Dae ye need a hand, lass?" he laughed, moving across the sand towards me, both hands outstretched.

"*Um*," I hesitated, my eyes shifting back and forth between the two men, "I'll be okay. Just a tiny accident…"

"Are ye okay?" Doughal pressed, grasping my hands and leading me closer to the castle.

"What in the world were ye doin'?" Ferghus finally exploded, his dark brows knitted in frustration, "yer soaked tae the bone!"

"Yes, I'm aware – "

"Easy, Ferg," Doughal reprimanded, "it isn't *her* fault. The tide can have a mind of its own…"

"*She's* the one with a mind of her own!" Ferghus cried, his face turning red, "I'll deal with this, Doughal. She's mah responsibility…"

"Na, na," Doughal said, dropping my hands and waving at Ferghus as if he was being dismissed, "Aam not busy at the moment; let's get the lass inside."

I had started to shiver and wrapped my arms around myself for warmth. Doughal noticed and quickly removed his great kilt and wrapped it around me. "Thank you," I murmured.

Ferghus rolled his eyes. "Bu choir dhomh bruidhinn rithe,[119]" he stated, his voice trembling.

"Nae need," Doughal said brusquely, shaking his head, "tha mi airson iarraidh oirre mo phosadh.[120]" He wrapped an arm around my shoulders and pushed open the hidden door. "After ye, Brigid," he said gallantly.

Ferghus trailed after us. "Ah think yer bein' hasty, Doughal."

[119] I should talk to her.

[120] I want to ask her to marry me.

"Not after everythin' ye told me this morn," Doughal argued as we made our way down the hall.

"Ach *posadh*?" Ferghus said incredulously, "*Thachair thu a-raoir*![121]"

Doughal led me into the sitting room and motioned to a chair by the hearth. "Sit here and I'll fetch a servant tae light a fire," he told me, brushing past Ferghus as he hurried from the room.

"Coimhead na tha thu air a dheanamh a-nis[122]!" Ferghus cried in exasperation. He knelt in front of the hearth and began to make a fire while I stood by the chair feeling awkward.

"I can't understand you."

When he stood, he towered over me and grimaced. "*Ah said ye'll be the death of me!*" His entire body was shaking.

"*Why*? It was an *accident*, Ferghus!" I responded vehemently, "I didn't do it on *purpose!*"

"Of *course* ye didn't!" he cried, shaking his head, "ye never mean any of it, dae ye? Ye make a man loove ye and it's all a big joke!"

"*What*? Who said anything about *love*?" I balked as I heard the flames begin to crackle.

Just then, Doughal returned with a servant. When he saw the fire was already lit, he motioned the man away. "Sit, Brigid." He came to the edge of the chair and frowned at Ferghus. "Go aboot yer day, Ferg. I'll watch over her now."

Ferghus sighed deeply. "Gu dearbh gheibh thu,[123]" he stated morosely before hurrying from the room.

---

[121] But marriage? You just met last night!

[122] Look what you've done now!

[123] Of course ye will.

"I don't want to ruin your furniture," I said softly, staring into the handsome face of Thor's twin.

Doughal smiled. "It can be replaced," he stated, his eyes studying my face intently.

I nodded and eased myself into the chair. "I'm sorry about all this," I apologized, unsure what else to say.

"Don't trouble yerself, lass; Ah don't mind," Doughal said firmly. He stared down at me, shifting his weight from one foot to the other. "Ah find ye bonnie, Brigid. I've always liked pretty things, but yer *exceptional...*"

My eyes opened wide in surprise. I hadn't expected *this* type of conversation after making such a fool of myself. "*Oh,*" I whispered dumbly.

Doughal laughed low in his throat. "Ah have mah faults, but Ah think mah prowess in battle and bein' next in line are favourable qualities."

"*Mmmhmm,*" I nodded, unable to tear my eyes from his.

"Aam set tae inherit Dunvegan; Ah can show ye the grounds so ye can see how extensive they are. Ah promise ye, there isn't a finer estate on all of Skye..." He looked at me meaningfully and stroked his beard as if trying to think of more talking points.

"The beach was stunning," I blurted and then realized how stupid my statement must sound given my present condition.

Doughal grinned. "Ye like tae swim?" he questioned, "I'll take ye out in mah boat too. We have an ambitious fleet. Dae ye like tae sail, Brigid?"

"I'm not sure," I answered honestly.

Doughal smiled at me. "Ferghus told me yer last experience wasn't a good one, but I'll help erase the memory by takin' ye anywhere ye desire. Ah have the means and experience as a seaman," he boasted, "and Aam a born leader. Ye'd naturally have a position of eminence by mah side, earnin' the respect of all mah kin. Ye'd never be treated the way Ferghus said ye were handled by the *MacDonalds*. Eh'd personally defend yer honour and lay down mah life fer ye…"

I blushed, feeling heat spreading through my body not caused by the blazing fire in the hearth. "Doughal, why are you telling me all this? Am I being quizzed later?"

Doughal gave a loud belly laugh and shook his head. "Nae, lass, there won't be a test." He suddenly grew serious; beads of sweat appeared on his brow as he knelt upon the carpet by my feet. "Brigid, if ye'll agree tae be mah wife, we can wed within a fortnight. I'll spare nae expense. I've met a few eligible partners, but ye outshine every single one with yer exquisite form and magical hair. Ah wish tae start a family and want tae dae it with ye by mah side…"

Silence filled the room as the gravity of his proposal sank in. Butterflies began to swirl in my stomach. I gazed down at his expectant face, feeling lightheaded. *"Doughal –* "

"Aye?"

"I'm afraid I'm feeling completely – "

"Honoured?" he suggested hopefully.

"Um, I was going to say *overwhelmed.*"

He wrapped his palms onto his knee and frowned. "Ye need time tae think it over?"

"Mmmhmm," I responded, barely able to get the noise out of my throat.

He sighed and pushed himself off the ground. "Ah guess it's understandable, given ye just met me. Dae ye want tae see the grounds first?"

"Would it be okay if I had a little time to myself?" I suggested in a squeaky voice, "I can't seem to focus…"

"Ah have that effect on women," Doughal admitted. He reached for my hand and helped me to my feet. "Don't take *tay* long; breakfast will be ready in an hour…"

He kissed the top of my hand and strode confidently from the room. I collapsed back into the chair, leaning forward with my hands wrapped around my head. I tried to practice my grounding techniques, to focus my breathing and calm my mind, but it was impossible. Doughal MacLeod had just proposed to me! What in the world was I going to do?

Chapter Twenty-Six:

When the nausea passed, I rushed from the sitting room, down the hall, and outside as fast as I could. I flew across the moat, away from the forest on either side of the castle, and ran for the hills on the western slope. I didn't stop until my lungs burned. I doubled over, gasping for air. It wasn't until I straightened and looked around that I saw the glistening water below. I hadn't realized Dunvegan was completely surrounded on three sides. The waves were rougher now, capped with white foam, and the beach on this side was rocky. Still, it was breathtaking; I felt dazzled by its surreal beauty. If I couldn't get home again, wasn't remaining here the next best thing?

"Ye shouldn't wander alone," a deep voice said behind me.

I turned quickly and then relaxed when I saw Ferghus. He'd changed into his green and blue kilt. "Oh, it's you," I said softly, turning back to gaze at the scene before me.

"Ye sound disappointed," Ferghus stated sadly.

"No, just relieved," I told him without moving.

"Here," he said. I glanced at his hand and saw he was offering me a muffin.

"I'm not hungry, Ferghus."

"If ye reject mah muffin, I'll get very angry," he teased.

When I looked into his peacock eyes, they were empathetic. I blushed. "You're making fun of me," I accused lightly and grasped the muffin from his hand.

"Nae," he breathed, staring at my profile, "Ah just don't want ye tae starve while ye think things over..."

I looked at him sharply. "What do you know?" I questioned.

"Gilda said she saw ye runnin' outside; Ah gathered ye might have been caught by surprise…"

I could feel my hands start to tremble again. "Take it," I said, thrusting the muffin back into his hand, "I'm going to drop it." I held my arms out for him to see; they were shaking uncontrollably.

The food disappeared inside Ferghus's great kilt and his hands were suddenly grasping mine; he gripped them firmly, turning me to face him. He didn't say anything, just held onto me while my body shook like a leaf in autumn. Tears started to escape my eyes; I cried openly in front of him, letting all the confusion and fear out until, finally, both the tears and the trembling subsided. Only then did Ferghus release me. "Ye'll be *okay*, Brigid," he said softly, "yer the strongest, most capable lass I've ever met. Ye'll be okay."

I shook my head vehemently. "I'm not ready for this!" I lamented, "I didn't ask for any of it! You said I'd be safe here. This wasn't part of the plan!"

Ferghus shifted guiltily. "Dunvegan is the best place tae keep ye safe," he responded, "but Ah didn't factor in mah brother's obsession fer beauty…"

I laughed ruefully. "He told me that himself, actually – that he likes *pretty* things…and a whole list of other attributes about himself. I asked him if I was being tested on the information later. I had no idea he was going to ask me!"

"Ah think he didn't know heemself until he saw ye this morn," Ferghus explained, "he knows the rules are different because yer not a servant; if he wants tae have ye, he needs tae marry ye…"

"This is all so he can have *sex* with me?" I inquired in a high-pitched voice.

Ferghus was silent for a few seconds, as if trying to decide how to respond. "It's a good deal, Brigid; ye'll get tae be the lady of all this," he said, gesturing to the view in front of us, "ye'll be the Chief's wife one day. It's an honour…" Everything he was saying sounded like a gift – like I was being offered a prize no one else could win, but his voice was laced with melancholy.

"Then why don't you sound happy for me?" I questioned bluntly, "why does it sound as if you know something you're not telling me about Doughal?"

Ferghus shrugged. "Doughal's Doughal."

"What does *that* mean?"

Ferghus sighed. "If ye marry mah brother, ye'll be the Chief's wife one day. Ye'll inherit everythin'. There's no shame in wantin' tae be cared fer. Ye'll have security and so will yer bairns. No one would blame ye, Brigid. It's a good deal…"

"You've said that already," I accused, "but it's all about what I would get *financially*."

"Nae, ye'd have the protection of the clan tay," he reminded me.

"But wouldn't I have that if I married someone else? I mean, not *now*, but in the future. If I stayed here, and married another man, wouldn't the clan protect me then too?" I pressed, remembering his statements when we were journeying to Sloane's.

Ferghus's cheeks coloured. "This is a good deal. Ye should take it, Brigid. Ye won't get a better offer…"

"*Answer my question!*" I cried, feeling my pulse accelerating, "you told me when we were on our way to Sloane's that your friends would protect me if you asked them to. You never said I had to marry a *Chief* to earn that! Why is it different *now*? Did I do something to change your cousins' loyalty to me?"

Ferghus avoided my gaze and stared at the gulls picking fish out of the water instead. "Ye have *all* our loyalty, Brigid," he said simply.

"Okay," I breathed, wringing my hands against my dress. I inhaled and then asked, "what did you mean when you said, Doughal's Doughal?"

Ferghus actually laughed. "He likes pretty things," he responded, "he *knows* hens find him handsome; they like his confidence and power. And he enjoys the attention." He shrugged. "Aam sure ye've noticed him tay; he can't keep his eyes off ye…"

"*It's all too fast!*" I exclaimed, "he *just* met me!"

"Why wait if ye know what ye want?" Ferghus responded, "Doughal and Ah may not see eye-to-eye on everythin', but he's shown me what happens if ye put things off…"

"What am I going to *do*?" I wailed, flopping down onto the grassy hill.

Ferghus hovered above me for a few seconds before sitting beside me. "Mirna will be excited," he said neutrally, "ye can ask her advice."

I shook my head. "*You* know me better; what do *you* think I should do? Pretend you're me; what would *you* decide?"

Ferghus's sympathetic expression wavered for a moment. "Ah can't tell ye what tae dae, Brigid," he finally answered.

"Why not?"

"Because Ah can't put mahself in yer place. Aam not a lass. Aam not an orphan. Ah was *born* here. Ah can't advise ye properly."

"*Fuck!*" I screamed into the air.

"*God's bones!*" Ferghus suddenly called.

I glanced at him quickly and then shouted, "*fucking hell*!"

"*Damn it*!" he cried, the corners of his lips twitching.

I couldn't help but smile at his ridiculous attempts to curse in English. "You're a *terrible* swearer," I told him.

"Ah have other talents," he stated, his eyes twinkling.

"Now you sound like Owyn."

Ferghus laughed. "Ah have very little in common with Owyn."

"I don't think that's true; you're both kind." Ferghus was quiet as he stared at my profile. I looked at him. "*What*? You *are*! I know you don't like him, but it's not *his* fault he was born physically weak. You just got a lion's share of strength; he got good eyesight – or whatever..."

Ferghus grinned. "Ye can tell Doughal ye can't marry him because ye want tae marry Owyn instead. It should make fer some cheery conversation at breakfast..."

"*Ferghus*! I don't *want* to marry Owyn! I wish Mirna could marry him, but that's another *issue*! I'm so upset right now. I thought you said I'd be safe here and now I have to make this *stupid* decision. I'm only *twenty-one* for god's sake!"

"Doughal's just tryin' tae do what God wants fer once," Ferghus said unexpectedly, "he doesn't want tae sin with ye. At least he asked ye tae dae things proper..."

"You were right – about the bolt," I confided.

Ferghus sat straighter on the hill. "*The bolt*?"

"Yes – last night. He tried to get into my room," I responded.

Ferghus's forehead creased. "And what happened?"

"I had already locked the door; I told him I was tired and in bed. He said good night and left."

When Ferghus didn't reply, I turned to stare at his profile and saw his eyes had turned stormy. His scar was pale pink in the sunshine. I studied his handsome jawline and let my eyes wander to the bare skin visible inside his tunic. "Ah should have sat on the *other* side!" Ferghus suddenly cried. He was glaring at me with flushed cheeks. "Ah guess I'll leave ye tae yer thoughts," he said angrily, and started to stand.

"*Ferghus!*" I exclaimed, "*please don't go!*"

He looked at me with wounded eyes. "Yer always makin' me feel not good enough. Doughal never lets up about it either, and – "

"What did I *do*?" I pleaded, "please stay and talk. You're always exploding at me! I didn't do anything *wrong*!"

He snorted loudly. "Yer always starin' at mah scar."

"No, I – "

"Don't try tae deny it, Brigid; Ah told ye before, Ah can't stand lyin'."

My cheeks flushed. "I'm not *lying*! You assume the very worst about a person and never give them a chance to explain!"

He gritted his teeth. "Why would Ah listen tae ye weave tales? People already talk about me; everywhere Ah go, Ah can feel them starin'."

My face flushed even more. "I – I'm not *always* staring…" I said lamely.

Ferghus levelled me with an incredulous glare. "Not *always*? But sometimes ye are?"

I inhaled deeply to gather my courage. "I guess. I don't mean to. I'm not trying to be hurtful. I just see you sometimes and forget I'm – "

"I've had enough of this conversation," Ferghus fumed, "just marry him and make some bairns. Ye'll be very happy." He folded his arms across his chest in resignation.

"I'm *sorry*," I said plaintively, "I don't stare at you the way you think. I'm not always looking at your *scar*, Ferghus. There are different *kinds* of stares you know…"

He snorted again. "Nae, there is only mockery, and yer the queen of it; I've never been looked at with such dislike by *anyone* else. Ah see yer eyes on me daily. Ye make a grown man want tae crawl into a cave…"

"Oh my *god*!" I breathed, tears burning my eyes, "*that's* what you think of me? That's what you think I'm *doing*?"

"Tell me ye didn't spend half our time walkin' tae Sloane's starin' at mah face?" he challenged, his strong chin jutting out in anger.

"I – okay – I was *angry* sometimes," I hedged, "I thought you weren't very nice to me at the start; tying my hands and yelling at me when I messed up your *rules* about the dress. I tried my best, but you pissed me off a little."

He shook his head aggressively. "Na, that's not what Ah mean; Ah mean studyin' it; thinkin' how ugly Ah am and pityin' me or loathin' me in equal measure…"

"*What*? None of that is true!"

"Fer fuck's sake, Brigid, it's tay late fer pretendin'. The damage is done!"

"There are different *kinds* of stares!" I protested, getting equally frustrated, "and you've stared at me too!"

His jaw dropped. "Nae, I've never done such a thing!"

It was my turn to snort. "Oh my *god*, you have too! Now who's lying?"

Ah *don't lie*!" he said defensively.

"It's a sin to tell lies, so why don't you just tell the truth about the staring and come clean?" I said, trying to use his own beliefs against him.

His face changed colour from bright red to white in a few seconds. He looked like he'd seen a ghost, or become one himself. His jaw twitched in anger, but he eventually answered. "Fine – I've stared at ye a couple of times, but only when Ah needed tae get yer attention tae tell ye somethin'." He finally met my gaze and his eyes were guilty.

"*Twice*? Come *on*! You've done it *loads* of times. There are different types of stares. People do it for different reasons."

"Such *as*?" Ferghus urged testily.

"Sometimes they're angry, but not always. Sometimes it's to get someone's attention, like you said. But there are other kinds. People stare when they're curious. Maybe they want to know something, but are too shy to ask. Or maybe they find someone attractive, but know they shouldn't say anything. Not every stare is mocking!"

Ferghus had listened intently to every word I'd spoken; now his body was still as we sat together upon the hill. I was careful to look straight ahead at the waves. After *ages* of silence, he finally shifted beside me. "Can Ah ask ye somethin'?"

I turned slowly towards him and nodded. His blue eyes were gentle and curious, all traces of hostility gone. "Yes, I'll do my best..."

"What did ye mean by wantin' tae know somethin'?"

I looked at him blankly. "I don't remember saying that..."

"Ye said, someone might be curious and want tae ask somethin', but be tay shy..." he repeated hopefully.

"Oh – that. I just meant someone might find another person *intriguing*, but they're not sure if it's okay to ask."

He nodded thoughtfully. "Aye." He paused, flexing his fingers back and forth a few times before continuing, "did ye ever dae that kind of stare?"

I was surprised by his question and bit my lip while I decided how to respond. "Sure, I guess so..." I finally answered.

Ferghus's eyes were piercing into mine now. "What were ye curious aboot?"

"It was no big *deal*," I said defensively, "I was just trying to *know* you better. I asked a few questions about Tristen, but you either got angry or quiet. I didn't mean to pry."

He nodded again. "It's a sore point for me; Ah hate talkin' about it."

"Sorry."

He smiled in understanding. "Ah shouldn't have assumed yer questions were all about me bein' misshapen..."

"Ferghus, you're not *misshapen*..."

He laughed sardonically. "Aye, Ah *am*...Ah wish ye could have seen me before; get a better first impression..." His voice was shy now.

"I saw a portrait of you inside the castle," I said, "your sister saw me staring at it."

Ferghus laughed low in his throat. "What kind of stare was *that* one?"

I laughed too. "Curious – intrigued. I'm not sure..."

"Curious aboot what?" he asked.

"I've wanted to know something, but thought it was inappropriate to ask you," I answered vaguely, my cheeks flushing.

"Dae ye want tae ask me now?"

"I don't think I *can*," I hedged, "you have so many *rules* and I don't want you to get offended."

"Ye can *ask*, Rosa; this time I'll know yer not tryin' tae misbehave," he suggested in a husky voice.

I suddenly felt like I was under a microscope, embarrassed for being curious about his injury for so long. "I just kept wondering what it looked like – " I stopped and laughed nervously before continuing, "I mean, I wondered how *far* the scar went. I don't know. I should just stop talking now."

I felt utterly ridiculous; my cheeks probably matched the colour of my hair. When I lifted my eyes to meet his, he was watching me closely. I wished I could read his thoughts. Was he angry or offended? Ferghus hesitated and then sat up taller upon the hill. "It stretches from here," he said, pointing to his cheekbone, "all the way tae mah ribs…" He grasped the bottom of his tunic and lifted it slowly to reveal the pale line that ran beside his broad chest and ended on the bone he was pressing with the tips of his fingers. I took it in, wondering how anyone could do that to another person – wondering how Ferghus had *survived* such a brutal attack – and wondering how he had thought any chance of happiness was eliminated because of a *scar* someone else had caused. "Yer starin' again, Rosa," he whispered.

I jerked my head up and looked into his curious eyes. "Sorry," I breathed, "you're beautiful – *oh god* – I mean – I was distracted by your ribs. It was an *accident*." I finally clamped my mouth shut when I realized I was babbling like an idiot. "*Fuck*." I placed my palm against my forehead and laughed in embarrassment.

"Doughal's not gonna let ye curse like that," Ferghus teased as he pulled his tunic back down.

"I'm sorry; I don't want to say *anything* else. I'm making a fool of myself!"

Ferghus laughed quietly. When I glanced at him, he was smirking. "Ye were right, Rosa…"

"About what?"

"There *are* other kinds of stares…"

"*Oh god*! I'm *sorry*! I shouldn't have asked you to show me!"

"Ye can ask God tae forgive ye," Ferghus suggested, his eyes still twinkling.

"You're making fun of me!" I lamented, "I can't ever look at you again. You *made* me tell you, and I *knew* I shouldn't!"

"Na, Ah didn't realize ye were intrigued about *that* until Ah saw yer face just now," he admitted honestly, "Ah thought it was just lads…"

"I'm not intrigued about *that*," I said, pretending to scoff, "I just –
"

"Just ask fer forgiveness, Rosa," Ferghus said, suddenly serious, "and I'll ask Him tae forgive me tay…"

"But you didn't do anything *wrong*," I said in confusion.

"Ah wish that was true," he said, "but I've been curious tay…"

His words hung heavy in the air. I blushed again. "I thought you *hated* me. You got so angry about the dress," I said, my voice quavering slightly.

"Ah don't *want* tae sin," Ferghus whispered, "but Ah dae. Ever since Ah met ye, Aam sinnin' *all the time*…"

"You *are*?" I inquired, my voice rising in pitch, "I'm *sorry*! I didn't mean to take it off – *or* to break your rules…"

"It's not just the frock," Ferghus interrupted, "Ah sin every time Ah look at ye…"

"You *do*?"

"Aye."

"But *how*? You've never done anything inappropriate…"

"Mah thoughts are…"

"They *are*?"

"Aye."

"*Oh.*"

"Ah think about ye at night, Rosa. Aam curious about things…"

"Like *what*?" I questioned, finally facing him. His eyes were different now; they were burning in a way I'd never seen before and it made my skin burn too.

"Ah shouldn't tell ye," Ferghus said, "it's wrong." He picked a handful of grass and sifted it between his fingers.

"You touched me – once – when we were coming here," I blurted.

He glanced at me sharply, his neck turning red. "How dae ye know that?"

"I woke up," I admitted sheepishly, "your arm was around me; I didn't know how to move it without waking you, but then you woke up. I pretended to sleep; I was nervous…" He blinked, clearly unsure what to say. "It's okay," I said hurriedly, "I shouldn't have told you."

"Aam sorry, Brigid," he apologized, "Ah shouldn't have done it…"

"No, it's alright," I said, unable to stop talking, "I liked it – I mean – *oh god* – I kind of hate myself right now…"

The desirous expression deepened. "Ye shouldn't say ye liked it," he whispered, but his eyes said otherwise.

"Okay," I mumbled as the air of tension grew, "I broke another rule? I won't tell you that again…Can you pretend I didn't say it?"

His lips twitched. "Aam not good at pretendin'; that sounds like *philosophy…*"

"*What?*"

"Ah like *facts*, remember?" he answered, his lips curling into a smirk.

"How do you remember every single thing I've said and then use them against me later?"

"Ah pay attention," Ferghus responded, "and Ah like the sound of yer voice…"

"You *do*?"

"Aye."

I fidgeted with my hands. "So what happens *now*?" I ventured.

"Ye get married?" Ferghus suggested, tossing the grass in his hands onto the ground.

"*Oh god*! I have to give him an *answer*!" Ferghus actually laughed. I glared at him. "It's not *funny*! How would *you* feel?"

He shrugged, his smirk growing. "Aam not a lass; Ah have nae *idea* what goes through yer minds – except fer a few things ye just told me. We both need tae spend some time prayin' later. Ye won't forget?"

"You don't care about me marrying *Doughal*?" I cried, feeling suddenly furious.

"He's mah *brother*, Brigid; he's goin' tae be *Chief* some day. Ah can't blame ye fer wantin' that life…"

"I never *said* I wanted it!" I protested, but Ferghus was already standing and brushing dirt off his kilt. He offered me his hand, but I shoved it away.

"*Brigid…*"

"Why did I ask you all those embarrassing questions? And tell you all those things I felt? You just wanted me to feel ashamed! You don't care how I feel *or* what happens to me! You just wanted me to say all that personal shit so you could *what*? – get off on it *later*? I fucking *hate you!*" I stood shakily to my feet and fled down the hill, grasping my skirts in my hand so I wouldn't trip. Tears streamed down my face as I raced for the castle entrance. Suddenly, Tristen MacDonald and all his groomsmen were looking like the lesser of two evils…

Chapter Twenty-Seven:

After splashing cold water upon my face and changing into a fresh gown, I entered the Great Hall with as much composure as I could muster. Thankfully, Mirna ran to my side immediately. *"Brigid*! Ah heard the *news*!"* she squealed, grasping my forearm and sort of hugging it as she pulled me towards the head table. "Come meet mah mum."

The Chief's wife stood when she saw us approaching. She smiled widely and nodded. "Nice tae meet ye, Brigid," she said in a heavier accent than everyone else in the family. I noticed how much Mirna resembled her mother.

"Thank you," I replied, forcing a happy smile onto my face.

Murtagh nodded also. "How are ye enjoyin' Dunvegan?" he asked, "is mah son bein' a good host?"

"Very much," I answered simply, "you have the loveliest views…"

Mirna giggled. "And things are about tae get even *more* enjoyable…"

"Mirna," her mother chastised gently, "let Brigid *absorb* the news; Ah remember how nervous *Ah* felt when Ah was in her position…" I blushed and wrung my hands.

"Come *on*, Aam *starved*," Mirna said, leading me to my chair as if I was her play thing.

Doughal's keen eyes followed me the entire way. When I was close, he stood and pulled out my chair. "Ye look bonnie," he stated as we all sat down, "Ah hope ye were able tae get some rest," he added pointedly.

"I was, thank you," I replied vaguely.

"Yer late, Ferg!" Mirna called suddenly, *"and ye tay, Ang!"* I forced myself not to lift my head in his direction. I didn't want to give him the satisfaction after having played me.

"Ye'll have tae excuse Mirna," Doughal said with a laugh, "she tends tae treat everyone with an equal amount of loove and scoldin'…"

I looked up into his pale blue eyes and smiled weakly. "It must be nice being so cared for," I found myself saying.

"Aye, tis," Doughal stated, "and if ye agree tae be mah wife, ye'll be part of this family tay. Ye can put the pain of yer past behind ye, lass, and enjoy everythin' yer heart desires."

"Where've ye been, Ferg?" I heard Mirna ask Ferghus. I focused on what the servants were placing in front of me.

Breakfast was an assortment of fresh fruit – mainly berries – oatmeal, and haggis. I forced myself to try everything, even the haggis, and it wasn't half bad. It had a rich flavour and reminded me of a stuffing one of my foster moms had made at Christmas. I could overhear snippets of Ferghus's and Mirna's conversation, but not enough to comprehend what they were discussing. Anghus had sat on the far side of the head table beside his mother. "What's your mom's name?" I asked Doughal.

"Lesley," he replied, "she was a Norman before she married mah father."

"Did she have to travel far?"

"Mah mum grew up in Bucholie," he told me, "which, compared, tae how far *ye've* come, isn't a long journey at all." I had no reference point for what he was talking about; everything here seemed *dreadfully* far, but that was simply because I'd been *walking* everywhere. The advent of paved roads to connect towns together, and the invention of the automobile, would completely revolutionize their way of life. I wasn't sure what year that would all begin, but I imagined the early nineteen hundreds. "Eh'd like tae take ye sightseein' today if that suits ye," Doughal said while he sipped his tea.

"The weather's been really good," I commented, "we hardly had any rain when we were travelling…"

"Must be *ye* who brought it," Doughal laughed, "it usually turns cold and grey now. Yer a beam of sunshine is what *ye* are." He winked at me and I blushed. I found it difficult *not* to react when he did that; he was a handsome man and he knew exactly how to charm a woman. I wasn't sure if knowing that he behaved this way with everyone would keep me out of danger, or if my argument with Ferghus would push me into Doughal's waiting arms.

After breakfast, Doughal led me to the beach where the boats were docked. He had arranged for several servants to prepare a galley for a pleasure tour of the area. He said as long as we stayed southwest of Dunvegan, we wouldn't be challenging anyone's territory. It all sounded rather complicated to me. Just as we were about to board, Ferghus came out of the castle with Anghus. I tried not to notice how handsome Ferghus looked in his kilt; I loved how his peacock blue eyes contrasted with his dark brows, always brooding, and how the muscles in his forearms rippled when he performed physical tasks. I loved the sound of his voice when he spoke in his own language, and the way he called me Rosa. I loved so many things about him and I hated myself for it. Suddenly, Ferghus's eyes met mine; I blushed and glanced quickly at Doughal, who was offering me his hand to help me into the galley. As I stepped tentatively inside, Doughal said, "are we teachin' our little brother how tae sail?"

Ferghus laughed. "Aye, and if he crashes, Brigid can rescue him from Nessie…" When I heard my name, I looked at him sharply. Ferghus grinned, causing me to blush and stare at the sail fighting for its freedom in the wind.

"Ah can *swim*, Ferg," Anghus retorted under his breath.

"It must be hard having two older brothers," I commiserated with a friendly smile at Anghus, "*I* certainly couldn't endure it…"

"Aye, tis, but they wouldn't treat *ye* the same way," he informed me.

"And where *is* Mirna?" I questioned, "does she not enjoy sailing?"

"She's gettin' fitted fer new frocks," Anghus stated.

"A sensible choice," Doughal said approvingly, "Mirna needs tae prepare herself fer her new life…" I knew his comment shouldn't impact me, but I suddenly felt nauseous.

"Dae ye want tae sit down?" Ferghus asked. I blinked, noticing his face directly in front of me now.

"Perhaps I should," I answered vaguely as we pulled away from shore.

"There's a seat fer ye here, beside me," Doughal interjected. He quickly intervened, offering his hand and smiling broadly at me.

"Thank you," I said quietly. I followed Doughal to the centre of the galley where he gestured for me to take a seat upon a long support beam. I had never been on a large sailing vessel before – just jet skis and a kayak once when Selma had invited me to her family's cottage.

"Dae ye see the seals, Brigid?" Ferghus asked. He pointed at several large grey shapes that slowly came into focus as we rounded the rocky beach.

I squinted to see them better, shielding the sun from my eyes. "*Yes!*" I exclaimed happily, watching as one waddled along the shoal and immersed itself in the water, "they're adorable."

Doughal swivelled sideways in his seat to address Ferghus. "Tha mi a 'smaoineachadh gu bheil thu air gu leor a radh.[124]" His voice was gruff.

Out of the corner of my eye, I saw Ferghus shrug. "Cha do thuig mi gu robh na roin gu math diomhair,[125]" he responded sarcastically.

"Tha mi a 'feuchainn ri eolas fhaighinn oirre nas fhearr,[126]" Doughal shot back. I wished he'd turn back around in his seat, because his broad shoulders and back were pressing into me. I didn't want such closeness.

Ferghus smirked. "Is docha gum bu choir dhut a bhith air sin a dheanamh mus do dh 'iarr thu a lamh.[127]"

"Eu-coltach riut, tha fios agam ciamar a gheibh mi na tha mi ag iarraidh,[128]" Doughal growled, his neck turning red. He turned angrily back to face the water, jostling me in my seat. "Mah apologies, Brigid," he said with forced cheerfulness, but his voice was laced with unresolved tension.

"Is something wrong?" I questioned cautiously.

"Nae," Doughal said dismissively, "just mah brother not knowin' when tae mind his own business…"

Ferghus snorted from the other side of the boat where he was standing with his muscular arms crossed. "Is e mo ghniomhachas a bhith a 'sgriobadh a h-uile cail a ghluaiseas![129]" he retorted.

"What's going on?" I inquired, "are we in danger?"

---

[124] I think you've said enough.

[125] I didn't realize the seals were top secret.

[126] I'm trying to get to know her better.

[127] Perhaps you should have done so before you asked for her hand.

[128] Unlike you, I know how to get what I want.

[129] You screwing everything that moves is my business!

Doughal patted my leg. "Nae, lass, mah little brother thinks it's wrong fer me tae admire yer beauty. His deformity has warped his view of courtship and – "

"*Falbh 's tarraing!*[130]" Ferghus shouted. I stared at his angry profile in shock.

"What's – " I began to ask, but Doughal had stood and was facing Ferghus with clenched fists.

"*Stad a bhith gad ghiulan fhein mar phaiste!*[131]" Doughal exclaimed, "can ye not conduct yerself in a civilized manner in front of Brigid?"

"A bheil thu a 'dol a dh' innse dhi gu bheil thu air na seirbheisich uile fhuadach?[132]" Ferghus questioned, his jaw twitching.

Doughal glanced quickly at me and then responded, "ni mi na tha mi a 'smaoineachadh as fhearr.[133]"

"Nae," Ferghus argued, "bheir thu aire dhut fhein.[134]"

"Would you please speak English?" I interrupted, staring up at them from my seat.

"Aye, if ye wish tae know everythin', Ah can oblige," Ferghus said, but he was still glaring at Doughal.

"This conversation is private," Doughal warned, "and it ends now..." He took a step towards Ferghus, his hands still clenched.

"Is that a threat?" Ferghus scoffed.

---

[130] Screw you!

[131] Stop behaving like a child!

[132] Are you going to tell her you've fucked all the servants?

[133] I will do what I think is best.

[134] You'll take care of yourself.

"Ah shall make ye even uglier," Doughal countered, "if ye don't shut yer gob. Ye have nae idea how tae speak in front of a lass."

Ferghus laughed sardonically. "Tis true; some of us have more experience than others. Why don't ye explain tae Brigid – ""

Ferghus wasn't able to finish his sentence, because Doughal launched himself across the row of seats at him. Ferghus sidestepped, but not quickly enough; Doughal shoved Ferghus so hard he lost his balance and came down on his hands and knees.

"*Oh my god!*" I cried, standing quickly to watch the altercation.

"*Stand up, ye coward!*" Doughal hollered. Anghus threw up his hands in frustration and came to stand beside me. Ferghus was halfway to his feet, but before anyone knew what was happening, he punched Doughal in the back of the knee. "*God's bones, I'll kill ye!*" Doughal yelled, reaching for Ferghus's collar.

Ferghus was too fast for him; he took a step back and steadied himself on the rocking boat. "Tha thu nad phrois ardanach! *Chan eil eadhon gaol agad oirre!*[135]" Ferghus spat at Doughal.

Doughal reached for Ferghus again, but Ferghus stepped backwards. "And Ah suppose ye dae? Is that what this is aboot?"

"Nae, Ah just don't want tae see ye abuse her trust," Ferghus responded, his cheeks flushed.

"*It's none of yer damn business!*" Doughal retorted, "yer makin' a rockit of yerself. Are we done?"

Ferghus chuckled. "A bheil thu a 'dol a thoirt suas Gilda?[136]" he questioned, his jaw defiant, "or is she a package deal?"

---

[135] You're an arrogant prick! You don't even love her!

[136] Are you going to give up Gilda?

Doughal's face turned purple as he threw himself at Ferghus. He crashed into him so hard, Ferghus toppled backwards. Doughal grasped Ferghus's tunic in time to prevent him from falling overboard. He hesitated for a fraction of a second, and then punched Ferghus in the face. I gasped and rushed towards them. *"Leave them, lass!"* Anghus urged from behind me, but I was too alarmed to listen.

Ferghus retaliated with two of his own quick punches to Doughal's cheek and chest. Both their faces were red, and they were panting. *"Stop it!"* I shouted, but neither one acknowledged I was there.

Doughal threw a heavy punch into Ferghus's ribs that would have broken an average man's bones. I was caught completely off guard, therefore, when Ferghus started yelling as he rushed towards Doughal and threw all his weight against him. Doughal smashed into me, but was able to steady himself on the edge of the moving galley; I, on the other hand, was not so fortunate. I flew overboard and plummeted into frigid blue-green water. I was shocked by the cold, and the weight of my dress. I kicked hard, trying desperately to resurface. At the same time my head emerged, a strong hand grasped my arm and another took hold of my waist. I blinked away the water and saw Anghus leaning down from the galley, a net in his hand. He was shouting, but I couldn't hear his words. I glanced to my left and saw Ferghus treading water with one hand, while gripping my forearm with his other. "Are ye alright?" he asked, his eyes panicked.

"Take Anghus's net, lass," Doughal encouraged. When I turned my head, I saw him on my right, pushing me towards the boat while trying to keep afloat with his free arm.

"You're both crazy!" I exclaimed as I reached for the net. Anghus managed to pull me close enough that I was able to climb a set of slippery wooden stairs leading up the side.

"Come, sit down," Anghus urged, gesturing to the bench. A servant already had a blanket ready to wrap around me.

Doughal climbed up the stairs next, followed by Ferghus. They stood dripping in the warm breeze, neither one speaking as they wrung water from their tunics and kilts. Ferghus ran his hand roughly through his dark hair to dry it. Finally, both men straightened and turned their attention to me where I was making a pool of water on the wooden floor. Doughal's eyes were guilty, and Ferghus's remorseful. Before either one could address me, I asked, "are there any sharks in that water?"

"Nae," Doughal answered first.

Ferghus was about to speak, but I held up my hand and he stopped abruptly. "That's too bad," I commented, "because you're both *bleeding*; they would have taught you a lesson you could both desperately use!"

Ferghus's jaw tightened and he turned to gaze over the gentle waves. Doughal cleared his throat noisily and responded, "Ah appreciate yer wit *and* yer advice; Ah apologize fer behavin' so regrettably..." Despite his size and strength, he looked like a chastised school boy after performing a prank, especially with the bruise already visible beneath his left eye.

I sighed and turned my attention to Anghus. "I think you're the *only* son who has any sense," I told him, "thank you for helping me."

"Oh, fer fuck's sake, Ah was tryin' tae help ye tay!" Ferghus exploded, turning angrily to face me.

"You threw me off a boat!" I accused.

"Ah did not!" he cried, his eyes flashing.

"Ah jumped in tae save ye," Doughal reminded me with a smug smile.

"Oh, *fuck off,* Doughal!" Ferghus lashed out, "Ah jumped in tay. Yer not the fuckin' hero here!"

"It certainly looks that way," Doughal countered, still smiling.

"Dae ye still want tae stop here?" a servant interjected suddenly.

"Aye," Doughal answered with a nod. He looked my way and said, "this is Rum Island; we can stop here fer a while. Dry off." He winked and sat beside Anghus. "We can start a fire."

"Why do they call it Rum?" I asked curiously, "do they make it?"

Doughal looked at me quizzically. "Make what?"

"*Rum.*"

"What's *rum*?" he questioned, his brow furrowed.

"A type of drink," I said slowly, wondering when rum had become widely known in this part of the world, "we drink it back home…"

"Ah," Doughal said with a nod, "a local favourite? Ye'll find horses on Rum, and lots of birds. I'll have the servants get a fire goin' and we can have lunch."

When we'd secured the galley, the servants began unloading supplies. Doughal helped me out, and Anghus and Ferghus trailed behind. "Ye can let go of her hand now," Ferghus muttered under his breath, his voice furious.

"Aam just makin' sure Brigid doesn't fall; we wouldn't want ye tae trip over yer feet agin and send her flyin'." Doughal winked shamelessly, and I blushed and focused on the hilly landscape in front of me.

"…murder ye mahself, Ah will…" Ferghus muttered behind us.

"Don't mind him, lass, he's always been a wee touched in the head…" Doughal joked, tapping his blond hair.

"*Fuck off!*" Ferghus cried, and marched away from us.

"Where's he going?" I questioned.

"Don't worry yer bonnie little head about mah gantin brother," Doughal laughed, "let's enjoy each other's company and take some refreshment." He gestured to the base of a ridge and called out to his servants, "set everythin' up there."

"*Oh my god!*" I exclaimed, sidestepping a patch of what had appeared to be seaweed from a distance but, up close, was actually a nest of some kind, "I almost stepped on it!"

Doughal paused to see what I was pointing at. "A pipit's nest," he informed me.

"Aye, but look – a cuckoo laid an egg tay," Anghus piped up. He was correct: one of the eggs was different from the others.

"I'm glad I didn't destroy it," I breathed as we reached the ridge.

"Dae ye see those?" Anghus asked, pointing into the sky above the hill.

"Yes, what are they?"

"Golden eagles," he answered knowledgeably, "and if ye had better shoes, Eh'd take ye up tae show ye the white-tailed eagle nests."

"You know a lot about birds," I told him. His face turned as red as his hair.

"Ah like studyin' em," he admitted, "they fascinate me."

"You could be a scientist one day," I suggested as Doughal motioned to a blanket that had been laid upon the ground for us to picnic on.

I took a seat and was joined on both sides by a MacLeod brother. "I'll probably get married and start a farm," Anghus said as the servants began passing around glasses of heather wine.

"Thank you," I said and took a sip.

"Science is fer people like Owyn," Doughal interjected, "scholars who can't make a livin' with their hands..." He had already drained half his glass. "Find mah ugly brother and take him somethin' tae eat," he said to the nearest servant who nodded and went to fetch a plate.

"I'll get it mahself," Ferghus stated from above us. I glanced up and saw him ambling down the grassy slope.

"Where did *you* come from?" I gasped.

"Mah brother is just showin' off, Brigid. Pay him no attention," Doughal teased.

Ferghus scowled and sat upon the edge of the blanket. "Nae, just gettin' some fresh air and exercise," he contradicted, his eyes piercing into me, "Ah find it helps give me a new perspective on things. Ye can relate, right Brigid?"

I couldn't tear my eyes away from his. "Mmmhmm," I whispered.

"Ye should have stayed away longer," Doughal said tersely as a servant handed him a plate of food, "we were discussin' married life."

I blushed scarlet and looked at my hands. "Anghus was just telling us what he wanted to do when he leaves home," I explained.

"Sounds like a sound plan," Doughal assessed, "maybe ye can move in together, since ye'll be needin' a place tae stay, Ferg..."

I felt my stomach start spinning as I blurted, "that was unkind, Doughal; Ferghus has just as much right to a happy life as any of you..."

"Aam right *here*, Sassanach; Ah don't need ye tae fight mah battles fer me!" Ferghus said defensively.

Doughal chortled. "Ah don't know about *that*; yer face looks sorrier than mine. Perhaps we need tae have another go?"

"Fine with me," Ferghus replied icily.

"Would you both stop it?" I exclaimed, my hands shaking so hard my wine spilled onto my dress. "*Fuck*! Now look what you made me do! Here – hold this," I said, pushing my glass into Anghus's hands and standing. "*I need a break*!" I stated to no one in particular and stomped across the grassy plain. I could hear angry voices behind me, but I didn't turn to acknowledge them. I was so pissed off, I could hardly see straight! Ferghus was always saying his cousins acted like 'bairns', but right now both he *and* Doughal were behaving like children!

I had no idea where I was going, but I could feel my frustration melting away in the breeze as I moved. I reached the base of another hill and wandered along it until the MacLeod brothers and their servants were no longer visible. I exhaled and stretched my arms over my head to limber up. I performed small arm circles and then larger ones. I tilted my head back and forth, and then did ten knee bends. Each exercise I performed released more stress until I had warmed up my entire body. I glanced behind me and, when I didn't see anyone, I began to perform Kata Naihanshin. It was a simple kata with quick arm movements that loosened my shoulder and elbow joints. I was on my third rotation when suddenly my fist connected with a man's open palm; I whirled to face the newcomer and saw I had hit Doughal. "*Oh my god*!" I cried, "I'm *so* sorry!"

Behind him were Ferghus and Anghus. "What were ye *doin'*?" Doughal questioned, his brow furrowed, "preparin' tae fight someone?" His tone was humorous on the surface, but I could tell from his slanted eyes he was suspicious.

"It's *okay*, Doughal," Ferghus interjected, stepping closer to us, "she didn't hit ye that hard, did she?"

Doughal glanced quickly at Ferghus. "Of course not, but that wasn't mah point," he retorted and then met my gaze again. "What were ye *doin'*?" he repeated.

"Just exercising," I explained, but I knew it sounded dishonest.

"I've never seen any exercises like *that* before," Anghus piped up, a hint of admiration in his boyish voice.

"Nae one asked ye," Doughal said dismissively. He stared at me for a few more seconds and then shook his head in confusion. "It wasn't very quine-like," he finally assessed, "nor was yer cussin' before. Ah have questions that need answers. What can ye tell me about yer family?"

"Drop it, Doughal," Ferghus growled, "Ah told ye everythin' ye need tae know before. We came over here tae apologize tae Brigid, *remember*?" His tone was so determined, my eyes opened wide in shock.

"*Apologize*?" I breathed, unable to think clearly.

"Fer all their squabblin'," Anghus told me.

"Ah said, be *quiet*," Doughal said, levelling Anghus with a glare that completely transformed his normally jovial expression. Anghus's face coloured and he hung his head in silence.

"Let's get Brigid somethin' tae *eat*, Doughal," Ferghus suggested.

"Ah guess," Doughal agreed warily, "Ah just think somethin' isn't right here. Ah can't put mah finger on it…"

"She was just exercisin' – tryin' tae forget aboot our nonsense," Ferghus explained. I noticed his eyes were clear and sympathetic.

"I'm sorry," I hurried to say, "I was just trying to clear my head before lunch. I shouldn't have wandered so far, or done anything to alarm you. We practice a different form of physical conditioning back home…"

"The *hens*?" Doughal questioned skeptically, "why would they need tae dae such rigorous training?"

"It keeps us healthy," I answered, knowing I was being vague again.

"Fer *what*?" Doughal pressed.

"Childbirth," Ferghus suddenly said.

I stared at him wide eyed, wondering if I should correct him or wait to see if Doughal would buy his explanation. "Hmm," Doughal murmured, "it seems an unusual practice. And the cursin'; Ah don't understand why ye speak so crudely tae yer superiors..."

I almost choked on my tongue, but Ferghus's fierce eyes told me not to argue. "I'm sorry" was all I said.

"Come and eat," Ferghus urged softly to end the debate, and started walking away. I quickly followed, and so did Doughal and Anghus. The crisis had been averted momentarily, and I had Ferghus to thank for it.

Chapter Twenty-Eight:

After a lunch of cold meat, cheese, and bread, and two glasses of wine to settle my nerves, we packed everything up and began a tour of the island. It was a rough terrain, wind-swept and rocky, but breathtakingly beautiful at the same time. We came upon a group of about twenty Rum ponies. They had long, shaggy manes ranging from white to black and all shades between. Some were napping when we approached, but quickly became skittish in our presence. "They're beautiful," I murmured as we wandered past.

"Brigid, there's another golden eagle." Anghus pointed to a large bird just landing atop the crest of a nearby hill.

"Do they nest all the way up there?" I asked.

"Aye," he answered.

"I wish we could climb up," I mused.

"Ah think ye've had enough exercise fer one day," Doughal commented gruffly.

Ferghus laughed low in his throat and I glared at him. "It's not funny," I accused.

"*Nae*, it's *not*," Doughal agreed.

"Ah thought ye looked very coordinated," Anghus mumbled quietly. I gave him a grateful smile.

"Is toil le ar brathair direach boireannach a bhith ag eacarsaich anns an leabaidh aige,[137]" Ferghus chuckled mischievously.

"Don't fuckin' start *that* agin!" Doughal exclaimed, his neck turning red.

"Whatever you're saying – don't," I chimed in, "or someone else might get shoved overboard on our way back."

[137] Our brother only likes a woman to exercise in his bed.

Ferghus guffawed loudly. "It's not mah fault mah brother's an arse."

I rolled my eyes and retorted, "I think you say things in your own language that aggravate him unnecessarily."

"Yer very wise, Brigid," Doughal assessed.

"What he's not tellin' ye, lass, is that – "

"*Ferghus!*" Doughal intoned threateningly, his pale eyes flashing.

"Why don't we head back to the boat?" I suggested, feeling exasperated, "the two of you don't seem able to get along for more than *five* minutes at a time…"

"Welcome tae mah life," Anghus said, rolling his eyes skyward.

"*Ye can fuck off tay, Ang!*" Ferghus said grumpily as we all headed back the way we'd come.

The ride back to Dunvegan was sombre. Doughal sat beside me on the wooden bench again, his thigh and bicep grazing me every time he spoke or breathed. I was so annoyed at the entire clan by the time we arrived that I pretended I had a headache and wanted to rest in my chamber until supper. I soon tired of the lack of movement, however, and escaped outside in the late afternoon. I wandered through the trees beside the castle, enjoying the shade and solitude while maintaining the ability to move freely at the same time. Eventually, I grew weary of the dim setting, and took to the hills overlooking the water. It was here where Ferghus found me for the second time that day. He didn't sit this time; instead, he gazed down at me with tired eyes. "Feelin' better?" he asked softly.

I laughed ruefully. "Not really," I responded, meeting his gaze.

"Dae ye really have a headache?"

"No."

"Ah thought ye told me ye didn't lie?"

I gaped at him. "Give me a *break*! You and Doughal acted like a pair of nit wits the *entire* day!" He watched my face closely, but didn't reply. I sighed deeply. "I *still* can't believe what happened on the boat. What in the world got into you?"

"Ye think it's *mah* fault?" Ferghus questioned, his eyes blazing with indignation.

"What else am I supposed to think?" I shot back, "you kept speaking so I wouldn't understand you. Then the two of you had a *big* fight and knocked me off the galley!"

Ferghus looked out over the water, colour creeping up the back of his neck. "Aam sorry about that," he admitted quietly, "it was not mah intention."

"Why didn't you speak *English*?" I pressed, not buying his apology, "you *know* it's hurtful when you exclude me!"

He glanced at me sharply. "Ah was tryin' tae defend ye, Brigid. I didn't want tae embarrass ye by sayin' everythin' plain."

My forehead creased in confusion. "I don't get it! What were you defending me *from*?"

Ferghus's cheeks had turned red. "Ah just want him tae respect ye," Ferghus stated gravely, "tae treat ye the way ye deserve. Yer a remarkable lass, Rosa; ye don't deserve tae be second best..."

I stared at him for a few seconds as I processed his words. "You think Doughal doesn't *respect* me?"

Ferghus shifted his weight to his other foot. "Doughal's Doughal."

"Why can't you just be honest and answer my questions?" I exclaimed angrily, "I answered all *your* stupid ones this morning!"

"*Fine*!" he cried, "what dae ye want me tae tell ye, Brigid? That mah brother likes tae sample every lass he meets? Will that make things *easier* fer ye – quiet yer fears and make ye less anxious about bein' a new bride?" His eyes were fierce as he spat the words at me.

My hands started to tremble in my lap. "So he doesn't respect me, and you don't think he ever will."

"He respects ye in his own way," Ferghus tried to explain, "he thinks ye should be satisfied with bein' the wife of the future Chief and not expect anythin' else."

"Oh, *really*?" I responded, lifting my chin in the air, "and what's he going to say when he realizes that means nothing to me?"

Ferghus frowned. "It shouldn't mean *nothin'*, Brigid. Ah understand Doughal's not the type of man ye deserve, but bein' Chief's wife *is* an honour. Ye shouldn't criticize it so harshly."

I rolled my eyes in exasperation. "I can't figure you out; one minute you're trying to save me from your promiscuous brother – the next you're angry I don't want to be his little wife. Which is it?"

"Doughal and Ah are very different, but we both know what an honour it is tae be Chief."

"Okay, I'm sorry; I just meant I've never *desired* such status. I'm not here to try to win some position that everyone else wants."

"Ah know."

"Then you understand why marrying Doughal is not what I want."

Ferghus shook his head. "Ye'd have security from the MacDonalds; an important position in our clan. Ye wouldn't have tae worry about anythin'. Ah told ye before – it's a good deal."

"You just finished telling me your brother would be an adulterer! That's the type of marriage you want for me?"

"Nae," Ferghus answered, "but Ah don't want ye unmarried and vulnerable. Eh'd rather ye be with mah brother than alone."

"Why *can't* I be alone?" I argued, "what's so wrong with it?"

Ferghus shook his head. "Ye can't live here alone; it's not our way. Yer a young lass of many gifts; ye need tae marry."

"Why can't I live with someone *else* then? I could get a job and pay rent…"

Ferghus smiled at me sympathetically. "Quine don't own *houses*, Brigid; yer suggestin' tae live with a man out of wedlock?" He raised his eyebrows at me.

"*No!*" I replied, "I didn't *say* that! I just meant, why can't I be alone for a while and *then* get married when I'm ready? I could stay at Dunvegan with Mirna…"

"Mirna's gettin' *married*, Brigid; and ye should tay." His tone was firm. "Doughal will want an answer – taenight…"

"*Oh god!*" I moaned, "I can't *marry* him, Ferghus; I don't care about him that way."

"Ye don't find him attractive?" Ferghus questioned curiously.

"No," I answered confidently, "I realize he's *physically* handsome, but I don't feel anything special when I look at him. He actually scares me a little…"

"Maybe that's just yer feminine sensibilities takin' over," Ferghus suggested, "anticipatin' the weddin' and such…"

"No, I don't think that's it," I said, "I think he intimidates me in a way that makes me feel inferior. I feel judged when I'm around him. Like I'll never be enough. Does that make any sense?"

Ferghus was quiet for a second and then he nodded slowly. "Aye, Rosa; Ah know all about that feelin'." We stared at each other for a minute and then Ferghus cleared his throat nervously. "Ah came out here tae say good bye tae ye; Doughal had father send me off again – scoutin' the area. They think it's necessary after what happened at Sloane's..."

My eyes opened wide. "You're *leaving*?"

"Aye. Tomorrow at dawn."

I was dumbfounded. "This can't be happening; we just got here. Doughal even said you were *late*! Why would he ask you to leave so soon?" Ferghus met my gaze, but didn't speak. His eyes were intense and I shivered. "Is it because of your argument – on the boat?"

"'S docha," he replied with a weak smile.

"Well, why don't I apologize to Doughal? Or ask him to forgive you for it?" I said, my mind whirling, "would he take it back and let you stay?"

Ferghus shook his head. "Nae, lass; he doesn't want me here."

"Well, can I come with you?" I asked desperately, feeling a panicky sensation building in my stomach.

Ferghus was surprised by my suggestion. "Why would ye want tae do *that*, Sasannach?" he questioned, "everythin' ye need is right here..."

"But you were helping me," I accused, "you promised to help me – and we just got here – and if you go, how will you know I'm safe?"

"Nae one will let anythin' happen tae ye, Brigid. Dunvegan is the safest place fer ye; the wild is no place fer a lass."

I swallowed the lump in my throat and tried to catch my breath. "I understand, but if it makes no difference to you, I'd like to come."

"It's not appropriate," Ferghus replied, his voice suddenly husky, "we can't be alone, Brigid – not after everythin' ye told me taeday..."

My eyes fluttered up to his face. "All I said was I was curious about your scar," I said defensively, "I don't see how that's so terrible. I won't ask any more questions, and I *won't* take my dress off to bathe. I'll do everything you ask – just please don't leave me behind."

"We *still* can't be alone," Ferghus said, his own voice beginning to tremble, "Ah dae not trust mahself. Yer safer here. Ye can bolt yer door at night and stay with Mirna durin' the day…"

"Why don't you trust yourself? You've never done anything shameful; I can't imagine you ever doing *anything* that goes against your rules…"

"*Brigid*," Fergus whispered, his head falling down as if he was in pain, "*please* – Ah have tae go and ye have tae stay; that's all there is tae it. I've struggled tae act in the proper way, but ye tempt me – all the time – ye tempt me. Ah can't be alone with ye. It's better this way…" The muscles in his jaw clenched several times as he finished speaking.

"Why won't you look at me? Have I done something to offend you?" I questioned, my voice rising in pitch.

"*Please*," he whispered, "take the deal, Brigid. Ye'll be safe. Ah want ye tae be safe…" He suddenly turned and fled down the hill before I had a chance to respond. Tears stung my eyes and I curled into a ball on top of the ridge and wept.

Chapter Twenty-Nine:

I finally managed to stop crying and stumble back to my chamber to wash my face. Mirna came to fetch me when it was time for supper. She was wearing one of her new dresses. "Dae ye like it?" she asked, twirling in front of me, "Doughal said he'll pay fer ye tae get some new ones tay."

"It's very pretty," I told her, but I couldn't bring myself to smile.

Mirna hooked her arm around mine. "Doughal's waitin' fer ye," she said, "he asked me tae check on ye…"

"I'm feeling out of sorts," I apologized.

"Ah feel that way sometimes – when Ah think about leavin' mah home. Yer just homesick, Brigid. It's normal."

When we entered the Great Hall, Doughal stood and came towards us. "How are ye feelin'?" he asked, "is yer head better?"

"Yes, thank you," I replied evenly, "I'm just tired."

"Help her tae her seat, Mirna," he instructed and we moved to the head table. Anghus was already seated, talking with his parents, but Ferghus's chair was empty.

When the servants came around to fill our wine glasses, I immediately gulped down half. Doughal glanced sideways at me and asked, "are ye sure yer okay, lass?"

"Mmmhmm," I mumbled as I swirled the burgundy liquid in my glass.

"Ah apologize agin fer what happened with Ferghus; he fancies himself above the rest of us," Doughal stated as bread and cullen skink were served.

"What was Ferghus so angry about today?" I asked innocently.

Doughal laughed. "He thinks he's an expert on matrimony, even though he'll never get married."

"Why do you think that?" I questioned.

Doughal shrugged as he took a bite of his soup. "He scares away every lass he meets. Ye've seen him. He's more frightenin' than a MacDonald…" He chuckled under his breath.

"I think he's become too self-conscious," I commented, "a person is more than just their physical appearance."

"Aye, perhaps, but it's the first thing ye see when ye meet someone; if ye can't stand tae look at em, then how can ye get tae matrimony?" Doughal broke off a large piece of bread and shoved it into his mouth.

"I think if someone took the time to get to *know* Ferghus, they would see his other qualities."

Doughal glanced at me incredulously. "*What* other qualities? Yer tay optimistic, lass. Ferghus is sanctimonious and intolerant. He'd spend his time moralizin' instead of makin' bairns…"

"He's loyal, isn't he?" I pressed, deciding the haddock soup was not my favourite thing in the world, "family means the world to him. He speaks so highly of his clan. He's also incredibly brave; he's risked his life for me more than once. Those qualities have to count for something…"

Doughal eyed me curiously in the candlelight. "Aye, he's loyal" was all he said before he bent his head and began to eat again. The rest of the meal passed in relative silence; we made small talk, but Doughal never brought up the subject of marriage or his brother again, until dessert, tea, and gin were served. "I've waited all day fer an answer tae mah question. Mirna wants ye fer a sister, Brigid, and Ah would be honoured tae have a bride as bonnie as ye…"

I pushed my pudding away and inhaled deeply. "I appreciate how you've taken me in – an orphan with no roots; it was very good of you and your family to accept me like this."

Doughal frowned and tipped his glass of gin back before saying, "*but*?"

"I'm just not ready to get married," I admitted, "I've never desired it."

"Yer twenty-*one*, Brigid; ye need tae get married."

I sighed. "Everyone keeps telling me that, but I don't *feel* ready. There's so much I haven't done yet."

"Ye can do those things with yer husband," Doughal stated, as if it was the most obvious thing in the world, "there's nothin' ye need tae dae that ye can't do with a man by yer side..." I knew there was no point trying to explain to Doughal that I might want to go back to school, or travel somewhere in my own time period, or go to a movie with Selma. When a servant passed by, I asked for more wine. Doughal shook his head and interjected, "she's had enough." My eyes opened wide as the servant nodded and walked away. How could he speak for me? I could feel my cheeks burning, but instead of exploding I clenched my hands in my lap beneath the table.

"I'm tired; I think I'll go to bed now," I said curtly.

"Ye don't want tae watch the entertainment?" Doughal inquired, "some music might cheer ye, lass..."

I felt like telling him that so might another glass of wine, but I bit my tongue and smiled sweetly. "Thank you, but I need to rest. Woman troubles you know..."

He nodded uncomfortably. "Okay, but please think on everythin' Ah have tae offer ye, Brigid. We can get married in a fortnight and start tryin' fer a family…"

"Good night, Doughal." I stood quickly and said good night to everyone else before climbing the stairs to my room.

Once I'd bolted the door, I gathered all the blankets I could find, including the curtains, and began knotting them together. I waited by the window, watching the night deepen and the stars appear in the sky. When all was quiet in the castle, I secured the first blanket to the closest bed post and pulled it taut. It seemed strong; I hoped it would hold my weight as I descended from the window. I climbed onto the sill and tossed the trail of blankets down, backing slowly out the window and inching carefully to the ground. When my feet were firmly planted, I exhaled in relief. Next, I entered the stables and led Selma from her stall. She seemed happy to see me again. I waited until I was well past the hills where I'd sat to watch the water before I climbed onto Selma's back and began to gallop away from Dunvegan. I wouldn't need the cover of trees until dawn, so I pushed her hard. When she tired, I slowed her to a light trot. We continued in this way for another *four* hours; I wasn't sure what time it was, but I knew dawn couldn't be far off. I was exhausted, but I didn't want to stop until I was well beyond the Fairy Pools. I dismounted and pulled Selma into the cover of thick woods. The starlight didn't penetrate this section, so it was slow going. My feet were beginning to ache, and I wondered how much longer I'd be able to continue without a rest.

An hour later, sunlight slowly began to filter through the canopy in thinner areas. Ferghus would be setting out from Dunvegan soon; I hoped my head start would be enough. If I was lucky, he'd have no idea I'd even left and would therefore not be looking for me. If I could retrace our steps to the narrow straight, but head northwest instead, I might be able to find Tristen, or one of his kin.

Two hours later, the trees began to disappear and the land gradually sloped towards several blue-green pools. I had successfully reached the Fairy Pools in record time. I led Selma to the edge of one pool and she began to drink. I splashed water on my face and cupped my hands to drink. Once again, I was astonished by how cold the water was. I rested on the grass for a few minutes but, when I began to feel as if I might fall asleep even while sitting up, I stood and reluctantly climbed onto Selma's back. I remembered Ferghus saying this area wasn't safe, so I galloped down the hillside and continued at a brisk run for close to an hour. Trees began to appear again and, when they were thick enough, I moved into their protection on the opposite side of the hill.

By this time, my stomach was beginning to growl. I had picked at my supper the night before and gone without any food since. I endured two more hours of agonizingly slow movement through dense forest. The sun was high in the sky. I wondered if anyone in the castle had noticed I was missing yet, and what their reactions would be. I wasn't their prisoner, so surely they wouldn't send anyone to bring me back. I had told Doughal I wasn't ready to get married yet; whether he accepted my decision or not was to be seen. My legs ached so badly they had started to tremble from exhaustion and muscle pain. I pulled Selma into an especially secluded area of the trees and secured her before falling into a deep sleep.

***

I awoke a few hours later both hungry and thirsty. I felt lightheaded as I stood, so I grasped Selma's lead tightly in my left hand and used my right to reach for slender trunks to steady myself. It was slow going again, as the paths were ill defined and hilly. It was cool in the forest, but I began to feel nauseous from exerting myself for so long without food and water. Eventually, a headache began that made all sensory stimulation uncomfortable. The cries of birds above me sent shivers down my spine. I stumbled along, scraping my knuckles against rough bark and falling onto my knees more than once. I continued like this for as long as I could, much longer than I ought. The already dim forest began to slowly darken and night insects began to send out their incessant hums. Finally, at around eight or nine o'clock, I couldn't continue. It was so dark I could barely see trees directly in front of me. I was almost too dizzy to properly tie Selma to a branch, but I managed with much fumbling to secure her · before I crashed unceremoniously onto the mossy ground. I crawled to a large conifer and hid behind its enormous trunk. I didn't know how to make a proper shelter, and I didn't know which berries or nuts I could safely eat. I had no weapon to hunt with, and I hadn't brought any containers to carry water. In short, I was ill prepared for this journey, but I had wanted to leave before anyone else in the castle was awake. To prepare for all eventualities would have taken more time and consideration – time I didn't want to spend in Dunvegan.

I tried several times to swallow, but my throat felt chalky. My feet were sore and my arms and knees had open scratches upon them. I knew if I didn't find food and water soon, I wouldn't have the energy to continue or go back. I needed a plan, but I was too weak to make one. I fell into an uneasy slumber that deepened with the night. I woke once to the sound of an animal scurrying through the underbrush, but was too tired to lift my head to identify it. More time passed, but I was too ill to track how much. The temperature dropped significantly. I wrapped myself into a tight ball, but still my shoulders shook and my teeth chattered. I passed an entire night in this dismal manner. When the sun finally rose, I felt as if I hadn't slept at all. Instead of feeling hungry, my body only registered sickness. I knew I should prepare Selma for further travel, but I couldn't lift my head; standing would have been impossible without risking collapse and injury. I moaned softly, clutching my pounding head. Why had I left Dunvegan? What had possessed me to begin such an arduous journey over unfamiliar and uneven terrain without food, water, or proper clothing?

A small degree of sunlight filtered through the thick branches, warming my hair enough to stop the shaking. That gave me enough energy to cry. My tears were short-lived, however, because I was too dehydrated and fatigued to continue. I felt an animal scurry past me, which made the hairs on the back of my neck stand; I hadn't considered what would happen if I couldn't make it out of the forest. Would predators sense my weakened condition and prey upon me? I had no weapon, so I rolled onto my side and grasped for a large branch or rock – anything to defend myself if necessary. The only thing I could find was a handful of pine needles. I wanted to cry, but I couldn't; my head ached too much to fume. The only action I could take was a fitful sleep. I woke to the sound of my own quiet moaning several times; other times, I thought I heard the sound of an animal close by. Eventually, night began to settle upon the forest once more. I hadn't had anything to drink since the Fairy Pools. Affecting me even more than thirst was the constant pounding in my skull. I clutched my head, but even pressure against my temples didn't assuage the pain. As all light faded from the forest, a dampness crept into my very bones, and my chest began to ache where I had been punched at Sloane's. I knew my teeth were chattering again, but I was too weak to even curl myself into a ball this time and it wasn't long before I passed out from exposure.

Chapter Thirty:

I'd been right about predators; something brushed against my legs some time later. I tried to push it away, but it had covered me so quickly with its fur, I couldn't escape. The animal was moaning, but the sounds were muffled. I could feel its body heat seeping into mine, erasing the previous chill that had enveloped me. My teeth stopped chattering, and the creature stopped making its strange, plaintive noises. I could hear breathing next to my face, but I was too tired to open my eyes. Suddenly, I felt something pressing against my lips. I tried to move my arms, but the animal was holding me too tightly. The creature was strong, and warm. Suddenly, cool liquid splashed against my lips. I gasped and the water stopped. I rubbed my moist lips together a couple times and opened my mouth. More water came, but this time I was ready for it. The liquid soothed my parched throat and didn't stop until I'd swallowed an entire mouthful. "*Mmm*," I murmured.

"Yer freezin'," a deep voice whispered next to my ear.

"*Mmmhmm*," I managed to reply.

"Ah searched everywhere fer ye," he informed me gruffly.

The heat continued to spread through me, eventually even warming the tips of my fingers and toes. "*Mmm*," I murmured again, flexing the fingers on my left hand – the ones not crushed beneath the animal's embrace.

"Dae ye need more water?" the voice asked.

"*Hungry*," I whispered.

"Not til morn," he told me, "it's tay dark now."

"Are you going to eat me?" I questioned, trying to open my heavy lids.

Silence.

"Will it hurt?"

"Even yer poor cuddie was thirsty; what were ye thinkin'?"

"*Hungry.*"

I heard the animal sigh heavily. "Have some more water." The bottle pressed against my lips again. I took another long swallow and smacked my lips together. I tried clearing my throat and it worked this time.

"Who are you?" I whispered.

"Aam yer husband," the creature responded, "at least Ah *should* be…"

***

"I'm too young to get married," I protested weakly.

"Yer the *perfect* age – and it seems like marriage is the only thing that will keep ye from doin' anythin' reckless. Maybe *then* ye'll actually listen tae me. What did Ah tell ye about travellin' without water?"

I found myself smiling in recognition. "*Ferghus?*"

"Who else did ye think it could be?" he asked tersely.

I laughed with difficulty. "*Doughal? – Tristen?*"

"*Tristen?*" he repeated angrily, "*nach leigeadh thu iomradh air ainm dhomh!*[138]"

"Did you just tell me to fuck off?" I questioned.

"Brigid – *fer fuck's sake!*" he cried, "Ah tracked ye fer *two days*! How could ye think Ah was Tristen?"

"I didn't," I assured him as my lashes slowly fluttered open. Ferghus's handsome face came into focus directly in front of me. He was curled on his side with his left arm wrapped around me; his great kilt was

---

[138] Don't you dare mention his name to me!

covering us. I blinked a few times, relieved to see him there. "Are you real – or am I dreaming?"

"What were ye *thinkin'*, Rosa?" Ferghus asked, his voice husky, "ye could have been attacked, or *worse!*"

"You were leaving me," I accused half-heartedly, "I had no choice."

"Ye could have stayed and married mah brother – been the Chief's *wife!*"

"You know I couldn't," I responded softly.

"Ye were reckless," Ferghus stated, ignoring my sentiment.

"*Yes,*" I admitted, "I *was.*"

Ferghus shook his head in frustration. "Doughal asked ye first; Ah cannot interfere."

"*You* met me first," I countered.

"Ye'd be happier with him," Ferghus said, but his tone was as half-hearted as mine as he continued to try to convince me of Doughal's superiority.

"*You're* the better man," I said, staring into his beautiful blue eyes.

"Nae, Rosa," Ferghus argued, "Aam broken. Ah might have been someone once, but – "

"You're someone to *me*! You think a *scar* changes that?"

Ferghus's jaw twitched. "Doughal's made a claim – Ah can't – "

"Oh, *fuck Doughal!*" I hissed, "I don't want *him!*"

I heard Ferghus's breath catch in his throat. He paused for a few seconds and then replied, "ye shouldn't speak about mah brother that way, Brigid. He's made a claim. Have ye answered him?"

"*Yes!*" I said in exasperation, "I told him *no*. I said at supper I couldn't marry him. He told me to consider it longer, but I already said *no*. How many times does he need to hear it?"

Ferghus eyed me warily. "Are ye sure ye said all that?"

"I'm not an *idiot!*"

"Ye came into the wild without water!" he countered, his lips curling slightly.

"Oh, *fuck off!*" I couldn't help smiling too.

"Are ye warm enough?" Ferghus asked suddenly.

"*Toasty.*" Without responding, Ferghus lifted the blanket and slid out, wrapping the edges back around me. I frowned as some of the heat dissipated. "Why'd you do *that*? It was so cozy!"

"Ye *know* why."

"Your *rules?*"

"Aye."

"You couldn't break them, just this once, on account of me almost freezing to death?"

"If yer not careful, people will think yer a temptress and burn ye at the stake," he said playfully.

"Aren't *you* cold?"

Ferghus shrugged. "I'll be okay. Eh'd make a fire, but ye picked an awful place tae set up camp."

"You're an asshole."

"Are ye not a *wee* bit grateful, Sasannach?"

"Yes."

"Ah was so worried."

"You *were?*"

"Aye."

"Thank you for saving me from Tristen."

"*Tristen*? Ye *saw* him?"

"No, I was going to *give* myself to him," I said sheepishly.

"*De fo shealbh*?[139]" Ferghus exclaimed, sitting rigidly beside me.

"I thought if I retraced my steps, I could get back home…"

Ferghus was breathing hard. "Ah understand yer homesick, but *Tristen*? Ye were safe at Dunvegan. Did ye not like it there?"

I hesitated. "It's a beautiful home. I've never seen such pretty views, Ferghus."

"*But…*?"

I sighed. "Your family is very nice. I really like Mirna, and your parents, and Anghus…"

"*Doughal*?"

"I don't want to marry him, and everyone wants me to. Even *Mirna* was excited. If I stay, I'll be letting everyone down. I can't bear it!"

Ferghus was quiet for a few seconds. I stared at the outline of his face in the darkness. Finally, he sighed. "Ah understand. Ah just wanted ye tae belong somewhere. Ah know what it's like tae feel displaced…"

"Couldn't *we* find a place? There have to be towns around…"

"Aye, but it's safer livin' with kin. And we can't stay under the same roof…"

"I could pretend to be your cousin," I suggested quietly.

"That doesn't help us, Brigid," he replied.

"Why not?"

"It would just be the *two* of us; Ah have tay many enemies, plus there's still the issue of not bein' able tae *live* together…"

139 What the hell?

"But I was going to pretend to be your cousin, remember?"

"Yer a *lass,*" Ferghus pointed out, "Ah can't live with ye!"

"You live with *Mirna,*" I stated.

"Mirna's mah *sister*; Ah cannot marry mah *sister!*"

"You can marry your *cousins*?" I exclaimed in horror.

Ferghus actually chuckled. "Not more than one at a *time*, Brigid. Ye haven't eaten in two days; Ah think yer delusional…"

"I'm *not* delusional!" I protested, "in my world, you can't marry your first cousins *ever!*"

"*Really?*"

"Yes, *really*! It's gross!" I informed him, wrinkling my nose in disgust.

"What if it's someone ye've never met and ye both grew up miles apart?"

"Not even then," I said firmly, "I'd never be able to get over the fact they were related to me."

"What if they were strong and loyal and wealthy?" Ferghus asked.

"Not even then. How could you ever be attracted to your *cousin*?" I wondered.

He shrugged. "It's better than marryin' a MacDonald."

"*I'm* a MacDonald…"

Ferghus was silent for a few seconds. "Then Ah guess Eh'd better kill ye – *right* – *now*…" He leaned towards me and pretended to grab my neck. I squealed in surprise and grasped his wrist.

"*You wouldn't!*"

"Aye, Ah would – most definitely. Death tae all bonnie, red-haired, MacDonald lassies," he growled as he slowly lowered his hand. I pushed up on it with all my strength, but it wasn't enough and I could tell he was hardly trying. I giggled. He quickly dropped his hand and cleared his throat. "Ye should get some sleep now."

"Okay," I said quietly. The air had become tense again. "Are you angry with me?" I questioned nervously.

"Nae," Ferghus responded gruffly, "only at mahself."

"*Why?*"

"Sleep now."

"*Ferghus…*"

He sighed. "Aam in *loove* with ye, Brigid and it's makin' me crazy."

"I don't think you're crazy, *exactly*," I teased, "more erratic and grumpy…"

He ignored my joke. "Ah should have asked ye tae marry me before we got tae Dunvegan, but Ah was tryin' tae respect yer wishes and move slowly…"

"And don't forget you were also busy yelling at me," I reminded him.

"*Brigid!*" he complained. I giggled again and he glanced down at me in the dark. "Ah loove that sound," he breathed, "is it awful Ah didn't want Doughal tae hear it?"

"Yes, you're an *evil* man, Ferghus MacLeod – positively heartless…"

"Aam bein' serious, Brigid."

"I don't think you're awful," I confessed.

"Dae ye forgive me fer bindin' yer hands? And overreactin' sometimes?"

"Yes."

"Ah know ye think yer tay young, but if ye change yer mind – "

"Yes."

"*What*?"

"I love you too."

"Ye *dae*?"

"Yes."

Ferghus clasped his hands in his lap and tried again. "So, as Ah was sayin', if ye change yer mind and – "

"I'll marry you."

"Ye *will*?"

"Yes."

"Yer sure ye don't want tae marry Doughal?"

I giggled. "I'm *very* sure."

"Ah don't think mah scar will get much better, Rosa. It's faded as much as – "

"I think you're very handsome, Ferghus," I told him shyly.

"Ye *dae*?"

"Yes."

Ferghus fidgeted for a couple minutes before nodding. "Okay, we'll get married, but Doughal will be angry."

"I'm sorry."

"It's mah own fault; Ah should have asked ye first. Ah assumed ye could never loove me, so Ah didn't want tae be humiliated."

"I'd never *humiliate* you, Ferghus."

"Ye rejected Doughal!"

"I know, but that's not the same as *humiliating* someone. I turned him down with *kindness*."

Ferghus actually laughed. "Ye know it's the same thing, right? Rejection *is* humiliating!"

"I didn't want to hurt anyone," I admitted honestly, I hope he'll forgive me."

"He'll take it out on me like he always does," Ferghus stated matter-of-factly.

"Oh, I don't want that," I said miserably.

"It's worth it, Rosa," Ferghus insisted, "now get some sleep."

Chapter Thirty-One:

Ferghus and I were married three weeks later. Gilda seemed relieved and helped make me a beautiful yellow tartan dress. It was strapless with a fitted waist and a ring of satin roses around the scooped neckline. The A-line skirt fell just over my shoes and was both elegant and practical for walking and dancing. The wedding took place at a small chapel on Skye; there were so many relatives that most only attended the reception at Dunvegan. I got to see Sloane, Nyle, and Owyn again. They were all very happy for us. To my relief, Ferghus's parents had been ecstatic about the news of our engagement; I think they were relieved their son had found a bride who loved and respected him. Mirna was overjoyed, and told me in private she was envious I was going to marry for love. I told her I thought she should speak to her parents one more time about her feelings for Owyn; she promised to do so the day after the wedding. Doughal had been mystified, believing it to be a ruse. Once he accepted the engagement was genuine, he began distracting himself with the servants again.

Lesley MacLeod enjoyed planning a grand feast. Every kind of meat and bread was served, as well as more than double the bottles of alcohol Sloane had provided for Nyle's birthday. I sampled everything, but felt a strange butterfly sensation in my stomach the entire evening. Everyone wanted a chance to tell me how beautiful I looked, or compliment Ferghus on his choice of bride. I muddled my way through a few traditional dances; I was embarrassed, but the numerous relatives seemed to enjoy the opportunity to teach me the steps. My feet were getting sore, so I sat at a table with Owyn and Mirna. Ferghus found me shortly after and greeted me with a smile that lit his entire face. "Ye've had enough dancin'?" he teased.

"I'm sorry," I said, but he just held his hand in my direction. I grasped it and he helped me to my feet.

"Thank ye fer comin', Owyn," Ferghus said politely to his cousin and then turned his intense gaze upon me, "ye sure ye don't want tae watch mah cousins drink tay much and make fools of themselves?" He winked.

My skin felt hot as I replied, "no, I'm good."

Ferghus laughed low in his throat. "As ye wish, Sasannach." He glanced at the table and reached for a bottle of heather wine before holding his free hand out to me. I placed my hand shyly inside his and he smiled. "We can go somewhere quieter tae talk," he suggested.

"Good night," I said to Owyn and Mirna before Ferghus tugged me gently towards the entrance to the Great Hall.

I observed his profile as he led me to the large stone staircase that wound to the top floor of the castle. He was wearing his dress kilt, but he had an elaborate tunic and fancy sporran on. "What kind of stare is *that*?" he suddenly asked. I was mortified.

"I wasn't – " I started to say, but stopped abruptly when I saw his blue eyes were twinkling. I blushed and stared at the torches flickering on the walls. I could feel my heart pounding inside my chest, but I didn't want Ferghus to know how afraid I was to be alone with him. I exhaled slowly and then said, "I've never been up here before…"

"Ah should hope not," he teased, squeezing my hand affectionately.

"Why's that?"

"It's mah home," Ferghus informed me.

"Isn't the whole castle your home?" I wondered.

"Aye, but the three of us have private sections," Ferghus explained as we passed two smaller chambers on either side of the stairs.

"What about Mirna?" I inquired.

"She'll move when she gets married."

"Don't *you* have to move? I mean – *we*?" I questioned uncertainly.

"Aye, we can talk it over – decide where we want tae make our home. Fer now, Doughal has agreed we can stay while we make arrangements."

"That was kind of him," I said as Ferghus pushed open a large wooden door at the end of the long hallway.

The room was twice the size of the one I'd been staying in. The stone floor was covered in fur pelts and there was a fire crackling in the hearth. Ferghus's bed was enormous, covering almost one whole wall. It also contained four posters and stairs leading inside, along with heavy velvet curtains. There was a small sofa in front of a large, curtainless window, and Ferghus motioned towards it. "Ye can rest yer feet and we can talk a while," he suggested.

I trailed behind, unable to form any intelligent replies. I perched upon the sofa and clasped my hands in my lap. Ferghus sat beside me and pressed the bottle to his lips. When he'd taken a drink, he offered it to me. I took the bottle gingerly, but rested it in my lap while I observed the rest of the furnishings. There was a wash stand with basin directly across from us, and several oil paintings of local nature scenes hanging upon each wall. "Did Mirna paint those?" I asked softly.

"Aye," Ferghus responded. He was watching me keenly and, after a minute, held his hand out. "Ah can take that." He smiled gently and I placed the wine into his outstretched palm.

"She's a talented artist," I commented to make conversation.

"Aye." I bit my lower lip, trying to think of something else to say. We'd never run out of topics of conversation before; why was this suddenly so difficult? Ferghus shifted sideways to rest the bottle upon the sill; when he turned back, he reached out and began to tentatively stroke my hair. I glanced at him in surprise. His fingers paused. "Dae ye mind?" he whispered huskily.

I could barely meet his gaze. "No, it's okay."

His fingers began their slow examination of my locks. "Yer hair's so bonnie, Rosa."

My eyelashes fluttered. "Thank you."

Ferghus smiled softly and cocked his head to the side to appraise me. "Yer quiet; is somethin' wrong?"

"No," I laughed self-consciously, "I just can't think of anything to say…"

"That's not like ye," he teased. He gently slid my silver headpiece off, placing it upon the sill too. "Did ye have fun taenight?"

"Yes," I answered, "everyone was patient with me."

"With the dances?"

"Yes."

"Ye did fine, lass," he told me sincerely.

"I tried. Where *I'm* from, there aren't any steps to memorize. It's a lot easier."

"Dae ye miss it?"

"The dancing?"

"Home," Ferghus said as he started pulling pins out of my updo.

"Yes, and no," I replied thoughtfully, "I miss my friends. I don't miss how busy the roads are, or how rude some of our customers can be…"

"It's quieter here?" Ferghus questioned as he found the last pin and ran his hand through my hair to touch the nape of my neck. Goosebumps emerged on my chest and arms, and I shivered.

"Much quieter," I answered, thinking about cars, and buses, and airplanes.

"Mmm," Ferghus murmured. When my eyes met his, his look was soft and intimate. He swallowed and said, "yer the bonniest lass I've ever seen, Brigid."

My cheeks coloured. "Thank you," I said quickly.

"It embarrasses ye tae hear it?"

"A little," I admitted shyly, "I'm not used to it."

"Ye did me a great honour taenight," he said, "Ah already pledged mah loyalty and protection in front of mah kin, but here, in private, Ah wish tae pledge mah loove and affection. Ah admire ye a great deal – more than I've shown…"

"*Oh.*"

Ferghus's fingers wandered down the back of my neck and came to rest upon my shoulder, which he stroked through the heavy tartan. "At first, some of the things ye knew and did frightened me."

"Like my katas?"

"Aye, and ye bein' from a country Eh'd never heard of."

"I never meant to scare you…"

"Ah know. I've come tae learn tae trust ye; ye've been honest with me about yer background and feelins. Aam grateful ye've been so patient with me."

"I'm sorry I wasn't very nice sometimes…"

Ferghus's fingers ran down my arm to my elbow, which he cupped in his palm. "We both made mistakes. Taeday we moved past them." He was touching me so gently, I felt momentarily speechless as I contemplated that no one had ever treated me with such reverence before. "The fire's almost out; dae ye need me tae relight it?"

I shook my head. "I'm okay."

"If ye change yer mind, let me know. Gonna be a cold night; the sky is clear…"

"Do you think everyone is still dancing?"

"Aye," Ferghus replied with a gleam in his eye, "Ah wouldn't be surprised if Nyle and Sloane get up tae some mischief taenight…"

"What kind of mischief?"

"They'll be goin' fer a swim in the wee hours, Ah reckon…"

"You probably wish you could join them," I teased.

Ferghus's expression changed. "Nae, Rosa, not at all…"

"*Oh.*"

"Aam happy right here – talkin' tae mah wife."

I flushed at the sound of the word on his tongue. "Wow, I'm your *wife…*"

Ferghus chuckled softly. "Aye, and Aam yer *husband.*" He set my elbow down and started kicking off his boots. "Ye can take yer shoes off; feels good tae relax…"

I slid my shoes off and flexed my toes. "You're right!" I laughed.

Almost instantly, the tension settled over the room again; a lazy playfulness was evident on the exterior of both our words and gestures, but underneath we were dancing around the obvious chemistry that buzzed in the air like honey bees overburdened with pollen. As night deepened, and the fire burned to coals, the stars were the only light source save one tiny stub of a candle flickering on the sill. "Should we save this?" Ferghus suddenly asked, "we can put it by the bed in case either of us needs tae light it in the night. If we let it burn tae nothin', ye may trip…"

"Oh, I didn't realize it was all you had," I answered uncertainly, my stomach suddenly beginning to tighten.

"Ah was careless – forgot tae ask fer more," he responded. He studied my face in the bouncing light, wet his fingers against his tongue, and extinguished the candle with a hiss. The smoke swirled into the air and escaped out the window. Darkness enveloped us and we sat side-by-side in silence for a time. Suddenly, Ferghus reached out in the inky space and ran his fingers, feather-light, against my own. I shivered again, amazed at the sensuality of that small touch. He repeated the gesture but, this time, he gently grasped three of my fingers with his and held on without breathing a word. I could feel my pulse beginning to accelerate and the skin on my decolatage began to burn. "Ah loove ye, Brigid," Ferghus whispered across the darkness.

I sucked in my breath and exhaled, "I love you too."

He slowly released my hand and began to remove his sporran. He placed it upon the sill and then silently lifted his tunic over his dark hair. He sat with the garment in his lap, as if uncertain what to do next. I could see the outline of his hard chest in the starlight, beside which ran the long, pale scar to the top of his dress kilt. He slowly lifted his eyes to meet mine. "Ye've seen *me,*" he said in a voice so low and husky I could hardly discern the words, "can Ah see *ye?*"

I bit my lower lip and nodded, unable to think clearly in the fog of slow-burning desire that had started to course through my veins like too much wine. "Aam curious," he murmured. He turned sideways on the sofa and placed both his hands upon my knees. He'd made such a big deal about his rules of touching, I felt positively dirty. I could feel my breath catching in my throat, breathing so shallowly for fear of showing him how truly anxious I was. I wondered if he could sense my apprehension. Ferghus cupped my knees and then ran his palms to my upper thighs. I could hear his breathing had accelerated too, which made me feel a little better. Suddenly, he stood from the sofa and held one hand out to me. I grasped it and he helped me to my feet. We stood in front of the open window, the soft breeze touching the back of my neck. "Does it button in the back?"

I felt flustered by his question. "Yes," I answered, my voice shaking.

Ferghus pressed his bare chest against me so he could reach around my forearms and unbutton my wedding dress. The material went slack; he gently tugged it down to my waist, and then knelt to help slide it all the way off. When he stood, I got goosebumps just from seeing the look in his eyes when he observed me in my corset. His movements were tender as his fingers trailed over my collar bone, moving outwardly until each hand came to rest upon the naked flesh of my upper arms. He lightly circled them and slid his hands towards my wrists. His eyes never left mine. "Can I have some of that wine now?" I heard my voice squeak.

Ferghus didn't reply; he just stepped even closer to me, reached around the back of my head for the bottle, and placed it into my right hand. He watched silently as I swallowed two enormous mouthfuls of the fragrant liquid. "Thank you," I said breathlessly.

"Aam not going tae have any supplies left," he whispered next to my ear. He pulled back and smiled softly. "Dae ye remember our long journeys through the forests?"

"Of course," I breathed, grateful Ferghus had broken the electricity with levity.

"Ah found ye remarkable," he confessed, his fingers finding mine in the dark.

"I felt the same about you," I told him shyly.

His eyes crinkled at the corners. "Ye were feisty and opinionated," he relayed, "Ah knew at once ye must be a true Scoottish lass."

"*Ferghus!*"

He chuckled low in his throat and wrapped his fingers more securely around mine. "*Come,*" he whispered, and pulled me gently away from the window towards the other side of the room.

At the foot of the stairs into his bed, he gestured for me to go ahead of him. I knew my cheeks must be scarlet, but it was much too dark for him to tell. I slid beneath the furs and watched as Ferghus slowly removed his kilt. He sat upon the edge of the bed, took two daggers out of his stockings, and cast them aside as well. When he climbed in beside me, he was stark naked and gloriously handsome. I had no idea what to do or say, but my eyes could see his handsome outline in the dim room and I knew I'd made a wise choice of husband. "I've never removed one before, so forgive me if Aam clumsy," he confessed as his fingers began to work the ties on the neckline of my corset. My heart was thrashing so rapidly, I thought he must be able to hear its every beat. Despite his inexperience, Ferghus managed to loosen the strings and pull the corset off me. His hand immediately covered my sternum as his eyes unabashedly moved over my body. "Bean ghaoil,[140]" he murmured, sliding his burning palm down to my navel.

"I wish I knew what that means," I whispered shyly.

"Bonnie beyond compare," Ferghus stated. His fingers found mine again. He lifted my arms above my head and pushed me back gently onto

[140] Loveliest wife.

---

the feather mattress. I had not imagined the desire and love I would feel for a man on my wedding night, but when he rolled on top of me and I felt every supple muscle in his thighs and chest pressing against my soft skin, it was euphoric.

Ferghus stroked my hair and gazed down at me lazily in the dark. "Aam goin' tae claim ye, Rosa," he told me unexpectedly. I almost choked, his words were so blatantly sexual. Did they mean the same in *his* world as they did in *mine*?

"You *are*?" I squeaked.

"Aye." He leaned closer and just barely brushed his lips against mine. His face was gone before I had time to react. I laid there with my mouth open, feeling ridiculous at the thoughts tumbling through my mind. He stared down at me, his fingers coiling through my hair now. Every gesture was slow and measured; he was patient and thorough while he explored my body. I began to ache for him to do what he'd said, but I wasn't sure if I was supposed to suggest it, or just lie there and wait for him to initiate its fruition. Suddenly, he bent his lips to cover mine, but this time they lingered for a few extra seconds. The kiss was G-rated by my *own* society's standards, but here, with him lying naked on top of me, I felt hot and desirous.

I reached out and placed the tip of my finger against the beginnings of the scar on his cheek. He froze as I trailed it gently down his chin to his collar bone, and then all the way down his ribs to his stomach. "Does it end there?" I asked.

"Aye," Ferghus said quietly, "ye've seen it all."

"Okay."

"Aam sorry if it bothers ye," he said gruffly.

"It doesn't." My palm was still resting against his stomach muscles. This time, I allowed my eyes to wander. He was holding himself up by his forearms and, as my fingers trailed along his hip and down the back of his thigh, I heard his breathing quicken. I glanced back at his face and his gaze was intense.

"Aam goin' tae claim ye, Brigid," he whispered for the second time. He almost sounded like he was in pain.

I nodded and leaned closer. The next thing I knew, he was kissing me eagerly. He threaded his fingers through mine and held my hand tightly beside his hip. I moaned softly against his lips, feeling as if my whole world was coming undone. I wrapped my free hand around the back of his head, pressing my chest as close to his as I could. I tried to play it cool, but I couldn't control my desire for him any longer. He suddenly pulled away and looked down into my eyes. He was breathing hard. "Ye make a lot of sounds," he commented huskily.

"*Oh god, sorry!*" I mumbled.

"Ah like it," he told me as he bent to plant small kisses down the side of my neck to my throat, and then continued along my sternum. I sucked in my breath as his lips grazed the side of my breast. He paused, gazing at my chest, before lowering his lips onto my nipple. When he began to suck, I gasped loudly and lifted my head involuntarily. Ferghus stopped and eyed me curiously. "Does it hurt ye?"

"No, no," I said in a rush, "it's good. It feels good…"

"Dae ye want more?"

"*Mmmhmm*," I breathed, biting my lower lip, "*please…*"

Ferghus's eyes were as eager as my own. He lowered his lips and began teasing my breasts again. I gasped and moaned, and pretty much made a fool of myself. Finally, I couldn't stand it any longer. My whole body was on fire. I slid my right leg up and wrapped it over Ferghus's back. He stopped kissing me and gazed up at me hungrily. "Ye hold nothin' back, dae ye, Rosa?" He slid his torso up my stomach and started to kiss me so deeply, I thought he was trying to possess my soul. I could hear the frantic sounds of my moans and the fierce, wet kisses we were sharing. Suddenly, without warning, Ferghus joined with me. I could tell it was unplanned, because he froze, his pupils dilated and his mouth gaping. "O mo chreach…[141]"

Ferghus's body was motionless, as if he wasn't sure how to proceed. I smiled up at him and ran my hand along the side of his cheek. "*Ferghus…*" I murmured happily. He smiled too and slowly the tension in his broad shoulders relaxed. He closed his eyes and leaned down to nuzzle my neck. I moaned as he gently pushed further inside me. I gripped his body with my thigh and held on tightly to the back of his head. His lips planted tiny kisses all along my neck and chin and then he started kissing my lips again. My eyes fluttered closed as he gripped the mattress over my head and began to make love to me. I gasped every time he moved deeper within me. I'd never imagined feeling so close to another person before. The pleasure suddenly reached an astonishing level. "*Ferghus…?*" I gasped, "oh my god, *Ferghus…*" I threw my head back against the pillows and started to cry out loudly.

He stopped abruptly and panted, "what's wrong?"

"Oh god, don't stop," I pleaded, glaring at him frantically, "for god's sake, *please don't stop!*"

Ferghus's eyes opened wide and he tentatively began moving again. "It feels *nice*?"

---

[141] Oh my God.

"Please!" I threw my other leg around his waist and moved my hips against him eagerly.

That was all the encouragement he needed. I climaxed again and, this time, he didn't pause. I dug my nails into his back and pressed my forehead against his shoulder as I cried. In my euphoric state, I didn't notice that Ferghus had stopped moving; he was groaning quietly in my ear, his chest slick with sweat. Our breathing was ragged, and we clung together for several minutes, still intoxicated from what we'd done. Finally, Ferghus stirred; I heard him inhale deeply as he pushed himself onto his forearms so he could appraise me. I was still nestled tightly against the bottom of his shoulder. *"Brigid?"* Ferghus whispered anxiously, "are ye okay? Did Ah hurt ye?"

I giggled inadvertently and laid back against the pillow. "No, you didn't *hurt* me." I sighed contentedly.

He studied my giddy expression for a moment and then the corners of his mouth relaxed into a proud grin. "It was all good?"

I giggled again and touched the scar on his cheek affectionately. "It was so much better than *good.* I *loved* it."

"So did Ah," Ferghus admitted. He lifted my hand and kissed my palm. "And Ah loove ye most of all," he added shyly.

"I love you too."

Ferghus kissed my palm again. "Can Ah ask ye somethin'?"

"Yes."

"The noises ye were makin', they were all happy sounds?"

"Yes," I laughed.

"Oh."

"Why – do they break your *rules*?" I teased.

"Nae," Ferghus responded quickly, his neck flushing, "Ah was just curious. Ye sounded like ye were cryin'; Ah thought Ah had caused ye pain…"

"You gave me the most incredible pleasure I've ever felt," I confided.

"Doughal told me Ah would hurt ye," Ferghus confided hesitantly.

"You talked about this with *Doughal*?"

Ferghus's cheeks flushed. "Aam sorry; Ah had a few questions." I was quiet for a minute. "Are ye angry?"

"No, just embarrassed. The thought of Doughal picturing me in *bed* with you creeps me out."

"Sorry," Ferghus said sadly, "Ah didn't mean tae – "

"It's okay." I ran my fingers up the length of his forearm and gently massaged his bicep with my small hand.

"Aam sorry, Brigid," he repeated earnestly.

"I know," I responded softly, "it's not your fault. We both had questions, but I didn't have a sibling to ask. I shouldn't be angry with you."

"Ah was nervous; Ah wanted tae be prepared – tae know what tae expect."

"Everything was perfect, Ferghus."

He exhaled. "Tis a relief it's over…"

I giggled. "I hope that wasn't the only time for us…"

Ferghus grinned shyly. "God has blessed me with an enthusiastic wife."

"*Hey!*" I pretended to be insulted, but I smiled too.

Ferghus grew serious again. "Taemorrow we can visit a site Ah picked out fer a home; if ye like it, we can make arrangements tae start buildin'."

"Is it far?"

"Nae, it's close tae Sloane's."

"That's a pretty part of Skye," I noted.

"Close enough tae home tae visit regularly; far enough from Doughal tae avoid conflict."

"You've thought of everything. Thank you," I told him. I pulled gently on his bicep and Ferghus laid beside me, pulling me against his chest so he could hold me in his strong arms.

"As long as Ah have *ye*, the rest doesn't matter," Ferghus said, "but ye have tae promise me *one* thing, Rosa..."

"What's that?"

"Ye have tae teach me yer katas," he said, "Ah can't have mah wife breakin' mah neck everytime we have an argument..."

I laughed. "Maybe one or two; I can't teach you *all* my secrets..."

The End

Alternative Ending:

I woke in the middle of the night still cradled in Ferghus's arms. I stretched, trying not to wake him, and slowly crawled out from beneath the furs. I had to use the bathroom, but it was too dark to see. I fumbled for the candle. "Ye okay?" Ferghus asked sleepily from the bed.

"Just need to go to the bathroom, but I can't see..."

"I'll get ye another candle; there are lots in the drawer..."

I turned to see Ferghus slowly sliding out of the bed and walking towards me. "I thought you said there weren't any more candles?"

Ferghus reached me and placed his hands upon my shoulders. "Aam sorry about that; it was a wee lie. Ah didn't know how else tae get ye into mah bed..."

I stared at him incredulously. "You pretended to run out of *candles* to get me into *bed*?"

Ferghus's cheeks coloured. "Ah didn't know how else tae ask ye..."

I giggled. "*Ferghus*!"

"*What*? Ah was nervous."

"You didn't seem nervous at all."

"Ah did mah best," Ferghus joked as he pulled open the drawer, took out a candle, and lit it, "I'll walk with ye."

"Okay."

We moved across the stone floor to the large, wooden door. Ferghus used his free hand to unbolt it and pull it open. It creaked on its heavy hinges. Ferghus held out the candle to illuminate the hallway, but there *was* no hallway; instead, there was only a small room filled with unopened boxes, cleaning supplies, and a large bag of coffee cups. We both stood frozen, staring into the dim supply closet. "*Brigid?*" Ferghus whispered uncertainly, "what is this place?"

"It's the shop where I work," I told him, my voice quavering, "what should we do?" I glanced at his shocked face. "Do we stay, or do we go?"

The End, #2

About the Author

J.G. MacLeod

    J.G. MacLeod has always been an avid reader and writer. As a child, she was drawn to putting pen to paper so that she could record the people and places she would create inside her mind. As a young adult, she earned a university degree in Honors English and history due to her keen interest in nineteenth-century studies.

    Ms. MacLeod then went on to graduate with a Bachelor of Education and has spent the past seventeen years teaching. She taught creative writing, English and social science for most of those years, but she has also spent time as a guidance counsellor and working with students with developmental disabilities. She loves encouraging students to find their own voices through writing and believes that every single person has a story to tell.

    Ms. MacLeod has three young children of her own and resides in southwestern Ontario where she lives for road trips and Lake Erie sunsets. She has a passion for travel and loved a recent visit to Huntsville. Ms. MacLeod dedicates time every day to the act of writing and loves the beautiful nuances of the English language.

Author Website: jgmacleod.com

Made in the USA
Middletown, DE
04 January 2021